W9-BCB-044

DISCARD

{ DELPHINE PUBLICATIONS PRESENTS }

Stitching LOVE

A NOVEL

They find themselves battling life's hurdles with a newly discovered secret weapon....each other

TISS DEVANE

DISCARD

Delphine Publications focuses on bringing a reality check to the genre Published by Delphine Publications

Delphine Publications focuses on bringing a reality check to the genre urban literature. All stories are a work of fiction from the authors and are not meant to depict, portray, or represent any particular person Names, characters, places, and incidents are either the product of the author's imagination or are used fictitiously, and any resemblances to an actual person living or dead are entirely coincidental

Copyright © 2015 by Tiss Devane
All rights reserved. No part of this publication may be reproduced, stored in or introduced into a retrieval system, or transmitted, in any form, or by any means (electronic, mechanical, photocopying, recording, or otherwise), without the prior written permission of both the copyright owner and the above publisher of this book.

ISBN: 978-0996084444

Edited by: Shelia Hood Bryant
Layout: Write On Promotions
Cover Design: Odd Ball Designs

Printed in the United States of America

R0442906482

Stitching LOVE

Chapter One

Skyla's Dangling Threads

The clock began blaring after only a few hours of sleep. I blindly felt around for it and hit the snooze button before slowly opening my eyes. For a moment, I didn't know where I was. But, after seeing my old Usher and Boyz II Men posters on the wall, I suddenly remembered the homemade sex tape that had landed me back in my childhood bedroom. The clock sounded again at 4:22am. I snoozed a couple more times then forced myself to sit up. Despite the fact that my life was unrecognizable, I still had to go on, especially for the sake of the life growing inside of me. Even though I hadn't shared the news with anyone, I was grateful for that life and felt comforted by its presence.

I hurried into the shower and afterwards entered into my normal routine of hair and makeup. But today, I took extra care to make sure every loop and layer lay in its proper place and each eyelash separated and curled just right.

Then, I pulled items from the Bloomingdale's, Neiman Marcus, and Saks Fifth Avenue bags I accumulated with mom last night until I was completely bedecked in a winter white Valentino wool pantsuit complete with a matching lace shell underneath.

To top it off, I slid on my Alexander Wang black and white booties and threw a white Chloe Paraty bag over my shoulder. But, it really wasn't me. I was more of a Cache/BCBG kind of girl and my idea of red bottoms was a red clearance sticker on the sole of any shoe from Macy's. Still, shopping with mom was fun and helped me kick Phillip where it would hurt him most—in his wallet.

After slowly examining myself in the mirror, I felt halfway presentable. Then the opinions of my two favorite critics ensued;

You go girl—you look like a million bucks! my quite inner voice whispered in my head.

Yeah, but too bad you only feel like an under the cushion penny with gum and Dorito crumbs all over it, my loud inner voice screamed.

I headed downstairs toward the door where I found my mom waiting for me. Her under eye bags revealed that she'd also had a restless night.

"Skyla?..."

"Ma, we already talked about this. I know, background is everything and you told me not to marry him."

"I did, but you never listen to me. Damn that Phillip! What was he thinking, showing us a tape like that? Your father and brother were ready to kill him!"

"Obviously he put in the wrong one, Ma. Don't worry. I'll find your anniversary party DVD when I go get the rest of my things."

"Okay, but why should you be the one to move out? That house is just as much yours as it is his."

"He can have it. I don't want it."

"That's just your pride talking."

"My pride got up and left halfway through the viewing of Phillip's porn premiere."

"I know you're hurt and embarrassed."

"Try devastated, Ma. I mean, I knew my marriage had problems, but I had no idea it was that bad."

"I know. Still, I don't think it would be wise to just walk away from such a beautiful home."

"It was never a home, Ma. It was a space that I resided in. Prisoners have that same provision."

"Well, that space has your name on it too. Phillip should be living on the street since he's just using it to tape himself screwing whores behind your."

"Ma, please. I'm not going back there and that's it!"

"Okay, well you look fabulous. Try to have a good day."

She kissed me on the cheek and gave me a consoling hug.

"Thanks Ma. After yesterday, it can't get any worse."

I grabbed my coat and headed off to work. I'd anticipated a much shorter commute downtown from my parents' southside of Chicago home. But the freshly fallen snow made the drive extra long and tedious.

Normally at a time like this, I listened to anything by Yolanda Adams on my way in. But today, I couldn't—couldn't cry, couldn't pray……and couldn't let this fool veering into my right side get in front of me;

"Hey! Don't you see me in this lane you idiot!!" I shouted at the stranger while laying on my horn.

He gave me the finger and sped around me.

Finally, I arrived at the Center for Research on the Economically Disadvantaged. CRED, was a 15-year study established by Princeton University that examined the effects of poverty on minority children and their families. I was the Project Administrator, which meant that I wrote proposals eloquently begging for money from private donors and grant-making organizations and once I received the money, I spent it on budgeted items. I also assisted my boss, Candice Jing, with anything she needed as the Project Director.

I enjoyed working at CRED. Unlike the greedy fat cats at the fortune 500 companies I worked for after college, CRED was run by a diverse group of academics mostly at the PhD level who seemed to give a damn about something other than their pockets.

I stepped off the elevator and took off my coat before heading down the long dark hallway leading to my office. Out of nowhere, a familiar male voice said,

"Damn, you've got a great future behind you!"

I turned around and saw Chase Foley slowly following me with a devilish grin.

"Good morning Mr. Foley," I replied, continuing on while checking my company issued Blackberry.

"It could have been a good night too if you would stop playin' games."

Chase was the company flirt. But while many found his demeanor lewd and vulgar, on a lot of days he was just what I needed—and not because he was the IT whiz who could retrieve permanently deleted files either. He was young, cute and silly with coffee bean brown skin and an in-your-face sense of humor. But I could have done without his jesting on this particular morning.

"My night was just fine Mr. Foley."

"That ain't all that's fine, comin' up in here with those tight ass pants on. I could just flip you over and lick..."

"How's your girlfriend doing? You know, the one you brought to the summer picnic. You do remember her, right?"

"Don't you worry about her."

"Somebody has to, since you seem to have completely forgotten her."

I entered my office and stood looking over the mounds of files and paper on my desk while Chase watched me from the doorway.

"Alright Skyla Richards. I'm gonna leave you alone for now, but you know I'll be back."

As he left I hung up my coat and chuckled. It felt good to feel my cheeks rise and form the shape of a smile again. Then, images of Phillip's on camera romp bombarded my mind and a gradual sense of despair crept over me again.

I felt like crying but still couldn't leak out any tears. They'd all been used up over the course of my six year marriage. There were so many red flags or in Phillip's case, full length red velvet curtains too thick to be overlooked. But somehow, I'd managed to ignore them all and last night was the culmination of my shortsightedness. Didn't he think I had fantasies about wild sexcapades too? Well, I did. But my marriage vows were the boundaries that kept them neatly tucked away in my head, safe from leaking out and spilling onto flat screen TV's and Youtube videos.

To dig myself out of the doleful mood I'd fallen in, I pulled the sonogram I'd been carrying around out of my purse. The early snapshot of my developing baby was the only thing sustaining me and I'd been clinging to it like a sea stranded sailor to a life raft.

As I ran my fingertip across its surface, I relished in the joy of knowing I'd be a new mother in seven months: albeit a single one now. Work was always a good remedy for my trials and tribulations. So I kissed my unborn child, put the sonogram away and began editing a stack of proposals I'd written.

"Uh, oh. I know that look," Bree, my BFF said from the doorway.

She was an accountant I'd met on my first day at CRED. We both loved fashion and fun and I considered her to be the slightly older sister I never had.

"What look?" I asked.

"That, my husband has pissed me off again and I gotta keep working to keep my mind off of his dumbass, look."

"Speaking of looks, you look great. Let me see." I motioned for her to come all the way in.

She strutted through the door past the leather couch and twirled showing off her winter white knit turtleneck and skinny cords tucked into matching high heeled boots. Standing at around

4'11", Bree was a naturally thin woman. Even though four inches taller, I still had to work to keep my size eight curves in check.

"I see you got the winter white email," I said.

"Well, you know what they say, great minds think alike. I love your suit. Your turn. Stand up and give me the full view."

I stood and slowly spun around, holding out my arms.

"Damn! Now I know you're pissed cause that's some expensive shit you've got on. I'm almost scared to ask what he did to deserve the dent you put in his credit card with that outfit."

Just as I was about to plunge into my Phillip saga, we were joined by another co-worker.

"Uh, hey sistas," Jonathan Bass peeked in and said.

"Uh, hey brotha," Bree teased.

"Sorry to interrupt. You have a minute Skyla?"

"We can talk later Sky," Bree said.

"You don't have to go Bree. It will only take a second," he assured her.

"Come on in Jonathan. What can I do for you?" I asked.

While Bree and I sat, he strolled towards my desk then stood gaping oddly at me.

"Sooooo????" I urged.

"Oh, um....I just needed one of those change of beneficiary forms, that's all."

"That's all? Deciding who gets your shit after you're gone sounds like a big damn deal to me. You adding or dropping?" Bree asked.

"Don't you think that's kind of personal Bree?" I said.

"It's okay Skyla. I'm adding my fiancée," he replied.

"So, the wedding is back on?" Bree probed.

"Ok Bree, please get outta the man's business."

"Well, I'm sorry Sky but everybody knows he's canceled that engagement more times than Oprah's been on a diet."

"Jonathan, please excuse her. You know how she is," I said.

"No, Bree's right. I have been pretty indecisive about the whole marriage thing. But not anymore. My mind is finally made up."

Suddenly, his cell phone began ringing. He answered it and walked over to the doorway and stood talking with his back to us.

As I got up to get the form, a warm, damp sensation gushed between my legs.

"Sky—what the hell?" Bree whispered, pointing at my crotch.

I looked down at my white pants and gasped at the sight of a huge expanding blood stain traveling down my inner thighs.

Bree grabbed a nearby roll of paper towels and immediately snatched some off and handed them to me. I didn't know whether to stuff them on the inside or try to cover up the growing stain on the outside.

Jonathan finished his call and was just about to turn around when Bree rushed over to him.

"Uh, look Jonathan, why don't I drop off that form later on," she said, nudging him through the door.

"But, I really need it today," he argued, trying to look back at her.

Meanwhile, a painful cramp had developed in my left side. My inner thighs became so drenched in blood that I had to remove both my pants and underwear and stuff most of the paper towels between my legs to stop the blood from flowing.

I found a pair of spare tights in my desk drawer and slid them on. Then I felt so light headed that I had to hold on to my desk for support.

Bree continued guiding Jonathan through the door. "Don't worry, you'll get your form," she told him. "Besides, by the time I bring it to you, you'll have probably changed your mind again anyway," she said, shoving him into the hallway and locking the door behind him.

"Oh my God! Sky, what's going on? Are you okay?" she ran over to me and asked.

"I think I need to go to the hospital!"

"I'll call 911!"

She grabbed the phone and began to dial.

"No! No Bree. I don't want that kind of attention. Not now," I said, doubling over in pain.

"Fuck that! You're having a medical emergency and I'm calling an ambulance."

"Bree, I said no!"

She reluctantly hung up while I hobbled over to my coat and sluggishly put it on.

"Thank God you wore a long, black coat today. Sky, just let me call an ambulance, please!"

"No Bree. Let's just go. I don't want to wait for an ambulance. Let's take a cab.

Go get your coat and meet me by the elevators."

"What? No! I'm not leaving you here like this."

"I'll be fine. We're wasting time!"

"Ok ok, I'm going."

I took what was left of the paper towels along with a full box of tissue and stuffed them in my bag. We met up by the elevators and rode down to the lobby as if nothing was happening.

Once outside, there wasn't a cab in sight.

"Fuck it. Wait here and don't move!" Bree ordered before bolting down the street. Five minutes later I heard screeching tires approaching. I looked up and saw her black Lexus barreling towards me as if she'd just robbed a bank. The door flung open and she yelled, "Get in…hurry up!"

I climbed in and we sped off to the closest hospital.

Hours later, I woke up in bed cloaked in one of those hideous hospital gowns with tubes running in and out of me. Bree was staring down at me through smeared mascara.

"Why didn't you tell me Sky?" she asked softly.

"Tell you what?" I groggily replied.

She glanced down, then back up at me and said,

"That you were pregnant."

I paused, studying her expression.

"Why did you say, were?" I hesitantly asked.

She hung her head and I knew I'd lost my baby.

Finally those tears that had been vacant for so long flooded my eyes and rushed down my cheeks. A piercing sense of loss clenched my soul and I began sobbing so hard that I felt my chest would cave in and suffocate me. Bree embraced me and began crying too. The doctor entered and handed me a box of tissue. After snatching a few, Bree went and sat in a chair in the corner.

I dried my eyes while the doctor began checking my blood pressure.

"How are you feeling?" the doctor asked. I didn't answer her.

"I know how hard this must be," she said.

What is it with all these people who "know" everything, I thought. Phillip said he "knew" how bad it looked after exposing his filth on film. And now this doctor chick was telling me that she "knew" how hard this was. Well, none of them knew anything. If they did, they would have known how futile those words sounded before ever uttering them.

"Mrs. Richards, you're young. You can have more children. Would you like for one of the nurses to call your husband?"

"I don't have a husband," I resignedly replied

Puzzled, she looked down at my wedding ring, then over at Bree who was looking just as confused.

"Okay. You try and get some rest. I'll be back to check on you in a little while," she said, turning to leave.

"When can I get out of here?" I yelled out, stopping her in her tracks.

She came back over to me and said, "Well, all of your vitals are good, but I would suggest you stay overnight just for observation."

"And what if I don't like your suggestion?" I replied.

She peered at me over her glasses.

"Well, then you're free to go after 8:00pm. Is that what you want to do?"

"Yes."

"Okay, I'll get your discharge papers ready."

Once she left, Bree came and held my hand.

"Did you call Candice?" I asked.

"Yes, but I just said you had a family emergency and had to leave early. She understood. Don't worry about work. You just try and get better. I don't blame you for wanting to get out of here. Hospitals are creepy as hell. Should I call Phillip?"

"I wasn't delirious when I said I didn't have a husband, Bree. And now, my baby is gone too."

"Okay, do you want to tell me what's really going on?"

"I will. Just not now."

"That's fine. I'll drive you home and come by tomorrow to see how you're doing. Maybe we can talk then."

"Thanks Bree. You've always been a great friend, but that won't be necessary. Can you just take me back to my car? I can get home from there."

"Are you sure about that?"

"I'm positive. I'll just see you at work tomorrow."

"Now Sky, I know you. I know how you like to use work as some sort of shield to ward off the evil drama dragon. But please, don't do this. Just take a couple of days off until you're ready to return to work."

"Thanks, but I'll be fine."

Once I was discharged, Bree and I got into her car and drove in total silence. That was one of the things I loved about her. We could be in each other's company and not have to say a word to be heard. She understood how badly I needed silence that night. And she gave it to me freely, allowing my mind to roam. I wondered what happens when the grand announcement becomes an honorable mention, or when a vigorous stream of hope instantly becomes a dried up well of dreams. Does the announcement become less important and the stream ineffective? I wondered what to do with my news—news of how new life and all the splendor that comes with it had suddenly turned into, what was.

Even though I hadn't told anyone, it was still precious news. But there would be no more excitement or expectation—just questions, sadness and anger that I didn't know what to do with yet. So I decided to just let it settle deep into the soil of sorrow were all hurts go and I would water it with denial until some seeds of healing could take root and spring forth.

Before getting out of the car, Bree made me swear to consider taking some time off. On the way to my parents' I realized she was right and called in sick the next day, even though I felt fine physically. Mom and dad just figured I was still reeling from Phillip's sex tape and thankfully didn't ask any questions.

Deep down, I knew I needed to journal—get some of my feelings out. But, the thought of engraving my pain on paper depressed me even further. Still, whenever I couldn't journal I could always muster up some sad ass, Chardonnay inspired prose:

How unique the styles of the partners we dance with to the tune of

"Acceptance"

Denial twirls us around leaving us breathless and dizzy

Then, anger cuts in picking up the pace with its fast and riveting movements

Next, Honesty takes us by the hand, dips us into reality and holds us close as we grow comfortable in its embrace then, gently hands us over to Courage

Courage grips us and whispers in our ear "follow my lead"

And in its eyes, we find the confidence to master a new dance to rhythms unknown

###

Even though it was hump day, I was in a terrible mood. At least I had befriended music again on my way into work. I couldn't listen to just any old song though. I only wanted to hear songs that reached down to the depths of my gloom and high fived my pain. So India Arie's, Good Morning, was the perfect choice followed by a chaser of, This Too Shall Pass, by Yolanda Adams. During the second selection, the absentee tears returned. I let them flow and connect with each word and felt a little better by the time I arrived at CRED.

The elevator doors opened and Sonya, our cheery, chatty receptionist was sitting at the front desk while a brown skinned woman with a pixie haircut stood screaming at her. As I approached, Sonya locked gazes with me.

"Oh God, I'm so glad you're here, Sky!" she said, eyes begging for succor.

"What's the matter?" I walked over and stood next to the irate visitor.

She scanned me up and down then growled, "Who the fuck are you?"

"Sky, I found her waiting in the lobby before anybody got here this morning. But she refuses to tell me what she's here for."

"That's because it's none of your business. I know what I'm here for and who I need to see."

"Well ma'am it's only 7:45am. We don't open for another 45 minutes," I explained.

"What are you gonna do, throw me out? Like I told your stupid ass receptionist, I'm not going anywhere. I'm staying right here. So you're both just wasting your time." She turned and headed towards the waiting area.

"I don't think we are," I said. "This is a private office and as such we have the right to know the nature of all office visits including yours. So, if you just tell us who you need to see, you can wait as long as you'd like."

"I told her that Sky, but she won't listen," Sonya said. The anonymous visitor came back over to us.

"Are you both deaf? I'm not going anywhere and don't have to tell either of you shit!" she shouted.

"Ma'am, you can't just loiter on private property. Either you tell us who you need to see or I'm going to have to ask you to leave and come back during normal business hours," I firmly said.

"I'm not gonna keep repeating myself!" she yelled at me.

"Well then, you leave us no choice. Sonya, call security," I instructed.

Sonya picked up the phone and started to dial. The woman reached over the reception desk and snatched the phone from her hand. I grabbed the woman's wrist, wiggled the phone away and gave it back to Sonya. Then the woman pushed me so hard that I lost my balance and fell to the floor.

"Don't ever put your hands on me you stupid bitch!" she screamed, placing her index finger just inches away from my nose.

As I stared into her eyes, I noticed they were hazel colored just like Phillip's which sent my mind into a fog of reminiscence. Suddenly, I was traveling back through his closet remembering all the gifts I'd stumbled upon that he never gave me. Then there were those dinner for two receipts I'd found that I was never in attendance at. I stood and tried to snap out of it but got trapped in my latest sting of loss and became swollen with rage.

As the woman continued screaming and cursing at me, spurts of spit shot out of her mouth and landed in random spots on my face. Suddenly, I felt my right arm rise and my fist collide with something damp and hard. It seemed like a dream and I only became fully aware of what I'd done when I saw her chasing her tooth as it rolled around on the marble floor.

"Sky!" Sonya shouted, running from behind the desk and grabbing my arms.

The woman held her mouth with one hand while scooping up her tooth with the other. Afterwards, she headed for the elevator but before boarding turned to me and roared, "This ain't over with bitch!"

Once she left, Sonya stood gawking at me then burst into laughter.

"Damn Sky! I've never seen you do anything remotely like that! What have you been reading, Act like a woman, think like a boxer?"

"What the hell just happened, Sonya?" I hazily asked.

"I don't know but I bet she'll think long and hard before she comes in here clownin' like that again."

Stunned, I stood there trying to wrap my head around what I'd just done.

"Aw Sky, don't look so worried. She deserved what she got. Listen, no one ever has to know about this. I'll make sure of it."

"Thanks Sonya. I'd appreciate that. I don't know what came over me. I haven't had a physical altercation since Tracy Anderson tore up the Father's day card I made for my dad in the 3rd grade."

"I just wonder who she came to see. Maybe she was a disgruntled study participant. Surely no one here would associate with a fool like that on a personal level."

"Well whoever she was looking for needs to do what I did and get out of that relationship as soon as possible."

"What? Are you and your husband breaking up Sky?"

I couldn't believe I'd just let that slip out. But the look on Sonya's face confirmed that I did.

"What? No. Um…I just meant that so many couples are breaking up and getting divorced nowadays."

"Uh huh," she replied, giving me the side-eye with folded arms.

I quickly went to my office, hung up my coat and plopped down in the chair. My eyes searched the room for remnants of Monday's tragedy but came up empty. I put my phone on forward and dove right into work. It was just about 11:30am when I decided I needed to hydrate.

On my way to the 3rd floor vending machines, a message from Phillip appeared on my Blackberry. What could he possibly want? I whispered, clicking on the message while continuing to walk:

"I can't seem to reach you at work and you're not answering your phone, so I decided to text you. Okay, I'm an asshole. We both know this. Please believe it had nothing to do with anything you did or didn't do. I know you hate me right now. You have every right to. But, think about it before you do anything stupid, Skyla. Aside from this little sex tape incident, you know deep down that no man will ever treat you better than me."

I bought a Sprite and on my way back to my office bumped right into another controversy. But at least this one didn't involve me.

"That's not what the bible says, Jonathan," Sonya said as I approached the reception area.

"You really need to expose your mind to other books besides the bible," he replied.

"Other books like what?"

"Like the Quran, the Torah or the Pāli Canon, perhaps."

"The Pali who? Nothing compares to the living word!"

"God you're rigid in your thinking!"

"Don't be using the Lord's name in vain!"

"Urgh!"

He abruptly walked away but while still in earshot of both me and Sonya mumbled, Simpleton.

"Atheist!" she hollered out in response.

Once back at my desk, I read Phillip's text a few more times then leaned back in my chair and slowly started to swivel. I did about three full turns before noticing my boss walking through the door.

"Stop daydreaming. We're having a meeting right now," she announced, closing the door.

She sat across from me with a stern look. But that didn't mean anything. She always looked that way even when she told a joke. Candice was a no-nonsense tall, Blasian woman with tiny hands and humongous feet. But, she was also a straight shooter with a keen sense of fairness that most everyone appreciated.

"Is everything okay," I asked, wondering if my version of Snapped had gotten back to her.

"You tell me. What's this I hear about you getting a divorce?"

"What? Who said I was getting a divorce?"

"Seriously Skyla, if you think Sonya can keep something like that to herself, then I've got a snow plow business to sell you in Miami."

"I don't really want to talk about it—only to say that I've finally had it and I'm ready to move on."

"Okay. Didn't mean to pry. I just want to make sure you're okay."

"I'm fine. You look a little peaked though."

She placed a manila folder she'd been carrying on my desk, then stood up and quickly sat back down.

"Are you alright?" I asked.

"Whoa…I got dizzy for a minute."

She gripped the arms of her chair and gradually slid all the way back.

"Let me get you some water," I said, turning to retrieve a bottle from the credenza behind me. As I turned back around she started coughing repeatedly. It sounded like she was choking and gasping for air at the same time. Suddenly, she buried her head in a nearby trash can and began to vomit violently.

"Candice! What's wrong?"

I got a couple of tissues from my purse and ran around to assist her.

"Ugh. I'm so sorry," she said, taking the tissues and wiping her mouth. "Guess I have some news for you too."

"You're not sick are you?"

"For now I am. But, I'll be much better in about seven months."

"What? You're pregnant?"

"Yep!"

"That's……that's uh, that's great Candice. Congratulations," I said, eyes tearing and voice trembling. I managed to compose myself enough to give her a hug.

"I'm really happy for you," I said.

"Aw, I can see that. I'm pretty excited! But, all this morning sickness is starting to get to me. I have a doctor's appointment in a couple of hours to make sure everything is okay. I'm just a bit nervous since this is my first child."

"That's understandable. Was there anything else you wanted to talk about?"

"In fact there is. Look, I need you to set up a disciplinary hearing for the latter part of next week. It's all in this file."

She pushed the manila folder towards me.

I opened it and skimmed through the complaint. Then my jaw dropped.

"Wow! Really? He seems a bit heady, but not at all like the type of guy who would go this far," I said.

"I know. Jonathan's always been respectful towards me. But we don't know what happened and we need to find out before he heads off to Princeton on our dime. So, check my calendar then email him and Angelica the date and time of the hearing. And as usual, you'll be sitting in on this with me."

I opened Outlook and examined our calendars.

"Why don't we do it next Friday so they can have the weekend to cool off and not have to deal with each other for a few days."

"Good idea. Go over the process with him and have him prepare a rebuttal by the end of next week."

She stood to leave and headed for the doorway then suddenly turned around.

"And Skyla, remember to maintain professionalism."

"Aren't I always professional?" I asked, wondering if she was baiting me into a confession.

"Look, you know how guys are. Not that you would ever get involved with anyone while you're still married, but you are kind of…well, vulnerable right now. Plus there's that no fraternizing policy we have."

"Thanks Candice. But trust me, you don't have to worry about that."

"Never underestimate the heart's desperate quest to heal itself."

"That's such a big job, way too big for a man to do. Only God can handle that one."

"Okay, but as a woman who's been through a divorce and is now on husband number two, I'm just warning you. Take it or leave it."

"Thanks, but I think I can safely leave it for now."

On her way out, she ran right into my next visitor.

"Well, look who's here. Come on in Jonathan. I was just leaving," she said as she stepped through the door then turned around and winked at me.

"I hope I'm not bothering you Skyla, but I really need that change of beneficiary form. Bree never gave it to me the other day."

"I'm sure she just got tied up. I can get it for you. But first, sit down. I want to talk to you about something."

"Okay, what's up?"

He sat across from me with his feet spread apart and his hands resting on his thighs. I took his copy of the complaint out and handed it to him then waited for his reaction. He didn't flinch. Instead, he just kept reading and without looking up said, "Now, I know you don't know me all that well, but come on Skyla." He looked me in the eyes and continued. "I'm not an idiot. Do you really think I would jeopardize my future and talk to my boss like this? I don't care what Angelica says, this never happened." He lightly flung the complaint back onto my desk.

"Well why on earth would she say these things about you Jonathan?"

"It's a long story."

"Then, I guess you'll be writing it over the weekend. You have to prepare a rebuttal by next Friday. I'll email you the time of your hearing once everything is confirmed."

"Go ahead and do what you gotta do. This too shall pass," he casually replied.

His last comment struck me as it confirmed the lyrics in the song I'd connected so deeply with on my way into work.

"That's a good attitude to have. Here, let me get that COB form for you." I stood and walked over to a nearby file cabinet. "I need to be more positive like you," I said.

As I began searching for the form, he came and leaned on the side of the cabinet with his arms folded and one leg crossed over the other.

"You look nice today. That dress fits you well in all the right places," he said, keenly examining me.

I shot him a look with a raised eyebrow.

"Aw man, I'm sorry. I hope I didn't offend you. Didn't mean to be talking all under your clothes like that."

"You didn't offend me, but good lord Jonathan—how old are you? Talking all under my clothes? I haven't heard that expression since my grandma passed away."

"I'm Twenty-Five, but people tell me I have an old soul."

"I'll say. Hmmm, I can't seem to find it. Let me try the next drawer. Forgive me. I'm usually not this disorganized. I'm just kind of off today."

"And why is that, if you don't mind me asking?"

"I don't mind. I've just had a lot on my mind lately."

"Matters of the heart?"

I paused and glanced over at him.

"Have you been talking to Sonya?" I asked.

"Seems more like you've been talking to Sonya and in true Sonya fashion, she talked to the whole office. So, are you really getting a divorce? I'm only asking because that's the one thing I've been so terrified of. It's why I've wavered so much in my own relationship."

I resumed looking through the files.

"Divorce is the result of an absence of true love and nothing to be afraid of Jonathan. I mean, no one wants it, but if it happens it's not a personal indictment of failure. You just have to make sure you and wifey love each other unconditionally."

"But that's just it. What looks like unconditional love can often be camouflaged as something completely different."

"Something like what?"

"I don't know—dependency, guilt, obligation or maybe all three."

"Sounds like you've thought about this a lot. And if you have to ponder that deep then it probably isn't true love. But, who am I to talk, given my current marital woes? Oh, here it is. I found it. Here you go."

I snatched the form out and handed it to him.

He looked it over and took a deep breath while I closed the drawer and leaned my back against the cabinet.

"Thanks Skyla, for the form and for the chat."

He rolled the form and his copy of the complaint up and stuffed them in his back pocket.

"We need to chat more often in the time I have left," he said.

"You mean before you dive into eternal matrimonial bliss?"

"Actually, I meant before I leave for Princeton. Guess it doesn't matter since they're happening practically at the same time."

"And when is that?"

"June of next year. You know, it's a peculiar place we're in, me and you. Think about it. You're moving out of something into the unknown and I'm stepping into something totally unfamiliar to me."

"Humph...you're stepping into something alright. I just hope it's not a bunch of bullshit."

He laughed, exposing his perfectly white teeth and a killer smile.

"I'm sorry for being so cynical. I didn't used to be," I said.

"It's okay. You're entitled to a little short term cynicism. Just don't stay there long. You're way too pretty and smart to become blinded by bitterness and miss a good man when he comes along."

"I'll try to remember that. I just keep telling myself that one day, I'll see the blessing in all of this."

"Did you two have kids?"

A knot formed in my throat. I looked down at the floor and swallowed hard to get rid of it.

"Um…no. We weren't blessed with any kids."

"That might not be such a bad thing. Divorce is often way harder on the kids than it is on the parents. So in your case, that's one less child who will have to grow up in a broken home or worse, potentially saddled with an abusive stepfather. To me, that is the blessing."

And with his last statement, the damn broke and water was spilling out of my eyes again. Despite his point, I still felt cheated out of motherhood and was a long way from ever viewing it as a blessing under any circumstance.

"Aw man, I'm sorry Skyla. I didn't mean to upset you," he said, soothingly rubbing my arms.

He darted over and partially closed the door, then rushed back over to me.

"Come here. I didn't mean to make you cry," he said, enfolding me in his arms.

I leaned in and settled my head on his chest while my tears soaked his beige, cashmere sweater. Even in five inch heels, the top of my head barely touched his chin. The more I cried, the more I felt the firmness of his biceps tightening around me.

He began stroking my hair with one hand while caressing my back with the other. I raised my head and his eyes met mine with a sincere look of concern. My tears slowed and I became lost in his comfort.

Before this day I honestly never paid much attention to Jonathan. But life had thrown me an emotional curveball that forced me to open my eyes and admit that this man gripping me was fine.

He was about 5'10 with a thin, but muscular build. His kinky, curly black locks and goatee neatly framed his face and when he smiled his warm brown eyes took on an oriental shape and almost disappeared into his smooth, reddish brown skin.

The only thing I knew for sure about him was that his work at CRED had earned him a future opportunity to pursue a doctorate degree from Princeton. He even looked the part with the rimless glasses he wore.

Now we were frozen in each other's path, unwilling to relinquish the embrace. His sympathetic gaze suddenly turned passionate and when we were as close as we could get, he guided his lips towards mine and I closed my eyes.

Chapter Two

Jonathan's Unraveling Seams

I was engaged to be married in six months, eleven days and five and a half hours. Yet, here she was in my arms with those haunting black opals looking up at me. Truthfully, I'd fantasized about this moment, but this wasn't exactly how I envisioned it. Still, I didn't care. This was an experience I'd longed to have with her, even if I'd gotten it by default during an emotional meltdown.

We'd shot the morning breeze at the coffee machine and at different office functions, but I honestly struggled to ignore her beauty every time I saw her. But now, in this moment, I could allow my eyes to travel the smoothness of her honey colored skin against the back drop of her shoulder length hair and explore the curvature of her breast and hips until our chemistry naturally united and formed an undeniable bond. Then, the door swung open.

"What the hell is going on in here?"

Skyla and I scattered to opposite sides of the room when Chase burst in.

"Aw, come on, not you!" he said, playfully stumbling around while holding his heart with both hands.

"Damn Jonathan, I thought you were my boy! So this is why you won't give me a chance Skyla? You're cheating on me with him?" he joked.

Skyla began to giggle. Seeing her smile brought a smile to my face too and soon I was cracking up. Chase had that ability. Although uncouth at times, he could always be counted on to deflate a situation and lighten it up by saying something outrageous.

"Nothing's going on man. I was just making sure she was okay. That's all," I said.

"Well if you're gonna leave me Skyla, at least you're in good hands. I taught him everything he knows." He slapped me on the back while grinning.

"Chase, we were just talking," Skyla insisted.

"Y'all were talking all right, with body language."

"Come on man, let's leave her alone and go grab some lunch," I said, dragging him from her office. We got our coats and boarded an empty elevator. On the ride down, he stood smirking at me with his arms folded while shaking his head.

"What?"

"You know what, you slick bastard. I didn't think you had it in you," he said.

"If you're talking about Skyla, it's not what you think."

"Yeah, right. That's exactly what I told my girlfriend when she caught me up on the down stroke with her aunt."

"That's your life not mine."

"Man, just stop it. You think I haven't noticed the way you look at her?"

"Who doesn't look at her —hell, she's attractive."

"Yeah, but I look at her with lust, the same way I look at all women. But you, now your look says something completely different."

"Ok, whatever."

"Come on Jonathan. It's me, Chase, you're talking to. The last thing I'm gonna do is judge you. You're a grown ass, about to be married man. It's about to be a wrap for you so I don't blame you for trying to get with a Vet like Skyla."

"Vet?"

"Yeah, fuck that Cougar shit. She's a Veteran. And every time she walks by, my dick stands at attention and solutes!" he said, cracking himself up. "She may not look it, but she's got us by about five years. She's still fine though."

"That's not what I consider, older. In fact, if I had time, I could probably teach her a thing or two about life."

"Life? Man, shiid. I'd rather teach her how to handle my package with care." He grabbed his balls and howled with laughter.

Once outside, we started down the street towards the nearest Subway sandwich shop.

"Man, you're crazy. She's way too classy to ever consider fucking you," I said.

"I dun had classy chicks before. But, once I get those drawers off, I can turn a high class, sadity chick into a screamin', ebonics speakin' freak in no time. Have her washin' and wringin' my draws out with her teeth. But this ain't about me. It's about you and how you plan to spend your last days as a free man. You sure you wanna go through with it? I mean, are things really any better between you and Mia?"

"On some days, they are. But on most days, they're not, like today. We were supposed to meet and handle some business at noon, but she was nowhere to be found."

"That's fucked up. She wasn't always like that in undergrad."

"I know man. I've invested too much to turn back now though."

"But what kind of return will your investment yield, that's the question."

I sighed.

"I know. It's complicated," I replied.

The rest of the lunch hour was filled with wild chronicles of the many women Chase had screwed, was screwing or wanted to screw. But while his tales of coochie conquering were entertaining, my mind was still on my earlier encounter with Skyla.

As we headed back, we passed the Willis Tower and I started feeling a little sentimental.

"I'm gonna miss Chicago. Just think, this time next year, I'll be roaming the esteemed halls of Princeton University."

"Wow! I know I clown a lot, but I'm proud of you man."

"Thanks. It's not every day a brotha gets to go to Princeton. I feel blessed. Got any words of wisdom for me?"

"As a matter of fact, I do. Get all the pussy you can before you hear the click of the ball and chain fastening around your ankle. And, if you get a chance with Skyla, you better hit it and knock it out of the galaxy. Then, report back to your commander and chief."

We laughed as we stopped in front of our office building and went our separate ways.

Over the next couple of hours, I conducted three in-home interviews with various study participants and their families. But I honestly couldn't shake the experience I shared with Skyla and thought the best way to deal with it was to go and see my soon to be wife, quick!

The ride to Mia's place gave me a chance to put things back into perspective. There was probably always gonna be some alluring woman I wanted to get to know or some sexy chick I wanted to smash. I just hadn't counted on Skyla being both at this time in my life. But I'd finally made a choice to move forward with Mia and I planned to live with that choice, no matter how I was tempted at work.

I popped in my Tony Guerrero CD and let the tune, "Mysterie" flow through my ears.

###

Once at Mia's, I ran up the stairs and let myself in. I could hear her on the phone and traced the sound of her voice to her bedroom.

"Look, it has to be Cerulean Blue! I don't care if you have to dye the orchids the night before and put them in the damn dryer. I'm paying you a lot of money and I expect the shit to be done right! I will not compromise on this, Tom!" she screamed into the phone.

I went to the kitchen to get a Coke. While my head was still in the fridge, she came and embraced me from behind.

"You know I still don't think it's fair that you have a key to my place and I don't have one to yours," she whispered.

"You've had three keys and lost them all," I faced her and replied.

"So get me another one," she said, hugging and beaming up at me.

"Damn!! What the hell happened to you?"

I held her face and examined it closer.

She pulled away and went and sat at the kitchen table.

"Another incident at work. A few of the customers got rowdy and as always, a brawl broke out. When security tried to break it up I got caught in the middle and this time my tooth got knocked out."

"Babe, you've gotta get another job. I mean, last month you ended up with 12 stitches in your lip. The month before that, you broke your hand. Now, I know the hours work great with your casting call schedule, but maybe you should try working at a restaurant or some place a little more tranquil."

"Sweetie, the tips at restaurants are nothing like they are at bars. Besides, this will all be a distant memory when I get that Oscar someday."

She came and put her arms around my neck while smiling up at me. But, I couldn't get past the hole where her other front tooth used to be.

"Don't look at me like that. I've already made an appointment to get it fixed tomorrow," she said.

"Tomorrow? Mia we don't have that kind of money to keep paying for emergency services every time you...... Have you been taking your medication?"

"Here we go again. I told you I don't need that stuff. I'm not depressed and I'm not bipolar. I've just been suffering from a little PMS that's all."

"Baby, PMS is a temporary condition. What you have is more like AAB, cause lately you're always a bitch. Now I'm serious, you either start back taking your medication or..."

"Or what Jonathan, you'll leave me? Is that what you were gonna say?"

"Babe, if the medication helps then why not stay on it?"

"Do you love me Jonathan?"

"What?"

"You heard me."

"Of course I do."

"Then, where were you this morning? We were supposed to meet at your job and go put a deposit on the reception hall."

"We agreed to meet at noon, Mia. I was at the gym this morning. I told you last night I was going. So where were you?"

"You're the reason I'm like this, you know."

"Don't say that. Everybody has to deal with something and this just happens to be your cross to bear."

I wasn't even sure I believed those words anymore. I just wished we could go back to the way it was when we first met in college. She still had some residual issues from a past relationship, but she at least seemed normal. But after that night, she became a different person. I just couldn't bring myself to abandon her especially sincc deep down, I knew she was right. It was my fault. If only I hadn't stayed up studying for three days straight. I wouldn't have overslept the next night and would have been there to walk her home when she got off work from Target. After that, things were just never the same between us.

"What the hell is that? Is that makeup?" she screamed, touching my sweater.

I looked down and saw residue from Skyla's earlier breakdown.

"It is makeup! Why the fuck are you even here Jonathan? I can't do this anymore. Just leave. Get the fuck out!"

"Mia calm down." My Blackberry started vibrating through my pants. I pulled it out and saw an email from Skyla:

Call me, please. I really need to talk to you, the message read.

I only realized that I was smiling when Mia slapped it out of my hand, sending it gliding across the kitchen floor.

"Who the fuck is that? Probably the same bitch the makeup belongs to, isn't it. Just get out!" she screamed.

"You sure about that?"

"I said get the fuck out!"

I picked up my Blackberry and left without saying a word. Then, the slew of apology text messages began just like they always did after one of her tantrums. When I didn't respond to the first 17, she started calling non-stop. This had become a vexing pattern and I was growing tired of it. No matter how I tried to will us to be happy, things were just off between us. It was like we got caught in a subtle rainfall that grew into a tumultuous storm that neither of us was equipped to navigate. And even though I intended to weather the storm with her, my commitment was slipping and I felt it every time I was around her.

I was just about to turn off my Blackberry when I noticed I'd also missed a call from Skyla. I checked to see if she'd left a voicemail and she had. She sounded anxious and needy—not bad, annoying, stop fucking calling me, needy. But the, get over here and service me right now!—kind of needy.

I listened to it again and as the cadence in her voice rose and fell, I found myself heading back to the office in hopes of satisfying any little pesky need she might have.

Chapter Three

Pinning the Pieces Together

As I sat trying to focus on work, thoughts of Jonathan kept cutting in, interrupting my productivity. So what, he was engaged. He was still a man and that's what men do when presented with an opportunity. They take advantage of it. So, of course he was gonna try to kiss me earlier. But, what was my problem? Why did I want to kiss him back? Must be the grief. Yeah, that's it. I was just grief stricken and drunk with sorry. Figured I'd read a couple of self-help ebooks and listen to my Iyanla Vanzant podcasts and I'd be fine.

Who was I kidding. Though it had been awhile, I was starting to feel the early budding of lust and it felt good.

"Now that's the Skyla I know and love. What's got you staring all off into space like that?" Bree asked, entering my office with a garment bag. She folded it over an empty chair and sat across from me.

"Hey girl, you've been shopping already? Well, let's see what you got," I said, changing the subject.

"Oh, this? Well my friend, this is for you."

She passed me the bag and I gasped as I opened it.

"My pants!"

"I had them cleaned. Now they're just like new."

"Thanks Bree! I didn't know what happened to them and just assumed the cleaning people had thrown them out."

"Throw out a pair of Valentino slacks? I'd have their hands cut off. Now those panties, that's a whole other story. But what's a friend if she can't throw out her BFF's bloody underwear. I hope you don't mind, but I tried on your slacks."

"Now you know your size four ass can't fit my pants."

"I know, but I still had to try them on. I just wanted to see what they felt like. Anyway, I'm glad I could bring a smile to your face. You were so down the other day that I thought I'd never see that smile again. But you were sitting here with that goofy grin before I came in. So what's up?"

Before I could open my mouth, Candice rushed in.

"Hi ladies. Bree, I'm sorry but I really need to speak to Skyla alone. Do you mind?" she asked.

"Not at all. Talk to you later, Sky."

Candice closed the door and sat expressionless in front of me. I went around and took a seat next to her.

"What's going on?" I asked.

"Have you read Angelica's full complaint against Jonathan?"

"Yes, I have."

"And what's your gut telling you?"

"I don't know. I mean, he just doesn't seem capable of what she's accusing him of."

"Maybe not. But, they say he can be pretty aggressive in the field."

"Don't the analysts have to be a bit aggressive? They do go to some rough neighborhoods. Besides, just because someone's aggressive doesn't mean they would call their boss a fat, white bitch and threaten to kill her if she calls them again, now does it."

"Not necessarily. You have good judgment so I know you'll use it when you make the final determination."

"Final determination? What do you mean?"

"Well, there's more to all this morning sickness than I thought. I've been diagnosed with Hyperemesis Gravidarum."

"Oh God, that sounds awful!"

"It's a rare, but severe form of morning sickness and I've been ordered to go on bed rest immediately. That means you'll be assuming all of my responsibilities, immediately. You are now the Acting Project Director and Sonya's your part-time assistant. Aren't you glad I forced you to get that mediation certification from DePaul?" she asked, patting my cheek.

"So, will I be assuming your salary immediately too?"

"Well, not quite. But, you will receive a $35,000 raise, should you choose to accept this challenge. And, since there aren't any other options, congratulations on your promotion!"

"But I…."

"Wait, it gets better. Do a good job with this hearing and the acting part of your title goes away and you'll become the Project Director permanently. I'll still be with CRED, but only in a consultant capacity, so you'll still report to me."

"Is this a joke? Are we shooting some type of office themed reality show? Come on, where're the cameras?"

"This isn't a joke. It doesn't get any more real than this."

"Wow, this is a lot to digest Candice. So, what if I screw up the hearing? Am I out of a job?"

"Don't sabotage yourself with doubt. You have the skills to get to the bottom of what really happened. Use them. Then decide if Angelica is just full of shit, which we all know she can be. But it has to be proven. On the other hand, this organization and everything we do represents Princeton. We have a reputation to uphold and if we end up awarding a full scholarship to an erratic, hotheaded, asshole, then that would reflect poorly on your decision and the organization as a whole."

"So basically, you're saying Jonathan's fate hangs in my hands."

"And yours in his if you side with him, and he later turns out to be a jerk. Don't worry. I know you'll come to the right conclusions." She stood and pushed in her chair.

I rushed around to catch her before she left.

"But Candice, I don't think I can…."

"Stop it Skyla, just stop it. Stop talking yourself out of things you deserve. I've been watching you. You might not have a PhD, but you're just as smart as anyone else around here and you're a harder worker. So, I have no doubt that you can and will handle this. You've sat in on enough hearings with me to know what to do. Just read the material, listen to both sides and make the best logical decision you can make. Now, gotta go. Give me a hug."

She threw her arms around me and squeezed.

"You know you can always call or Skype me with questions. Your paperwork is being adjusted."

She stepped back, gripped my shoulders and while looking me straight in the eyes said, "You can do this Skyla."

"Thanks Candice. Take care."

I watched her leave and afterwards sat on the couch dumbfounded with my elbows resting on my knees and my hands clasped together. One thing was clear. In order to secure my new position, I would have to get to the bottom of what really happen between Jonathan and his manager. But to do that, I'd also have to get to know him better. Since destiny had already started the ball rolling on the latter, all I had to do was continue its plan. Seemed simple enough.

I went to the ladies room and when I came out saw Angelica waving me into her office. I entered and stood in front of her desk.

"Look, I know Jonathan's hearing is scheduled for next Friday. But I'm leaving town next Wednesday and don't know when I'll be back. So, let Candice know we'll have to move it up to Tuesday," she said.

"Absolutely not Angelica. You've already accepted the invite. You can't just change it and expect everyone to scramble to accommodate you. Plus, you know that's not sufficient time for him to prepare a rebuttal. And Candice is now on maternity leave, so I'm taking over her position."

"You?? Geesh. Affirmative action strikes again around here."

"What did you just say?"

"Nothing. Well, I have an emergency to tend to, so you'll just have to change it."

I looked into her beady little eyes and knew she was lying. She was an obese, olive complected woman with wild wavy brown hair shooting up all over her head. Her greenish, gray eyes were encased in a large, oval face and her chin extended to the top of her chest.

The last roll in her stomach protruded to her mid thighs and her daily wardrobe seemed to be filled with oversized black tents. Some co-workers even complained that she had a fowl body odor. She'd earned a reputation for being crass, but I'd managed to escape any run-ins with her….until now.

"What kind of emergency?" I asked.

She paused for a minute then looked at me as though I was committing a crime simply by asking.

"It's private."

"Angelica, this is serious. If you're going to change a disciplinary hearing, we need a valid reason."

"Ok, they're gonna cut my mother open and yank out her gallbladder. That valid enough for you?"

"Umph, hope it goes well. I guess we have no choice then."

She smiled, quadrupling her already tripled chin.

Once I returned to my office, I called and emailed Jonathan to inform him of the change. Then, I went back to the file that housed the complaint against him and reviewed it from all angles. Still, none of it made any sense.

The clock on the wall read 7:30pm. While checking my Blackberry to see if Jonathan had responded yet, another text from Phillip popped up:

Look, this is stupid and I don't have time for this shit! If you don't call me or come home by the end of next week, I'm filing for divorce!! Is that what you want????

I quickly typed, Do whatever the hell you gotta do! but before sending it, got up and stood looking out the window behind my desk. The sky had grown dark amidst the lighted high-rise office and residential buildings lining the surrounding streets. Suddenly, a male voice said,

"Nice view from back here…,"

I jumped and turned to find Jonathan observing me from the doorway. I was surprised by the sudden surge of happiness I felt and couldn't stop myself from smiling.

"You scared me. How long have you been standing there?" I asked.

"I'm sorry, didn't mean to get you spooked. I got your messages."

He began walking slowly towards me then stopped in front of my desk.

"It sounded urgent so I came back to see what you needed. Is everything okay? You wanna talk about this morning?" he asked.

"We do need to talk. Not about this morning though. That can wait."

"Well, I'll be around for another six months."

"In that case, we shouldn't waste any time."

He licked his lips and grinned mischievously while joining me in front of the window. We gazed out at the skyline in silence. He reached back and cut my desk lamp off leaving only the city scene outdoors illuminating the room.

"Sometimes, I could just look up at the stars all night," he said, staring at the sky in wonderment.

"You have that kind of time?" I asked, looking up at the sky.

He turned to me and with a piercing look replied, "I make time for beautiful things."

I could feel myself blushing and started fidgeting with my Blackberry.

Just then, he leaned into my neck and inhaled deeply.

"Damn, you smell good," he whispered, allowing his lips to brush lightly against my earlobe.

My palms started to sweat as he moved closer. I quickly turned to cut my lamp back on and dropped my Blackberry. He bent to pick it up and placed his face as close to my leg as possible, blowing on it while slowly standing. My flesh tingled as the warmth of his breath traveled up my calf and reached my thigh.

"Here ya go," he said in a low tone, handing it to me.

I clumsily took it, inadvertently hitting the send button on the earlier reply I'd typed Phillip. But I didn't care.

He sat on the edge of my desk and swallowed my hand with his while drawing me between his legs.

"What did you want to talk about?" he asked, taking his fingertip and gently sweeping a portion of my hair behind my left ear.

"Oh….um, um…" My brain searched for words while my eyes became stuck on his lips. "It's Angelica," I said.

His mouth began moving closer to mine.

"Yeah, what about her?" he asked, continuing to come closer.

My heart started racing and I felt weak.

"She…she's gotta do something," I mumbled.

"Something like what?" he whispered, lips lightly grazing mine. I wanted to pounce and run away at the same time. I took a step back, but he quickly caught me by my waist and pulled me into his arms. Suddenly Candice's warnings were in my head and helped to free me.

"Look, the schedule for your hearing has changed," I said, untangling myself and starting towards the couch.

I sat down and hooked my legs into a tight fold. He came and sat next to me with one arm resting atop the couch. I moved over, pushing myself as far away from him as possible.

"You don't have to do that. I won't bite, unless you want me to," he said, smiling seductively.

I couldn't help but grin back.

"I don't want you to do that," I said.

"What do you want me to do?"

"I want you to go to Princeton and become a world renowned… whatever it is you're trying to become."

He chuckled.

"A child psychologist," he replied.

"So you like kids."

"Love kids. They're one of the most important things in life. So many of them grow up in turmoil though and just end up becoming dysfunctional adults, thus repeating the cycle and polluting the world."

"Well, maybe you can prevent a lot of that from happening."

"That's the goal."

"And a noble goal it is."

Our conversation stopped and we sat gazing at each other. His eyes found their way to my breast and he began staring at them as if trying to summon them to pop out of my dress with his mind.

"You really are beautiful, you know that," he said, scooting over to me.

"Thanks. You're kind of fine yourself. But we should probably talk about what really happened between you and Angelica."

Despite my efforts to redirect his focus back on his hearing, his eyes were taking a road trip over my body with his latest stop landing on my lips. And even though we were technically committed to other people, I couldn't help imagining him making a pit stop in one particular area.

Chapter Four

Wrinkles & Creases

As Skyla's plump, reddish lips spoke to me, I kept my eyes on them and wondered what else they could do. Suddenly, she stopped talking, drawing my attention back to her eyes. Our glance turned into a stare and then became intense—so much so that she abruptly broke the vibe between us.

"The hearing is next Tuesday instead of Friday because Angelica is leaving town on Wednesday," she sprang to her feet and blurted out.

"What? She can't do that! Can she?" I jumped up and said.

"She doesn't know when she'll be back, so I'm afraid she can. These cases have to be reviewed within two weeks of the complaint so this is the only time she can meet."

"But, I'm not prepared!"

"Well, you need to get prepared."

"What did Candice have to say about this? Was she cool with this?"

"Oh, that's the other thing. I'm now responsible for the disciplinary hearings. Candice had to take some time off."

My mind began to race as I nervously rubbed my forehead. I stared at the floor and felt myself starting to pace. Suddenly, I stopped as what she'd just said sunk in.

"You???" I scoffed.

Now I was really panicked. I mean, if Angelica were a dude, then maybe Skyla's pretty face, plump ass and cleavage could help me out. But now that Candice was gone, the only thing that could possibly help me win Angelica over was a slab of ribs.

"Relax Jonathan."

"Look, I know you've sat in on these things and taken notes before, but you don't know how to…."

She shot me a look of warning.

"I mean, I just hope you can be objective," I said.

Suddenly I realized I was coming unglued in front of her and felt naked. But, her expression softened and her compassionate eyes told me it was okay to fall apart and I believed them. She came over to me and touched my arm.

"I know this is a sudden change Jonathan, but you have to use your energy to focus on coming up with the best rebuttal possible. Angelica isn't the most credible person, so I'm willing to help you as much as I can. And, as far as being objective, that certificate on the wall over there confirms that I'm quite capable."

Just as I was coming to grips with the fact that I wanted this woman in various ways, my desire had suddenly been joined by my need for her as well. I listened to the passion in her voice and trusted it. Trust was an emotion I'd grown distant with and it felt comforting to get acquainted with it again.

She suddenly became aware of her lingering touch on my arm and took a step back. Refusing to release the connection, I moved closer and stopped just inches away from her. I wanted to say something, but my words remained hidden. She looked up at me as if trying to read my mind, then turned and headed for her seat. My eyes followed the rhythm of her every step until she sat down.

"Thank you Skyla. I could really use some help right now." I sat down across from her.

"Have you written anything so far?" she asked.

"No, I haven't had time."

Just then, her stomach growled.

"Sounds like you haven't had time for some things either," I said.

"The day just got away from me."

"Why don't you let me take you to dinner so we can talk about this more."

She looked at me with distrust. But, after a brief pause her expression changed to a look of benevolence.

"I guess that would be okay," she softly replied.

She grabbed her purse while I got her coat and helped her put it on.

"Do you like Mexican?" I asked.

"I love Mexican."

"Good, 'cause I know this nice little Mexican restaurant not too far from here."

"What's the name of it?"

"Casa Diego."

"I've been to Casa Diego and it is far from nice. In fact, it's a complete dump, but the food is good."

As we left her office side by side, I purposely slowed my pace and took the long route to my cubicle.

"So, where did you work before CRED?" I asked.

"At Buford & Schmidt."

"You're kidding—the Ad Agency on Jackson and Clark?"

"That would be the one."

"I worked across the street at the Chicago Alliance for Community Unity. It was a small non-profit and I was one of their community organizers. What did you do at Buford & Schmidt?"

"Well, they lured me into the position after college with promises of becoming a senior copywriter within a year. But instead, I ended up licking envelopes and unwrapping sandwiches for their corporate lunches."

"Yeah, that's corporate for you. Sometimes they think that's all we're capable of. And before that, where did you work?"

"Before that I wrote press releases for Kipling & Sadler, a small PR firm ran by a bunch of overly caffeinated women in need of a good lay."

Suddenly I stopped walking.

"Off Michigan and Wacker?" I asked.

"Have you been stalking me?" she replied with a smile.

"Not intentionally. I took a couple of public administration classes in that same building at the Kellum Institute of Learning."

We continued walking without saying a word.

"It's really strange that we've been in such close proximity, yet remained strangers all this time," she said.

"Yeah, it's almost like we've been moving towards each other until the universe finally allowed us to meet."

Once at my desk I got my coat and briefcase. She surprised me by walking all the way into my cubicle and looking around while standing really close to me.

She began examining the strewn of framed photos on my desk.

"Is this your mom?" she asked.

"Yep, that's her."

"She's absolutely gorgeous. Does she live here in Chicago?"

"She passed away when I was very young."

"Aw….I'm so sorry, Jonathan," she said with a genuine look of sympathy as she put the picture down. Now she was standing so close that her arm was touching mine.

"And what about this one. Is this your Grandma?" she asked.

"Very good. It is."

"I can see the resemblance between all three of you."

Then she zeroed in on another photo. She picked it up and held it so close it almost mashed her nose. Suddenly, she looked flustered, like she was about to become ill.

"You okay?" I asked.

While pointing at the picture she timidly asked, "Is this your fiancée?"

"Yup, that's Mia."

Her mouth dropped open as she continued staring at the picture. She pushed it far away from her face then moved it right in front of her eyes while gaping at it. Finally, she hesitantly said, "She wouldn't be in need of some urgent dental care, would she?"

"How did you know? Do you two know each other?"

Just then, she put the picture down and backed up nearly tripping over the trash can.

"Um, I just remembered I have some errands to run so I better go. I'm really sorry Jonathan," she said, darting off towards the elevators.

"Errands?—at 8 o'clock at night?" I began chasing behind her.

"Maybe some other time."

"What about tomorrow night then? Or maybe we could do lunch if you're busy in the evening."

"I don't think that's a good idea."

"Well, wait. Skyla, would you wait a minute!" I grabbed her arm.

She looked down at my hand, making me aware of how tight my grip was.

"I'm sorry." I let go and held up both hands. "What's the matter? Did I say or do something?"

"No Jonathan. It's late and I've really got to go."

She boarded an empty elevator then disappeared leaving me both confused and intrigued.

Chapter Five

Smoothing Out the Wrinkles

The next morning, I purposely took the train to work. That gave me a chance to review the barrage of threatening text messages Phillip continued to send. Plus I needed time to think—to figure out if God had looked down on my life and decided he either needed some entertainment or I needed a challenge. Or maybe he wanted to stretch me to see if my heart, mind and soul would recoil back to their original positions after being toyed with and shattered. Maybe they weren't supposed to go back and instead I was meant to go forth with all of my recent calamities and become someone new. But who would this new woman be? And why, pray tell, was Jonathan Bass becoming part of that newness?

I continued this inner rumination while dragging myself through the motions until hot coffee overflowed onto my hand in the office lunchroom.

"Shit!" I screamed, dropping the cup.

"Well, good morning to you too, Sky. Doesn't sound like a woman happy about being promoted. Congratulations!" Sonya said, whizzing by me and placing her lunch bag in the fridge.

"Thanks Sonya. I guess I should say congrats to you too."

"Thanks boss!"

She threw her arms around me and hugged me enthusiastically.

"Everything else okay?" she asked.

"No, but I'll survive."

I went to the sink and ran cold water on my hand.

"That's right. We strong black women always do," she said.

"Thanks for the reminder."

"Girl, you don't need a reminder. God is on your side. Like I told you the other day after the uh....incident, I got you. But, every time I think about what happened I just crack up."

She burst out giggling again.

"You wouldn't be laughing if you knew who the victim was."

The laughter stopped and her eyes popped open.

"Shut up! You know?"

I dried my hands and nodded yes.

"Well who is it?"

"Since you are the first line of defense, I guess you should know in case she comes back. It was Jonathan Bass's fiancée."

"OMG! Those two do not need to be together."

"Why do you say that?"

"'Cause, I mean he's cool and all. But he can get kinda crazy too."

"Sonya, are you saying that because you witnessed it or are you just repeating gossip?"

"Both. You can't trust no man who doesn't believe in God and reads all them philosophy books he be readin'. Then, wanna come up in here and argue with me about the holy trinity and whether or not Jesus was just a prophet or the Messiah."

"So this is personal. But have you ever seen or heard him like—curse anybody out?"

"No, I've never seen him do anything like that. That's what he has the crazy fiancée for I guess. Why are you asking?"

"No reason."

"Well, have a good day boss," she said before exiting.

As I approached my office, I could see Bree rearing back in my chair with her feet on my desk. As soon as I walked in she jumped up, rushed around me and locked the door.

"Okay, I'm not letting you out of here until you tell me what the hell is going on. I knew something happened between you and Phillip, but why in the hell do I have to hear from the ghetto grapevine that you're getting a divorce and got promoted? I'm supposed to be your girl."

"I'm sorry Bree. I've been meaning to talk to you. God knows I need to talk to someone about everything that's been happening."

"Well, I'm not just, someone."

She took a deep breath and sighed then dropped down in the chair in front of me.

"Alright. Give me the tea," she said, folding her arms.

"Okay. Phillip is an un-rehabable dog. I guess I've always known it but I kept waiting for him to mature and get it out of his system. That's never going to happen.

So, I have to leave him before his actions turn me into someone I hate."

"But, do you still love him?"

"What does it matter? Marriage requires way more than love."

"Well, that's true but…"

"Bree, my mind is made up."

"Okay. What about the miscarriage. How are you dealing with it?"

"I'm not. Don't know how to just yet."

"You know what you need? A girls night out where we can just throw on some sexy dresses with no panties on and let our titties hang out while throwing back some Mr. Funk's punch."

"Now, that sounds like fun. Let me know when."

"Next payday, after I get my new weave."

"Ok, it's a date."

"Now in the meantime, do you need me to do anything?" she asked softly.

"Yes, you can help me find a place to live. If I have to spend one more night scrunched between my parents watching reruns of The Jeffersons, I'm gonna scream!"

"Woo, that would drive me crazy too. We gotta get you outta there. And I know just the place. There's a vacant townhouse in my subdivision, so it's as good as done. Hell, you could probably move in this weekend."

"Please don't get my hopes up Bree. Just talk to the property manager and let me know what they say."

"Well, he's gonna say yes because I'm fucking him."

"Breeeee!"

"Don't Breeeee me. We got a pretty good thing going on."

"Oh lord, please tell me he's not married."

"I would, but that would be a lie."

"Bree!"

"Now Sky, you've never judged me before. Please don't start now."

"I won't. I just know I could never date a married man and wish you felt the same. I want you to find some nice, single guy to go out with."

"Me too. Where are they? You got any you can loan me?"

"What about Chase?"

"Chase who? Chase Bank? 'Cause I know you're not talking about that idiot Chase Foley in IT."

"That's exactly who I'm talking about."

"I'm gonna let you in on a little secret. I test drove that ride and the engine ain't all that. Just roars loudly."

"What? Are you saying you slept with Chase?"

"Yes ma'am and it was the worst. I swear, sometimes I wish there was a tutoring school like Sylvan or Huntington where the no-fucking brothas could go and learn how to hit it right-maybe even a Can't-Fuck Anonymous or something."

I laughed until my side hurt and tears were streaming down my face.

"Why do you think he goes around talking about his dick like it's his invisible best friend all the time. Insecurity, my sista," she said.

"Oh wow. I don't think I'll ever be able to look at him and keep a straight face anymore. When did you…"

"A long time ago. A bunch of us went out for drinks after work. I had too much Mr. Funk's punch and woke up in Chinatown with eggrolls on my head, if you know what I mean. It's funny that no matter how much you've had to drink, your body can still recognize bad sex."

"You're too much!"

"Well, I better go. You better do some work too so those checks can keep rolling in."

"I know. Oh, don't forget to find out when I can see the townhouse."

"I know it's soon but what about lunchtime today? You can trail me out there."

"That would work if I'd driven today."

"No problem. I'll just drive and we can get something to eat on the way back."

"You sure?"

"Positive. I'll call Michael and let him know we're coming. Trust me. This is going to work out perfectly."

When noon rolled around, Bree and I drove out to the Stone Village Townhomes in Forest Park. We were both in a chatty mood, so the ride went quickly.

"Congratulations on your promotion. That's fantastic!" she said.

"Thanks girl. I feel a bit overwhelmed, but I'll manage."

"I bet your bank account isn't overwhelmed."

We laughed and high fived each other.

"So where does this Michael and his wife live?"

"In one of the townhomes in my subdivision."

"Aw, Bree—don't you think that's a little too close for comfort."

"No, it's convenient as hell and it saves on gas."

"Aren't you worried at all about the wife finding out?"

"If she does, that's his problem, not mine. I'm not married to her."

"Woo, girl. That's cold."

"It may sound cold Sky, but it really isn't. It's very simple. She treats him like shit and makes him feel like a dumb schmuck and I make him feel like he just won the lottery."

"And what about you, how does he make you feel?"

"Like there's hope."

"How can dating a married man give you hope?"

"I won't be dating a married man forever. One day, I'll meet a single man who wants to be committed and I'll be married and miserable, just like you. But, until then, I'm going to bask in my freedom and continue my thrice a week trysts with Michael. I'm going to enjoy his company and allow him to enjoy mine when I feel like it. And I'm going to keep letting him take me on weekend trips to Vegas and long vacations in the Bahamas."

"You deserve so much more."

"Oh please Sky—let's not even talk about what I deserve, what we both deserve. You didn't deserve to be underappreciated and for Phillip to treat you like crap but he did. Life doesn't operate on the deserve system. You have to grab your happiness by the balls and take it."

"I just still believe that two people can fall in love and honor and respect each other for the rest of their lives."

She looked at me then rolled her eyes.

"You really are an incurable romantic aren't you," she said.

"Yep."

"So, you would do it all over again—this marriage thing."

"You're damn right I would. Phillip was just one asshole. All men aren't like him. He didn't recognize me as a gift. But someday God will regift me to the right man who'll see me as a blessing."

When we arrived at the gated community, Bree pulled up and parked in a reserved spot right in front of the management office.

"Won't you get a ticket if you park here?"

"I'm fucking him, remember."

We entered the office and were greeted by a gorgeous light skinned woman with curly, sandy brown hair.

"Hi Bree," she said, smiling and standing to hug her.

"Hey Stacy. I want you to meet my good friend Skyla Richards."

"You can call me Sky."

"Nice to meet you Sky."

"What are you doing here? Isn't it your day off?" Bree asked her.

"Michael had to go handle some repairs at one of our properties in the City so I'm in charge. Gives me a chance to check and make sure he's not screwing things up around here. He should be back any minute."

"Good. Sky is interested in that vacant townhouse on Peekoe street and I was hoping he could show it to her."

"Well I have keys, I could show…."

Just then a six foot something man with the smoothes dark brown skin I'd ever seen walked through the door. He was just as striking as Stacy and I was starting to wonder if they both moonlighted as models.

"Hey Shorty," he said, bending and greeting Bree with a firm hug while lifting her off the ground.

"Hey big guy," Bree responded. "Sky. This is Michael. Mike, this is Sky."

"Please to meet you Sky. Bree's told me a lot about you," he said, his large hand gripping and shaking mine.

"Likewise," I said.

"I was just about to show Sky the townhouse on Peekoe. She's interested in renting it," Stacy said.

"Oh, no problem baby. I've got my keys. I can take them over and show her. You go on and go. I'll see you later at home," he said.

"Okay," she replied then stood on her tippy toes and kissed him on the cheek.

Afterwards, Bree and Michael watched her leave while exchanging eager grins with each other. Once she was completely out of sight, Michael slid his long, arm around Bree's waist and pulled her to his side. Then, he bent down and kissed her passionately.

"Come on Sky, I'll take you all over in my truck," he said afterwards, holding the door open for us.

I climbed into the back seat of his white Lincoln Navigator while Bree sat next to him in the front passenger seat. As soon as we pulled out of the parking lot, Bree scooted over close to him and he put his arm around her. Maybe their unabashed affection was all a ploy to purposely get caught. And if that was the case, I didn't appreciate being part of their scheme and wanted to get this over with as quickly as possible. While they grinned and whispered to each other, I ignored them by checking my Blackberry.

Soon, we pulled in front of a row of red-bricked, three story townhomes encased in light gray A-frames.

"Well, here it is," Michael said as he parked and undid his seatbelt.

He got out and began rummaging through a set of keys. Bree and I walked behind him and she hooked her arm into mine.

"Well, what do you think?" she asked, giggling like a little girl.

"He's fine, I will say that. But he's married Bree."

"Urgh....," she said, dropping my arm. "There you go again. How about we not have this conversation."

"Well, you asked."

"You're right. I won't do it again."

By the time we reached the townhouse, Michael had already opened the door and gone in.

"Now this is one of the newer models Sky. I haven't actually been in one of these," Bree said.

Now I was worried. I'd always admired her townhome. But if this place was a dump and I had to hear, Well, We're Movin' On Up....,one more night I was gonna go insane!

We stepped in and I gasped while looking around.

"This is absolutely beautiful," I said, slowly turning and examining the space.

The main level had vaulted ceilings with floor to ceiling bay windows overlooking the front yard. The sunken living room and recessed lighting gave the place a modern-techno kind of feel and the pale yellow walls added just the right splash of brightness.

The hard wood flooring flowed into a cozy kitchen with granite countertops, light oak wooden cabinetry, stainless steel appliances and a breakfast bar with stools underneath. Across from the fridge was a cutout overlooking the living room. The dining area was just off the kitchen and was enclosed by French patio doors. Through the French doors was a small fenced in patio housing a gas barbeque grill and a charming little outdoor fireplace.

On the other side of the fence was a community pool and sunbathing area.

"I'll take it!" I said.

"But you haven't even seen the rest of it. This place is way nicer than mine, so I'm sure it's gonna cost a grip," Bree said.

"Don't worry, I can handle it," I replied, pulling out my checkbook and a pen.

"Oh I forgot, you're Ms. Baller now," she said.

"Don't hate."

We giggled like nine year olds jumping double-dutch at recess.

"I'm glad you like it. Our motto is we want you to love where you live," Michael said.

I couldn't help but snicker as he and Bree were taking that motto way too literally.

"It's $1175 a month. I knocked off $200 cause you're Bree's friend. We require two months security down. I'll collect it when you finish your paperwork. Let's go back to the office and get started," he said.

"Aw baby, we've got to get back to work. Can she just take the paperwork with her and I'll bring it back with her check once she completes everything?" Bree asked.

"You know I can't say no to you," he replied then bent down and gave her a slow, sensual kiss.

"I'm just gonna head to the car. Thanks for your time Mike," I said as their kiss lingered.

The two of them finally joined me and we headed back to Bree's car then back to work.

"What time is it?" Bree asked as we drove.

"Almost 2:00pm."

"Whoa, I don't think we'll have time to stop and eat."

"That's okay. I'm not that hungry anyway. Let me ask you something."

"Shoot."

"What do you think about Jonathan Bass?"

She began to cough.

"Ennngaagggeed, Jonathan Bass? I know Miss, I would never date a married man, is not inquiring about Jonathan Bass!"

"Well, he's engaged, not married and I just wanna know what you think about him. That's all."

"He's fine and sexy as hell. Intelligent too. But he seems way too intense to be a good rebound guy. Something about him makes me nervous for you. I just don't want you starring in his real life version of Stevie Wonder's Rocket Love video. You know—take you high up, then drop your black ass down to the cold, cold, world."

"I love that song. But I definitely don't want to be the video ho in that scenario."

"Well, stay away from him. Right now, you need a nice, simple man that you aren't attracted to."

"Who says I'm attracted to Jonathan?"

"Well you just did by getting so defensive."

We pulled into our office parking lot and headed back to work. Before parting I gave her a hug.

"Thank you girl. You've done so much for me over the last couple of days, I don't know how to repay you," I said.

"Oh, I'll think of something," she replied before heading to her office.

Since our trip to my new potential home took longer than expected, I closed my door in hopes of catching up on the day's work. Just as I fell into a grove, someone began pounding on my door. I immediately felt anxious and imagined it was Phillip. Then I heard Jonathan angrily yelling my name on the other side of the door.

Chapter Six

Tightening Loose Threads

I sat at my desk trying to concentrate on my case load. But the thought of being under the same roof with Skyla and not getting an explanation for why she ran off the night before was eating at my brain. I needed her to face me and tell me what the hell happened. But my pride wouldn't let me just walk into her office and ask. So, I resorted to roaming the floor in hopes of bumping in to her.

As I got near the reception area, the subtle notes in her perfume found me and I began following its scent.

"Oh, Hey Jonathan."

"Hey Sonya."

I breezed past her and continued with my hunt.

"How's the wedding plans coming along?"

I was more use to heated debates over religion with Sonya so her affability startled me and made me stop.

"Everything's coming along just fine. Thanks for asking."

"Now, when is the wedding again?"

"It's June 28th of next year."

"Oh. Well she'll have plenty of time to get that tooth fixed before then."

Her comment puzzled me and she grew jittery.

"I mean....uh....well, everybody wants their teeth to look nice in wedding photos, right?" she asked in a panicked tone.

Suddenly, my mind synced her statement with Skyla's disappearing act and I knew the two had to be related.

"What do you know, Sonya," I brusquely asked.

She stood up and leaned in close.

"Okay, look Jonathan. She didn't mean it. But, your crazy fiancée came in here and started yelling and cussing at us.

And…well…she's under a lot of pressure and she just snapped. But it was your fiancée's fault. I mean—Skyla would have never taken it that far had your fiancée not put hands on her first."

Now everything made sense and I immediately felt uptight.

"Jonathan, please don't say anything. If you do, she could lose her promotion, thus causing me to lose mine and it really wasn't her fault."

I turned and began walking towards Skyla's office as fast as I could without running. I hadn't quite figured out my approach yet. But, she was gonna have to tell me something.

When I got there, her door was closed. I gave it three hard thumps as if I had a search warrant. She didn't answer.

"Skyla! Open the door!" I yelled, causing our surrounding co-workers to look up and take notice.

Finally the door slowly swung open.

Damn. Why couldn't she be cross-eyed, bucktoothed and baldheaded. Then I could hold on to the confusion and fury I felt.

But no. She had to be fixing those black opals on me in a tight, nipple outlining, white blouse and a black pencil skirt that gripped her lower silhouette.

"Yes Jonathan?" she said with one hand holding the door, and the other placed ever so femininely on her hip.

"Are you busy?" I calmly asked.

"Come in," she replied.

While prancing to her seat in burgundy stilettos, my eyes became stuck on her frame and I almost forgot why I was there.

"You wanted to talk to me?" she said, leaning to one side in her chair with one leg crossed over the other.

"Uh, yeah," I replied.

Now I had her. But the last thing I wanted to do was give her a reason to feel justified by blowing up at her. I had to play it cool—disarm her with my charm—get in her head and play hockey with her thoughts.

I closed the door and stood leaning on the back of one of the chairs in front of her desk.

"How are you today?" I asked, flashing her my best mack daddy smile.

"I'm okay."

"Just okay? Well, you look lovely as usual."

She smiled wide and bashfully lowered her eyes.

"You should smile more often. You light up the place when you do."

"Thanks Jonathan."

"You know, it helps that you have really nice teeth too. Teeth are important. Take mine for instance. It took a lot to get them this straight."

She began squirming around in her chair as her smile wilted. Now it was time for the coup de grace as I continued;

"I remember taking that picture when I was little—you know the one where even though your two front teeth are missing, your ass is still cheesin' like there's no tomorrow. Aw man, thank God they grow back before we're grown. That would be fucked up to have to walk around as a grown ass adult missing a front tooth, now wouldn't it?" I said with a straight face.

She jumped up, snatched a file folder off her desk and stumped over to the file cabinet with an irritated look.

"If you've got something to say to me Jonathan, then just say it!" she barked, yanking open one of the drawers.

"I'm just saying…,"

"You're just saying what, huh?"

Her voice grew heavy and her eyes began to water.

"You don't know….." she said in staggered breaths while turning her back to me. With one hand on her hip and the other rubbing her forehead, she began sobbing.

Ok, this was going horribly wrong.

"In front of my entire family I found out my husband was cheating. Then, I miscarried. Then, your fiancée was yelling, cursing and spitting in my face and I just lost it, okay!" she said, voice trembling and quivering.

She turned around and grabbed a tissue and while wiping her eyes said, "You happy now?"

I immediately felt like the biggest asshole on the planet and instead of feeling compassion for my betrothed, I switched teams in that instant and wanted nothing more than to comfort Skyla.

"Aw, baby I'm sorry," I said, folding her in my arms.

Once again, she was using one of my sweaters as her personal handkerchief.

"Come over here, let's sit down." I took her hand and lead her towards the couch.

I locked the door and sat first then pulled her next to me by her waist. I placed my arm around her and she cushioned her head against my chest.

"Let's just sit here for awhile," I said, stroking her hair.

I let about 20 minutes pass so her emotions could air out. The tears were still flowing, but much slower and her breathing had returned to normal.

"So, you lost a baby, huh."

She nodded her head yes and I gently kissed her forehead.

"Nobody knows except for you and Bree. It happened the day you came in here for that COB form."

"Ahh. That's why Bree kicked me out."

She nodded yes again while the tears slowly continued.

"Baby I'm so sorry. I wish I could have been there for you."

It sounded ludicrous, but it was true. I mean, I barely knew her. But with the little sharing we'd done I felt closer to her than I'd felt to Mia in years.

She stood and got another tissue then fixed her makeup in the full length mirror on the back of her door. I sat helplessly watching her, leaning forward with my elbows on my knees.

"You're still fine. You don't need to do that. Why don't you let me take you to dinner tonight."

"I don't need a sympathy meal Jonathan."

"It has nothing to do with sympathy. You promised me you'd help me with my rebuttal. I've got problems too sista."

She chucked.

"Jonathan, you're about to go to Princeton. You know how to write. You don't need me."

"That's true, I mean the part about knowing how to write. But, you know how to mediate, so I do need you."

She took a deep breath.

"Okay. I'll go to dinner with you, but not tonight. Let's go tomorrow night instead. Where do you want to go?"

"Well, you know I'm just a young brotha out here trying to make it on an analyst's salary so is Burger King okay?"

That drew a hardy laugh out of her.

"Sure, if that's the best you can do," she replied.

"You know I'm kidding. Let me surprise you."

"Okay."

I got up and stood behind her and felt compelled to put my arms around her waist. She caught me off guard by covering my arms with hers as we studied our union in the mirror.

"We look good together," I said, then kissed her on the neck.

"Tell that to your psycho fiancée."

"Let me deal with that. You gonna be okay?"

She untied our knot and went back to her chair.

"I'm gonna be fine. But, thanks Jonathan."

"Anytime. I mean that."

"I know you do," she replied with a half smile.

I wanted to stay, but knew it best that I left.

On my way home, I ignored the repeated calls from Mia. I felt incensed and embarrassed that she went and acted a complete fool at my job and I wasn't ready to talk to her. I was hoping she didn't pop up at my place because I didn't want to see her either. I mean, this was getting to restraining order levels and I just didn't know what to do about it. But I knew I had to calm down before I bumped up the statistics by becoming another black man with high blood pressure. I popped in my Najee CD and let Romance the Night settle my mind.

Chapter Seven

A Flattering Fit

Thank God it was finally Friday and this horrendous week was coming to a close. What made it even better was that the organization had recently declared Fridays, Jean day, and I felt quite relaxed in my Lucky Sofia Skinny jeans. Friday was also my designated filing day, so I cranked up the playlist entitled, filing music on my computer and dove into the first stack on my desk. About a half hour into it, my phone rang.

"Hello."

"How are you today Ms. Richards?"

A smile immediately spread across my face as I turned the music down.

"I'm fine Mr. Bass. How are you?"

"I didn't ask how you looked. I asked how you are."

"That's original."

"Well, seeing as how you're an old lady I had to hit you with one of those throwback lines from your era."

"Whatever."

"What do you have on?"

"A black blouse and some jeans."

"Stop lying."

"I'm not lying."

"You do remember we're going out tonight."

"I know, but it's blue jean Friday and I wanted to be comfortable, so I brought my clothes for tonight."

"Ooh. I totally forgot about blue jean Fridays."

"Are you working from home today?"

"And miss a vision of you in jeans, not a chance. I'm gonna make a quick trip in just to see you."

"You don't have to do that Jonathan. You already have to come back to pick me up tonight. I don't want you to have to make two trips. That'll be too much."

"There's no such thing as too much when it comes to you. And, that's not a throwback line. That's a fact."

"If you insist."

"I'll see you shortly."

"Drive safely."

My cheeks were aching after I hung up from all the constant smiling. I hadn't experienced that in a long time and was surprised that he was having that kind of effect on me so soon.

I partially closed the door and turned the music back up. Now, a jam was playing and I couldn't resist putting my hands on my knees, poking out my ass and twerkin' to Beyonce's Baby Boy. Soon, I became swept up in the beat as I threw my hands in the air and swayed to the music while shaking my hips.

I shimmied over and examined my moves in the mirror then bounced back over to the file cabinet and started singing while still moving to the rhythm.

"Wow, look at you! Don't stop now," a familiar male voice said, startling me. I turned around and Jonathan had his hands in the air too as he danced close to me and starting singing Sean Paul's parts of the song. He took my hand and held it up. As I slowly swirled in front of him, his eyes remained locked on my jeans. I felt embarrassed but also flattered by the attention.

"Damn, guess I won't be working from home on Fridays anymore," he said over the music.

"Why not?"

"And miss you giving out free lap dances in jeans, I don't think so."

I turned around and danced with my back to him as he moved in closer, lightly tapping against me.

Suddenly, the music stopped.

"Uh, excuse me. How come no one told me we were holding Soul Train auditions today?"

"Oh, hey Bree. We didn't even hear you come in," I said.

"Yeah, I could see that," she replied, staring at us with rebuke.

I glanced at Jonathan from the corner of my eye. His focus was still below my waist as he folded his arms and licked his lips.

"Well, hello to you too Jonathan," Bree said.

"Huh, oh hey Bree," he replied without lifting his eyes.

"Alrighty then. Sky, call me when you uh, get free," she said before leaving.

While I walked back to my chair, I could feel his stare following, only releasing me when I sat down.

"So, Mr. Bass, can you give me a hint as to where you're taking me tonight?"

I cut the music back up a little.

Before he could answer, the phone started ringing.

"Hello."

"You're on dangerous ground. You two are really playing with fire," Bree cautioned.

"What are you talking about?"

"Sky, I'm serious. Not only could I see it, but I could feel the heat between you two. Please be careful."

Thanks for your concern, but I'll be fine."

I got up and went and stood by the window as Jonathan continued bobbing his head to the music. While adjusting the blinds for more light, I whispered into the phone,

"It's just a little harmless flirting, that's all."

"In case you didn't know, that's how most train wrecks start. Look, I know you began dating Phillip at a young age and now you want to play. I get it. But I don't think you know what you're getting yourself into. I just want you to find a less complicated playmate, that's all."

"I'm not getting into anything. I can't really talk right now, but I'll call you later. Bye."

Jonathan was now sitting on the edge of my desk. I sat down in front of him and leaned forward with my chin resting on my fist. He leaned in close as well while smiling.

"Now, where were we? Oh yeah, you were going to give me a hint about tonight," I said, turning down the music.

"Well let's see, we're going to get high and possibly dizzy. Then, we're going to eat."

"Are you taking me to a Reggae spot?"

"Nope."

"Your weed smokin' cousin Pookie's house?"

He laughed. "Nope."

"To the…."

"You're just going to have to wait until tonight. But I see you're really curious. That's good. I like that."

He got up and stood in front of my desk with his hands in his pockets.

"Can I have a hug before I go?"

At the moment, I didn't see any harm in it…..until his biceps were wrapped around me and our eyes were hooked into a yearning gaze while his hands caressed the small of my back.

"I can't wait to see you tonight," he whispered, making me feel flushed.

I had no ready response. I just stood there fixated on his lips while my hands found their way into his hair.

He slowly began loosening me. But I wasn't ready to be freed. So I clung a little tighter until I felt like initiating the release.

"I'll be back at 7:00pm. Be ready," he said, stepping back and dragging his hands over mine before backing out of the doorway with a confident but furtive grin.

Maybe Bree was right and we were playing with fire. But at this point, the gas cans were full and we had a lifetime supply of matches. Still, I didn't see a need to call 911 just yet.

The hours floated by nicely. Then I looked up and noticed it was 5:45pm. I suddenly felt panicked and started straightening up before proceeding to select one of the two dresses I'd brought with me to wear to dinner. But I was having trouble deciding. So as usual, the unsolicited advice from my two inner commentators began:

Wear the one that covers you the most. It will appeal to his intellect, allowing him to get to know the real you, my quiet voice started.

Intellect my ass! Put on the short, hip huggin' one with the plunging neckline. The man is 25 so no matter what you wear, his attention is gonna be on your knockers, my loud voice shouted.

You don't want him to get the wrong impression. You want him to like and respect you for you," my quiet voice softly reasoned.

Hey, Mother Teresa—did you see the way they were bumpin' and grindin' to the music earlier? I'm afraid it's a little too late for first impressions. So, go ahead and use this second impression to show him what you're really workin' with! my loud voice screamed.

The next thing I knew, I was zipping myself into a sleeveless, mid thigh, spandex black dress with a v-shaped lace bodice while my loud voice sang a victory chant and did the Cabbage Patch in the background.

To balance the hoochie with a little class, I threw my hair into a low, side chignon with opposite side front bangs and accented the total look with small, crystal earrings. I toned down the makeup a bit and lightly re-spritzed myself with perfume. But, the black stilettos were a must.

Butterflies began boxing in my stomach and I couldn't wait to see him again. I wrapped my shoulders in a sheer, black nylon scarf and sat waiting while listening to soft jazz. To settle my nerves, I decided to take another stab at a spreadsheet I was having trouble balancing earlier. After refiguring the numbers, I was still $6.29 off. I felt frustrated and began tapping my desk repeatedly with a pencil before noticing a pair of black men's shoes walking through my door.

All of a sudden, I felt subconscious like a 16-year old prom bound girl desperate for her date's approval. I wanted him to speak first and continued drumming my pencil on the desk while staring at the spreadsheet.

I could see him from the corner of my eye just standing there gawking at me. Was he really going to make me do this? Judging from the forced silence, yep—he was. I turned my head slightly to acknowledge him. Damn!!! Time for a silent prayer:

Dear gracious and merciful Father, please forgive me for not wearing any panties tonight. Help me to keep my dress down and my tongue in my mouth. Please keep us both and keep our hands on anything but each other. And, if either of us should happen to trip and land on top of the other, let us quickly regain our balance and part ways immediately. Amen.

The scent of his cologne was now traveling up my nostrils while he sat on the edge of my desk with a sexy grin.

"You have no idea how you're affecting me right now, do you?" he said.

I didn't realize I was smiling back until it was my turn to speak.

"If the butterflies in my stomach are anywhere near similar to what you're feeling, then I have some level of awareness," I replied.

He took and kissed the palm of my hand then held onto it.

"Don't be nervous," he said gently pulling me to my feet.

I let the scarf drift off my shoulders and land in my chair before grabbing my purse and allowing him to lead me over to the door. I released his hand as he retrieved my coat. But when I stuck out my arm to slide it on, he shook his head and threw it over his other arm.

"We're not outside yet. Just let me enjoy your appearance a little while longer," he said, locking and closing the door behind us.

Suddenly, he grabbed me by my waist and said, "Let's commemorate the moment," before pulling out his phone. "On the count of three say, sexy and smile." Then he proceeded to count while holding his phone in front of us and snapping a picture.

"Ahh, now that's nice. Look," he said, showing it to me.

"That is nice. Send me a copy."

"I will."

His large fingers merged between mine. As we walked towards the elevators, he tilted his head behind me and said, "What a wonderful sartorial choice you've made tonight Ms. Richards. You never cease to look anything less than stunning. Makes me want to see what you're like when you're all sweaty and dirty," then winked.

"Thank you Mr. Bass. You look quite dapper yourself. I love the tieless black shirt on you and the charcoal gray suit fits you perfectly."

"Thank you."

"Where's your coat?"

"In the car."

"You're going to catch pneumonia."

"I'll be fine," he replied, pressing the elevator button.

Once it came, he allowed me to board first then stood peering down and smiling at me.

Goosebumps began forming on my arms and my nipples sprouted out. My loud inner voice's earlier prediction suddenly came true as he couldn't take his eyes off of them.

I nervously slid my clutch purse under my arm and folded my hands together. He threw my coat over his shoulder and unfolded my hands then began massaging the backs of them with his thumbs.

"You sure are frisky for a man about to be married in six months."

"There's just something about you that collapses my boundaries and scrambles my judgment."

He took his index finger and moved my bangs out of my eye.

Once off the elevator, he finally helped me slip on my coat. But before taking one step towards the parking lot, clasped my hand again as we walked.

"So, you're still not gonna tell me where we're going," I said.

"Nope. You're just gonna have to be patient and wait."

He opened the passenger door of his Silver Jeep Cherokee and I slid in and unlocked his door. Soon as he got in he turned and retrieved a large shiny black rectangular box with a huge elaborate red bow from the back seat.

"This is for you," he said, handing it to me.

My eyes lit up with surprise as I undid the bow and opened it.

"Oh my God Jonathan, these are beautiful," I said, examining two dozen long stemmed red roses accented with white calla lilies.

"Read the card.....out loud," he said.

"Okay:"

Whatsoever things are beautiful, that gives light its shine; whatsoever things are lovely that gives flight its rise; whatsoever things are everlasting that gives fate its mission, I ask my love, which one are you?"

My eyes began to water as I looked over at him. He was grinning at me as if he expected an answer.

"You like it?"

"I love it. Thank you so much Jonathan. That was very sweet."

Now my guard was bending and I wanted to thank him in several ways. He took the box and placed it on the back seat. Then he slowly reached over, grabbed my seat belt and buckled me in.

"Safety first," he said.

His hand was clutching mine again as he took quick glances at me while pulling into traffic. I couldn't contain my excitement and grinned back like I was about to board the Screaming Eagle at Six Flags.

As we drove, we seemed to be getting further away from downtown and I didn't recognize the route at all. We pulled into a gas station and he parked and undid his seat belt.

"Are we lost?" I asked.

"Nope. Be right back."

Minutes later, he returned with a brown paper bag.

"What's in the bag?" I asked.

"Guess."

"I don't know—a half pint of Hennessy and some Tops?"

"What?"

"Well, you said we were gonna get high and possibly dizzy."

He laughed.

"Neither Ms. Richards."

He turned over the bag and a pack of Extra sugar free gum fell out. He opened and unwrapped a stick and tossed it in his mouth.

"You can't be the only one with fresh breath," I said, holding out my hand and waiting for him to give me a piece. He unwrapped another stick and held it to my lips. I opened my mouth and he placed it on my tongue then slowly drug his fingertip across my bottom lip.

As we pulled back into traffic and began driving towards downtown, he grabbed my hand again. It started snowing lightly causing him to slow down.

"Tell me about your family," he said.

"Well, my dad drives a bus, my mom is a nurse and my older brother is a musician and singer."

"Oh God, you're the only girl and the youngest? You're spoiled as hell."

"But not rotten."

"I guess I'll have to keep up the tradition then."

"You don't have to do anything."

"But see you every day."

He kissed the back of my hand then squeezed it.

"What about you? Tell me about your family," I said.

"There's not much to tell. My life was a cesspool until my grandparents intervened when I was ten. My grandmother is a retired postal worker and introduced me to my first love, books. And my grandfather was a carpenter by trade."

His mood suddenly turned somber and I didn't quite know how to shift it back into happy gear.

"Well, everything happens for a reason. Sometimes, we can't see God's plan. We just have to trust that he has one and it's usually to help people who've gone through similar experiences as us."

His silence became deafening, but I was determined to break it.

"Do you see your grandmother often?" I asked.

"Not as often as I'd like since she took in and started raising a relative's kids. That's Momma G—always rescuing and taking care of somebody. I still manage to talk to her once or twice a week though."

"That's good. Family is really all we've got."

"I'm starting to believe that."

We were on Michigan and Chestnut when he turned into one of those self-park parking garages. After taking a ticket and quickly finding a spot on the ground level, he got out and came around and opened my door. This time, he put on his coat.

As we started down the street, it hit me like a sack of potatoes. I'd lived in Chicago all my life, but had never been to the top of the John Hancock building—especially to sit and spin while eating at the Signature Room.

"Can I just tell you again how gorgeous you look?" he asked.

"You may, but this is the last time tonight. You don't want me to start questioning your true intentions."

"You can question them all you want. I'm prepared to be quite honest about my intentions with you."

He covered my hand with his then shoved them both into his coat pocket.

"Oh? And what are they?" I asked.

He stopped walking and we stood facing each other as snowflakes lightly sprinkled us. While looking into my eyes he said, "To show you how you should always be treated so you'll never settle for anything less."

I could have just passed out right there in the middle of Michigan Avenue. But, the ground was cold and wet and I didn't have on any panties, so we kept it movin'.

Finally we were there. We boarded an empty elevator and stood side by side. After we'd reached the 45th floor with no joiners, he stepped in front of me and slid his arms around my waist. We rode in silence while he smiled and held me. I beamed up at him while silently talking my arms out of embracing him and my lips from ambushing his.

The elevator dinged once when we got to the 95th floor and he turned and exited first, holding the door while I stepped off. He took my hand and led me into the slowly rotating restaurant.

The candlelit tables coupled with the wintery cityscape outside of the floor to ceiling windows lent an extremely romantic ambiance to the atmosphere as he took charge of the night.

"Jonathan Bass, reservation for two," he said to the blonde maitre d' standing behind the podium in the entryway. I stood behind him marveling at how his confidence superseded his age.

"Right this way Mr. Bass," the maitre d' said, leading us to a window table for two with menus in hand.

"Jack, your waiter will be with you shortly. Enjoy," he said before returning to his post at the podium.

Although the maitre d' had pulled out my chair, Jonathan took my coat and waited for me to be seated before trekking to the coat check.

I sat looking over the menu while taking a couple of sips of water. He returned, opened his suit jacket and sat down. I pulled a tissue out of my purse and deposited my gum in it then held it to his lips for him to do the same.

"So, what will it be? Black-eyed peas and ham hocks?" he joked.

"I think we're a little far North for that to be a menu item."

"Seriously though, what's your favorite food?"

"I love Mexican. Love the Cantina Grill down on Twelfth Street. But I can be flexible. In fact, Taco Bell has an under 300 calorie Fresco menu that I could eat from every day."

"Ah, Se Senorita."

"And what would your favorite dish be?"

"Spinach Lasagna. Not that frozen crap. Homemade."

Just then the waiter appeared at our table and rattled off the specials for the evening.

"I'll just have the Herb Roasted Chicken," I said.

"And I'll have the Chorizo Stuffed Pork Chops."

"Very good. And what will you have to drink?"

"I'll have a glass of Joel Gott Unoaked Chardonnay," I said.

"Wonderful. And you sir?"

"I'll have a glass of Rutherford Hill Merlot."

"Excellent choices," the waiter said before disappearing.

Our pupils were glued on each other again as the flicker from the candlelight casted shadows on our smiles.

"So were you surprised?" he asked.

"Pleasantly surprised and shocked actually."

"Have you ever been here before?"

"Nope. You're my first."

"Good. I want to be your first for many more things to come, starting with this."

He sprang from his chair and walked over to the live pianist seated in the middle of the restaurant. He whispered something in his ear and on his way back, the pianist began playing and singing a song I'd never heard before.

Jonathan was now standing at my side with his hand extended.

"Dance with me."

"Jonathan, nobody else in here is dancing."

"Don't be afraid of new experiences," he said in my ear.

And with that, I was gripping his hand, gliding to the center of the restaurant where we ended up next to the piano. He held me close and looked into my eyes. As we slowly moved to the music, he asked "Do you know the name of this song?"

"I gather from the course it's, Can't Get Started With You?"

"That's right. There're so many things I want to do with you, so many experiences I wish we could share. But, like this song says, I can't get started with you."

"We can always dream."

"I've been dreaming. But my dreams are no longer vivid enough. I want you live and in color, the way you are now."

The lyrics and rhythm of the song hinted that it was from a different time when neither of us were probably born.

"Okay, that's not exactly what most guys your age have in their iTunes playlist. And Franklin D and Garbo are decades ahead of both of us. So, how do you know a song that ancient?" I asked.

"I know a lot of things and good music, not that shit they play over and over again on the radio, is timeless. I want to reveal many things to you, but.."

"Let me guess, you can't get started with me." We chuckled.

The song ended and he took my hand and led me back to our table. To our surprise and my extreme embarrassment, everyone in the restaurant was now smiling at us. Even the waiter was standing at our table displaying a goofy grin as if he wanted an autograph. And Jonathan was loving it, so much so that I thought he was going to take a bow.

"You two make such a lovely couple. How long have you been married?" the waiter asked as we sat down.

Jonathan smiled back at him and said, "When you love each other the way we do, you don't count the years. You count the memories."

"Aw, that's so sweet. Your meals will be out shortly."

I picked up my glass of wine that had been placed on the table and took a huge gulp. Jonathan gave me a fiendish smile and took a sip of his wine too.

"So, let's not forget why we're here," I said.

"We're here because the universe wants us to be here."

"I think the universe probably wants your hearing to go well so you won't lose your job along with your opportunity to attend Princeton."

"That's not going to happen."

"And how do you know?"

"Because you're not going to let it happen. I have every confidence in you Ms. Richards."

Just then, the waiter returned with our plates.

"Careful, they're hot," he said, sitting our entrees in front of us.

By now, I was famished. But instead of grabbing chicken parts and gnashing meat from the bone like I was at some sort of medieval times festival, I used my silverware and cut small portions and delicately placed them in my mouth.

Jonathan cut his food then kept his eyes on my lips as we ate.

I took another sip of wine.

"How's your food?" he asked.

"It's delicious. Want some?"

"I would love to taste your meat," he replied with a devious grin.

I couldn't help but smile and shake my head while cutting him a piece of chicken. He placed his hand around mine and guided it to his lips, slowly lifting the chicken off my fork with his tongue.

"Mmmm, now that's good. I knew it would be. You want to taste mine?"

"No thanks."

"Come on. You know you want to. It's really good. Try it," he urged, cutting me a sizable chunk and placing it to my lips.

"Now, take it in slow and swallow, so you can really savor the flavor," he said, sliding his fork into my mouth.

"You were right. It's delicious," I said while chewing.

"See, I told you. You want some more?"

"No thanks, really. You go ahead and enjoy it."

We continued conversing between bites until I finished first. Even though I was still hungry, I saw no need for him to know what a devourer I could be and had only eaten half of what I'd ordered.

He took his time and had one pork chop left before putting his fork down.

"Man, that was good. We must do this again Ms. Richards."

"Don't you have a wedding to help plan?"

"My time is limited, this is true. But I'm sure we could find some spare time to see each other again."

"Spare time, what's that?"

"It's after work, on weekends, before work—anytime that isn't sucked up by responsibility."

"I know what it is. I just don't have a lot of that these days."

"What are you doing this weekend?"

"Moving."

"So, you're really leaving your husband?"

"Yep. My way of giving back to the community."

"You're strong. Most women want to be married so bad, they would have just stayed no matter what was going on."

"Well, I'm not most women."

"Oh, I'm well aware of that. Perhaps I can help with the move."

"I've already blackmailed my brother into helping me."

"Well, I'm sure you have something that'll need assembling. I'm very handy. Maybe I could drop by on Sunday and help put something together or uh, fix something that's been broken."

"Thanks, but if I have any energy left, I plan on going to church on Sunday. That's a good place to start when fixing broken things. But, I guess you wouldn't know anything about that cause I heard you don't even believe in God."

"Who told you that? I absolutely believe in God. I'm just not sure he needs the son and the holy ghost as his two sidekicks."

I gasped loudly, placing my hand on my chest.

"Blasphemy Jonathan Bass! You're going straight to hell."

"And I'm taking you right with me. That way, I can get to know you better before I enter into the fiery gates."

I sat all the way back and finished my wine.

He sat gazing at me with one elbow hutched over the corner of his chair while slowly turning the stem of his wine glass with his other hand.

"I'm curious, what do you do when you're not working?" he asked.

"I teach job readiness skills in the hood in conjunction with the Park District two nights a week. And, I volunteer at a local nursing home every other Saturday."

His eyes lit up and he smirked at me.

"You really are an angel on earth," he said.

"I wouldn't go that far. And how does a young man such as yourself keep busy when he's not at work or with said fiancée?"

"Well, you know I'm still in school finishing up my Masters at the University of Chicago."

"I didn't know that."

"Yeah, I'm almost done—just got a few more credits to get before officially qualifying for the doctorate program at Princeton."

"I thought you'd already been accepted."

"I have. But, it's still contingent on me finishing up a few credits and of course completing my internship at CRED."

"Speaking of CRED we still haven't talked about your hearing. So I guess we'll have to get together again after all. Maybe Monday over lunch."

"That would be wonderful. It's a date."

"Engaged men can't date."

"What do you call this?"

"This was a business dinner," I said, leaning forward and folding my hands on the table.

He chuckled then took and held both my hands.

"Dear, sweet Skyla—my little delusional angel you," he sneered.

I smiled at him and began gently stroking the back of his hands.

"You're sitting here holding my hands with your calls forwarded to voicemail and I'm the delusional one?" I scoffed right back.

He spread my fingers apart with his and began rubbing between them.

"The truth will set you free and the truth is lovely lady, this was a date."

I drew my hands from his and folded them in my lap while the waiter cleared our table.

"Did you want to take these home?" the waiter asked.

"Yes please," Jonathan replied.

Once the waiter left, he turned his focus on me with rapt attention.

"You seem apprehensive. Don't get so bent out of shape about it. In some cultures that's what the engagement period is for—to see if the woman you're affianced to is worthy of the prize," he said.

"And what backwards culture would that be? The man is never the prize. The woman is. She's the blessing."

"Says who?"

"Says the bible when it says he who findeth a wife findeth a good thing. It says nothing about a husband being a good find."

"So, you're a bible basher. Well, I don't have time to deprogram you tonight, but perhaps we can debate the bible some other time."

Just then, our waiter reappeared with doggy bags and dessert menus.

"Care for anything else?" he asked.

"Everything sweet I need is already at this table. But what about you love? Would you care to order something?" he asked, pulling out his Amex card.

"No thanks, I'm fine."

"Just the check then Jack. Thanks."

"Thank you for a wonderful evening Mr. Bass. I thoroughly enjoyed every moment of it."

"You're quite welcome. Looks pretty messy outside. I'll trail you to make sure you get home safely."

"You don't have to do that."

"It's no trouble. I actually like to drive."

He picked up the check and examined it.

"Even so, that would be a mighty long drive seeing as how you live all the way west in Oak Park and I live in the City."

Oh, shit. Now the wine was talking and there was no way out of this one.

He stopped signing the check and put down his pen.

"How did you know I lived in Oak Park?" he asked.

"Okay, I confess. I peeked through your personnel file."

He began laughing hysterically.

"I just needed to do a little investigating before we went out," I said.

"It's okay. That's actually kind of flattering. Look, I take safety very seriously so I feel responsible for your safety as well. If it makes you feel any better, I promise to just make sure you get in and leave right afterwards."

"How about I just call you when I get home and let the phone ring once," I bargained.

"It's a deal."

We left the restaurant and started back towards the parking garage hand in hand again.

We stopped at the corner and while waiting for the light to change, a homeless man stumbled up to us holding out a mug. He wearily asked us for some change and looked as though he could pass out at any moment.

"Sorry sir, I don't have any change but here, you can have this," I said, shoving my styrofoam container in his hand."

"Bless you ma'am, thank you so much. God bless you," he said, bowing repeatedly.

As we continued walking Jonathan bent down and kissed me on the cheek. I turned around to see where the homeless man had gone. He was sitting in the middle of the sidewalk enjoying the meal I'd planned on having for lunch the next day. Suddenly, I felt compelled to do more.

I snatched Jonathan's container from his hand and trotted back over to the homeless man.

"Here sir,' I said, handing him more leftovers.

As I walked back, Jonathan was waiting for me with a shocked look on his face.

"Close your mouth babe," I said, patting him on his jaw. I grabbed his hand and tugged him towards the garage. "I'm sorry, I hope you don't mind," I said.

"It's okay. I was just a little taken aback, that's all."

"Don't be mad at me."

"I could never be mad at you especially for impromptu acts of kindness. But damn, I kinda wanted that other pork chop, love—had my Louisiana hot sauce all ready for it."

"Tell you what. I'll make you some homemade spinach lasagna to make up for it."

"Uh oh, can you cook?"

I playfully punched him in the arm.

"Of course I can cook."

"Yeah okay, we'll see. You better not try to feed me none of that Stouffer's stuff either. I want the real thing. I'll know the difference."

Although we were just getting to know each other, everything about our connection felt natural, almost as if it had happened before.

Once in his truck, he reached for my hand and I reached back. His touch just felt so right that I couldn't resist.

"Man, I don't want this night to end. You sure I can't trail you home?"

I had to give it to him, he was tenacious.

"I'm positive. I'll call you when I get in. I promise."

"I'm gonna hold you to that promise."

We arrived at the office parking lot and exchanged a friendly hug.

"Here, don't forget these," he said, handing me my box of roses.

"Thanks again Jonathan," I said with a kiss to his cheek before getting into my car and pulling off.

As I drove with a fixed smile, my mind mulled over the details of the night. Jonathan was right about one thing; I definitely got high and dizzy, but not from one of Chicago's most famous landmarks. I couldn't stop thinking about the way he walked, talked, smelled and smiled. Had he belched and farted I would have been floating off of those fumes too.

Once at my parent's house, I opened the door and rushed in, leaving my roses in the car. Mom and dad were in their usual spots on the sofa cackling at George and Weezy's antics.

"Hello beautiful parents," I said sticking my head between them from behind and giving each a smooch on the cheek.

"Well, aren't you in a good mood," dad turned to me and said.

"Sure are," mom replied, inquisitively grinning at me.

She turned all the way around and examined me closer with a mother's eye.

"Where've you been all dressed up like that? That's not what you had on this morning when you left for work," she said.

"Aw Helen, leave the girl alone. She probably just went out with friends after work. Ain't that right baby girl."

"That's right Daddy."

"Well, it sure is good to see you smile again. So do whatever makes you happy sugga."

"Thanks Daddy," I replied, then kissed him again before racing upstairs to do what made me happy.

Once in my room, I locked the door and morphed out of my dress, liberating my village feeders. I found some comfortable panties to slip on then pulled Sadie and a pen out of my purse. I couldn't wait to talk to Sadie as I lay on my stomach and settled into my nightly routine. No matter how bad things got—how humiliating, painful or embarrassing the events, Sadie never judged, joked or told anyone. For that, I was committed to talking to her.

But tonight, I finally had something good to report as I began spilling out the details of my night onto her ruled, white pages.

Afterwards, I dialed the number Jonathan had given me earlier.

The phone was answered on the first ring.

"Blake's Pool Hall, Blake speaking."

"Jonathan? Is that you?"

"Hey, any of you guys in here named Jonathan? Nope, sorry lady. No Jonathan in here. Say, you wouldn't be one of the butt naked strippers we're waiting on would you?"

I recognized his voice and caught a serious case of the giggles.

"Hey lady, I wouldn't be laughin' if I were you. You've got a bunch of angry, anxious men here waiting to see some booty shakin' so I suggest you get your ass over here as soon as possible."

"Jonathan, quit playing."

"What's up, love. How come it took you so long to call me?"

"How come you answered? Thought we agreed to just let the phone ring once."

"You know you wanted to talk me. Now, answer my question."

"I wanted to get comfortable, you know—change clothes, relax a little."

"You could have done all of that with me. Maybe then you'd turn into one of those butt naked strippers Blake and his boys are waiting on. I could have made it rain on you."

I cracked up.

"Tonight was magical," he said.

"I agree."

"When can I see you again?"

"Monday at work."

"That's your story and you're sticking to it, huh."

"Yep."

He sighed.

"But I miss you," he said softly.

Truth was I missed him too, but I wasn't about to let him know that, especially while laying there half naked and horny.

"What are you doing?" I asked.

"Listening to music and getting ready for what I'm gonna do once I let you go."

"And what might that be?"

"The usual hygiene activities, then a little reading and some meditation."

"On your hearing no doubt."

"On a lot of things. The hearing being one of them, you coming into my life being another."

"You might want to pray on that last one as well."

"Prayer is a given. But when we meditate, we silence all the chatter in our heads and listen for God to talk back."

Hold up—you mean there is a way to hogtie and duck tape the mouths of those two blabbering commentators in my subconscious? I gotta try this meditation stuff.

"You there?" he asked.

"Oh yeah, I'm here."

"Thought maybe you'd fallen asleep on me."

"Never. I find you quite fascinating Mr. Bass."

"Likewise Ms. Richards."

Just then, I yawned.

"Go to bed and get some rest. I'll call you tomorrow," he said.

"Okay."

"Good night, love."

"Jonathan?"

"Yeah."

"Thanks again for a memorable evening."

"Play your cards right and they'll be many more to come."
"Oh yeah, how many?"
"As many as I can squeeze into the next six months."

Chapter Eight

The First Stroke of the Needle

I awoke the next morning to some idiot blowing his horn like a crazed maniac outside. I looked out the window and saw my brother, Drew parking a large U-Haul truck in front of the house. "Dammit, I over slept!"

I quickly washed up and rushed downstairs with a scarf still tied around my head. Now Drew was coming through the front door.

"You ready?" he asked.

"No, but let's go anyway."

"Are you sure Phillip isn't gonna be there? I really don't feel like whoopin' nobody's ass today," he said.

"I'm not sure about anything when it comes to him. I just know that he's usually at his office on Saturdays."

"Okay, let's do this," he said as we left and headed to the place I used to call home.

Over the next eight hours, we made three trips between my old house and my new one which were about 20 minutes apart.

Finally, all my stuff had been setup in the new place and it actually looked like a home. It's amazing what I'd gotten Drew to accomplish by threatening to tell my parents how dad's car really caught fire and how mom's Cartier watch ended up in the toilet when we were kids.

Now I was exhausted. Jonathan had called three times and I finally had time to return his call and couldn't wait to hear his voice.

The first call went straight to voicemail and I actually felt a twinge of jealousy. I waited 15 minutes before placing the second call which rang repeatedly, making me nervous. Suddenly, Ritz Crackers and pimento spread were on my mind, but I refused to kill my anxiety with a midnight snack. So, I waited 30 minutes before calling again.

"Finally I'm out of my misery," he said on the third ring.

"How are you?" I asked with girlish coyness.

"Better now. How did your day go?"

"Busy. I'm just now finding the time to call you back."

"Okay, I guess I can forgive you. I missed talking to you today."

"I missed talking to you too."

"If that's really true, you can make it up to me by preparing that home cooked meal you promised me after giving my vittles to Benny the bum."

"I said I would and I will."

"When?"

"Soon."

"That's not good enough. I need a date."

"Jonathaaaan….."

"Skyyylaaaa. You know you want to see me too."

"Maybe."

"Well, what about tomorrow?"

"We already discussed this. Tomorrow is Sunday."

"Very good. Move to the head of the class. You still going to church?"

I wanted to, but knew I was way too tired to make it to the 8:00am service. And as usual, if I didn't make it at 8:00am, I wasn't going to make it at all.

"I doubt it," I replied.

"That settles it then. If you want, I can pick up the ingredients and we can cook it together."

"No, I promised you a home cooked meal and I meant it. I'll text you my address."

"What time?"

"Sixish?"

"I'll be there."

"Oh, and don't forget to bring whatever notes you've written on your hearing. Unlike our date the other night, this dinner will be strictly business."

"If you say so. Sleep well."

"You too."

Before zonking out, I Googled, lasagna recipes and found one that seemed simple enough on Cooksillustrated.com. I'd just throw in a couple of spinach leaves, and voilà!

I stretched out, shut my eyes and tried to fall asleep. But the thought of seeing him again outside of work had me feeling wired, like I'd just guzzled a Grande Espresso from Starbucks. Then the phone rang. I answered without even looking at it.

"You can't sleep either huh," Jonathan said.

"It's just taking a little longer tonight."

"That's cause you can't stop thinking about me."

"Wasn't nobody thinking about you Jonathan Bass. I was just laying here trying to fall asleep and then the phone rang."

"You can lie to me, but don't lie to yourself. You wanted to hear my voice again just as bad as I needed to hear yours."

Did he say, need? Okay, now he was spittin' game. But, it wasn't gonna work on me.

"How's your fiancée holding up?" I asked.

"You mean the one you mollywhopped?"

He started laughing, but I didn't join him.

"I'm sorry baby. You got to admit the shit is pretty funny," he said.

"I don't think it's funny at all. Doesn't it bother you that I'm the one who put that hole in her smile?"

"Not in the way you think it does. Look, I'm not going to have too many more conversations with you about her. But, I see how much this is bothering you. I've thought about it and what happened wasn't your fault. The things that drove her to do what she did happened long before you two ever laid eyes on each other. So stop feeling bad about it. I don't want to waste anymore of our time talking about her."

"You really don't see it do you—the fact that there is a, her, to even talk about makes this whole thing so inappropriate."

"As far as I'm concerned, I'm still single and you're becoming single. This isn't a coincidence Skyla. Two people with the chemistry we have don't just stumble upon each other without some purpose behind it. We collided during this narrow window of time for a reason and I plan to find out what it is. I think it would be beneficial for you to know as well."

If I were ever facing 15 years to life, I would want him as my lawyer cause if that was his closing argument, then I'd surely be found, not guilty!

"Now can we please talk about something else, like what you have on?" he asked.

"I don't think you really want to talk about that."

"Yes I do. Tell me."

"A pair of lavender boy shorts."

"What material?"

"The kind that clings to every nook and cranny."

He took a long pause.

"And what else?" he asked.

"Nothing else."

The phone was silent again.

"Hello," I said.

"You're right. Maybe we should just say goodnight and talk tomorrow."

"Okay. Have a good night."

"You too, love."

###

The next day after breakfast, I went to get the rest of the ingredients I needed to make Jonathan want to smack his grandmamma. I couldn't believe how excited I was and actually felt something I hadn't felt in years, joy.

On my way into the store another text message from Phillip popped up:

It's 12 noon. You have exactly 1 week from this date and time to bring your ass home! If you don't, I'm filing for divorce and you won't see a penny!!! Understand me? NOT ONE FUCKING RED CENT!!! I know you're having some sort of breakdown, but hopefully you're not stupid enough to walk away from the best thing that's ever happened to you. Remember, ONE WEEK!!!!!

I didn't respond nor did I delete it. When I got home, I worked out then took a nap before getting up to cook. A few hours later, I got dressed and put on something sexy, but comfortable before slipping on a pair of high heeled wedge flip flops. Just before heading downstairs the phone rang.

"Hello."

"Hey pretty lady."

"Hey handsome man. You calling to cancel on me?"

"No way. Have you started cooking yet, cause there's a thick plume of black smoke that's got traffic backed up for miles. Is that you over there burnin' up stuff?"

"Very funny Mr. Bass. I don't burn food."

"Yeah, we'll see. I'll be there in about 45 minutes. You need me to pick up anything?"

"Nope. I've got it all covered."

"Alright. See you shortly, love."

"Okay. Drive safely."

I hung up and smiled at my new name. Lately, babe had been replaced by love and I liked it.

I freshened up my makeup, made sure the toilets and sinks were clean and then focused on the rest of the house. As I scurried around straightening up in preparation for his visit, I felt absolutely giddy. Not long after, the doorbell rang signaling round one of another battle in my head between my quiet and loud inner voices.

Don't do it. Don't open that door. If you do your life will forever be altered, my quiet inner voice whispered.

Shut up goody two-shoes! Her life ain't going that great now so, what does she have to lose? Nothing! Girl, you betta open that door. Don't keep a fine man like that waiting, my loud inner voice screamed.

The doorbell rang again.

You have free will to change your mind and make a different choice. You don't owe anybody anything," the quiet inner voice chirped.

You deserve this! And as far as free will goes, you should use it to turn her volume all the way down and answer that door! the loud inner voice roared. And with that, my inside loud mouth won again. I opened the door and my eyes landed on Jonathan's smile.

"Good Evening, love," he said, stepping past me carrying a slim, brown paper bag. The scent of his cologne gripped me as I closed the door and followed the movement of his khakis.

"You might want to chill this," he said, handing me the bag.

I removed a bottle of Joel Gott Unoaked Chardonnay from it.

"You remembered. Thanks." I went into the kitchen and placed it in the fridge while he sat on the sofa.

"I know how much you enjoyed it the other night, so I decided to restock you," he said.

"I picked you up some Rutherford Hill Merlot, 'cause I remembered how much you liked it."

"Thanks, love."

"Where's your coat?" I asked, walking back into the living room.

"In the car. Nice place you've got here. Can I get the grand tour?"

"Sure."

"You look beautiful as usual."

"Thanks Mr. Bass. You look pretty snazzy yourself. I love that shirt. What would you call that, sage green?"

"I think it's more of a moss color."

"Well, it looks really good against your skin. Let's start from the bottom."

He followed closely behind me as I led him to the basement.

"It's half finished, but it's great for storage," I said.

"And for working out too I see. I've seen these things on TV," he said pointing to my Air Walker exercise machine.

"I love it. Unlike a treadmill, I don't get bored on it so I use it more often."

"I can tell. How often do you work out?"

"I try to do it at least three times a week along with floor exercises with free weights daily."

"You don't know how much a brotha appreciates a sista who makes an effort to take care of herself."

"Well, it's important. Even if I don't lose a pound I just feel better in my own skin."

"I hope you're not trying to lose weight. I think you're perfect—thick and thin in all the right places."

"Thanks Jonathan. I can tell you get your work out on too and you look great."

"Thanks."

"Ok, now back upstairs."

I began trotting up the steps in front of him.

I showed him the patio and the third floor before we returned to the living room.

"Dinner will be ready shortly. Make yourself at home." I went into the kitchen and slid out of my shoes, then took some romaine lettuce and tomatoes from the fridge.

"Where're your sounds?" he yelled from the living room.

"We couldn't fit the system in the truck. So, I'm sure it will become a casualty of the divorce war."

"Now, that's cruel."

"It is. I find it very hard to exist without music."

"Don't worry. Got iPod, will travel. I'll be right back."

He left and returned a few minutes later with his iPod and a pair of mini portable speakers."

"You were really serious," I said while washing the lettuce.

"When it comes to music, I don't play."

He connected the two together and found an outlet to plug the speakers into. Soon, Eric Benet's, The Last Time, filled the air. The fact that he'd chosen a song of such romantic depth surprised me and once again he struck me as a man twice his age which captivated and frightened me.

I turned around and he was standing right in front of me.

"Let's dance," he said, taking my hands and drying them with a towel before leading me into the living room.

As the music surrounded us, he held me close and I clinched his body right back. Now, I missed my heels but he didn't seem to mind as he gently rested his head atop mine. As we moved slowly to the music, it felt like the world had shrunk leaving room for only us two. This was some silver screen shit and I wanted to see it through until the credits rolled. He began rubbing my back and my fingertips responded by caressing the nape of his neck. I could feel his growing stiffness pressing against me as he raised my head with the crease of his finger and moved his lips towards mine.

"I better finish dinner," I said, stepping away from him. As I walked back to the kitchen, I felt his eyes gripping my every move.

While finishing the salad, I peeped through the kitchen cutout and watched him. He caught me looking and came and stood close to me. Suddenly, I remembered the doctor's warning to wait at least two weeks before having sex. And I felt pretty confident that I could comply, until he was behind me kissing my neck. I grabbed the bottle of wine he'd bought from the fridge and shoved it into his chest.

"Here, open this," I said, taking a corkscrew from the drawer and placing it in his other hand. While he uncorked the wine, I got some wine glasses from the cabinet and placed them on the cutout ledge. He filled each glass half way then took a sip before sitting on one of the stools beneath the cutout.

"That sheer white blouse over the lacy white camisole is really striking a chord with me. And the black mini gives you a kind of naughty school girl look," he said, eyes perusing me up and down.

"Thanks." I took the pan of spinach lasagna out of the fridge and placed it in the oven before joining him. We sipped slowly while looking into each other's eyes. Then, just as I turned to open the refrigerator door again he caught my hand and drew me close, taking my wine glass and sitting it on the ledge next to his. Suddenly he was pulling me up on his lap leaving my legs dangling over his thighs. As his mouth seized mine his lips felt firm, yet giving. Our tongues gently tussled while his hands roamed below my waist. Then his eyes widened and he froze.

"You don't have any panties on," he said, looking surprised.

"Is that a problem?"

He grinned and removed his glasses, placing them next to the wine glasses.

Our tongues resumed their dance while he unbuttoned my blouse and maneuvered under my camisole where he found my hardened nipples waiting for him. His large fingertips greeted and delighted them before roving between my legs. While he rubbed my most tender spots, I undid his pants, put my hand inside his boxers and reached for his erection.

Suddenly, I glanced down in shock. I felt tricked! Hoodwinked! Bamboozled! For years, I had bought into the universal notion that one size fits and satisfies all and had remained a virgin until marriage. Now at age 30, my fingers were just discovering that a man could be hung like he was as both hands lost the battle to fit around his girth.

He smiled then whispered, "Don't be scared of it."

Now, my blouse and camisole were sliding off my arms and past my ears. My kisses traveled his neck as I unbuttoned his shirt and helped him yank it off completely. With hurried assistance from me, he pulled his wife beater off and threw it on the floor too. Then, he stood with me still on his lap and took a few steps back until my back met the cold sensation of the refrigerator door.

He extended my arms above my head, firmly cuffing my wrists together with one hand. While holding me against the fridge with his weight, he softly kissed my breast, tongue tending to my nipples. Then he pulled a condom from his pocket, ripping it open with his teeth. We kissed hungrily as he pushed his pants and boxers down, unleashing his erection. He rolled the condom on, then released my wrist, hooking his hands into mine. I could feel myself slowly expanding while he pushed himself inside of me. Then he stopped.

"Do you want me as much as I want you?" he whispered, breath whisking against my neck.

"Yes."

"Then say it."

"I want you Jonathan…I want you so much."

As we kissed, my moisture gushed around his hardness and I wanted to give and get at the same time. My moans kept pace with his thrust and his eyes glowed with excitement as if my every whimper excited him more and more. I completely shut my eyes, then he became still again.

"Look at me!" he demanded.

I did, eyes begging him to continue. His length swirled around my walls as he plunged into me deeply until my body exploded. I groaned loudly, staking my fingernails into the back of his hands and was completely out of breath when I heard him mumble, "My turn now."

His fingers caressed my delicate places while his strokes grew more vigorous. I kissed his chest as he grunted and groaned with every push. Then with one final shove, he filled me to capacity and screamed, shit!" I held him close while his body wrenched and trembled, before settling. As our heat cooled, I lightly sprinkled his face with kisses.

"I guess it's true," I whispered.

"What's true love?"

"That most house fires get started in the kitchen."

We laughed between pants and afterwards, he stepped completely out of his khakis, boxers and shoes and began carrying me up the steps with my legs and arms still wrapped around him.

He unzipped my skirt, making me aware that it was still on before lowering me and tossing it onto the floor. He gently pushed me down on my bed and stood looking down at me.

"I'm gonna use your lavatory," he said, disappearing while I lay wrapped only in the memory we'd just created.

Once he returned, we laid in each other's arms with our eyes pasted on one another. He held me tightly while my fingers stroked the hair just above the nape of his neck. I'd discovered its texture was slightly different from the rest of his mane and liked playing with it.

While gazing into his eyes, I said, "You didn't eat my stuff."

"Be patient. I'm gonna eat your stuff."

"I'm talking about the lasagna I made for you."

"So am I. Get your mind outta the gutter."

We burst into a loud guffaw.

"Let's take a bath together," he said.

"Okay."

"I'll run it while you go get some towels. You like it hot?" he asked, heading to the bathroom across the hall.

"Can't you tell," I replied, rolling out of bed behind him.

"There's some bath oil in the cabinet," I yelled out while pulling towels off the shelf of the hallway linen closet.

"Is it scented, cause I don't wanna be smellin' like daisies and cantaloupe."

"Don't worry, it's unisex."

As the water started to run, he hollered, "Where're your candles?"

I took the towels, a long handle lighter and several multi wick candles into the bathroom and placed the candles on a glass table next to the tub. I lit them before heading downstairs to get our wine glasses and the bottle of Merlot I knew he liked. Before heading back, I checked to make sure the oven had automatically shut itself off. The last thing I needed was to burn the food, like he'd teased earlier.

When I returned he was already in the tub with his legs spread apart. After filling both glasses, I took his extended hand and sat between his legs, leaning my back against his chest. He wrapped his arms around me in a firm embrace and I laid my arms atop his in an equally gripping hug.

"So, you came bearing condoms, huh. That was a tad presumptuous, don't you think?" I said.

"No more presumptuous than you runnin' round here with no drawers on."

I chuckled.

"Ok, that's fair."

"I don't know why you insist on pretending that you don't want this as much as I do."

"You're engaged Jonathan, that's why."

"That has nothing to do with you. I keep telling you to let me worry about that. By the way, are you on anything?"

"Anything like what? Crack?"

"You know what I mean silly. Like birth control."

"Oh, so you think this is gonna happen again."

He began playing with my right nipple.

"I know it's gonna happen again and again," he said.

"Well you can keep wishing on a star cause I'm not on anything and don't plan to be because this was a fluke—a one hit wonder—something we both had to get out of our systems. Lightning is not gonna strike twice between me and you Jonathan Bass."

"Ok, you keep telling yourself that. Seriously though, you need to get on something, 'cause I don't do the pull out thing and condoms can break."

"Did you hear what I just said?"

"I heard you, but that was for your sake not mine. You're trying to convince yourself that it won't happen again, even though you want it to. Look, what happened tonight was great, but it's not just the sex between us. It's kinetics—that energy in motion that ignites our heat and draws us together. We're being joined by an uncontrollable force that transcends time and reaches way beyond the attraction or passion we feel for each other."

His comments scared me because I knew they were true. I couldn't stay away from this man if someone paid me to. The more I saw him, the more I wanted to be in his presence. The more I learned about him, the more I wanted him to reveal. And, working together only exacerbated the situation.

"What's really bothering you? I'm not having sex with her if that's what you're worried about."

"Why not?"

"So, that is what you're worried about. Well, let's just say she has issues in that area."

"And you're willing to wait until she works through those issues?"

"For now I am, but who knows."

This might not be such a bad thing, I thought. Perhaps unstable Mable could provide just the right amount of buffering between me and him to keep us from being soldered together any further. Plus, he'll be leaving soon and this will all be just a distant, wonderful memory once he's gone.

"What did you think of me the first time you saw me?" he asked.

"I don't remember."

"Aw, I'm hurt Ms. Richards. I remember you very clearly. I was attracted to you the moment I saw you. I've been involved with beautiful women before, but you—you just struck me hard. It was your first day at CRED and you were standing at the coffee machine in a fitted burgundy dress. I politely introduced myself and asked if you were from Chicago. You said yes, but when I tried to continue the conversation, you just gave me that, get the fuck outta here, look and I left you alone."

That was him? Geeze, I thought he was some random weirdo that wandered in off the streets.

"I do remember that. You told me you were born in Texas but that your grandmother pretty much raised you. Then, I got nervous."

"Why?"

"All my life people have just walked up to me and told me things—things I really shouldn't know and it just freaks me out. I thought you were about to go there."

"You shouldn't be freaked out by that, love. People do that because you have an aura of openness about you that disarms and frees them from the fear of being judged. It's also part of that kinetic energy that pulls me towards you."

"So, you've been checkin' me out since then? That was two years ago."

"I've admired you since then. I wasn't really checkin' you out because I saw the ring and knew you were married."

"Well, that's about to change."

"How do you feel about that…I mean about him?"

"It's really strange. I'm sure I loved him. I had to have loved him because he was my first. But I swear I can't remember the feeling. All I feel now is emptiness when it comes to him."

"Maybe that's where I can come in and fill you up."

There he goes again—talking to me like he's free, single and ain't goin' nowhere.

"What about you? How do you really feel about, what's her name?" I asked.

He chuckled.

"You know her name. Well, I kind of feel like I cajoled someone into taking a cruise with me. Then when we hit rough waters, I tumbled and landed at the feet of a creature far more suited to be my traveling companion."

"Must of hit a helluva current. What cruise line was this, Carnival?"

He howled so hard his laughter echoed throughout the entire floor.

"Well, is this creature willing to be your travel mate?" I asked.

"She won't admit it, but deep down she is very willing."

"Maybe she's afraid."

"Of me?"

"Of you switching mates mid cruise."

"She has nothing to fear. In fact, she should have faith in the waters that are gently rocking us towards each other."

"I think I need a drink."

I sat up and took a sip of wine. Then, while looking in his eyes, downed the whole glass before sitting it back down. Then I belched.

"Excuse me. I'm sorry, "I said, resuming my place in his arms.

"It's quite alright Ms. Richards. You're human. That's why you're here with me."

He reached for his glass and finished his wine.

"Jonathan, what happens to her?"

"Who, you?"

"No, your original cruise comrade."

He sighed.

"I don't know. All I know is that I'm not going to be denied the pleasure of spending time with you before I leave."

He guided my lips to his and kissed me fervently.

My nipples were on display again. He noticed and began massaging them with the palms of his hands.

"I see you're cold. Let's get out," he said, moving the drain stopper with his foot.

I scooted up and stood while he got out and held his hand for me to join him. He took a towel and dried me from head to toe before drying himself and wrapping the towel around his waist.

"After you," he said motioning for me to exit the bathroom first.

I reached for a towel, but he guided me away from it.

"Uh, uh. I want to watch you walk," he said with a crooked grin.

I obliged him and when I got to the bed, he lightly flipped me over on my back before taking off his towel. He was fully erect again as he parted my legs with his body and kissed me everywhere, lingering down below on my fragile folds. Soon, he made me into a liar as we did it again and again.

Chapter Nine

A Straight & Perfect Stitch

I hadn't been home an hour before I found myself wanting to feel her body next to mine again. Her scent was still all over me, easing the pang of withdrawal I'd started to feel as I lay thinking about her. Our time together was nothing I could have imagined and yet way more than I'd anticipated and I wondered if she felt the same. So I picked up the phone to find out. To my surprise a voice was already on the other end.

"Hello, Hello—Jonathan?"

"Oh, hey."

"Hey. Remember me, your fiancée? I sat in front of your house practically all night and you never came home. Where've you been and why haven't you returned any of my calls? Is everything okay?"

"Everything's fine. I was out helping a friend with a problem. And I've been really busy with school and work. You know how it is."

"Well, since we're gonna be together forever, I guess I can be a little more understanding."

"How've you been?"

"Fine, except I miss you. I know our last fight was all my fault, but let me make it up to you by taking you to lunch today."

"Uh, today's not good Mia. Gotta prepare for that hearing tomorrow."

"Oh shit, I forgot all about your hearing. Well, what about dinner then?"

"I'm probably gonna be tied up tonight as well. Sorry babe. Can I get a rain check?"

"Sure, anything for you."

"Thanks. I really gotta go. I'll call you later."

"Okay, I lo...."

I hung up before she could finish. My life was growing more complicated by the second and I felt immersed in guilt. But not for the obvious reasons. My conscious had twisted so far in Skyla's favor that I somehow felt I was being unfaithful to her instead of Mia.

I looked at my watch and it was just about 6:00am. Skyla was sleeping so peacefully when I left that I decided not to wake her. But I figured if she wasn't up by now she'd be up soon, so I went ahead with my original plan.

"Hello," she answered sounding slexy; both sleepy and sexy.

"Wake up sleepy head."

"I'm on your mind already?"

"Well, you know you talk in your sleep. I heard you all the way over here. You were screamin' my name and hollering, oooo Jonathan—don't stop. I said, let me call this woman and wake her up before her neighbors call the police on her."

She cracked up.

"You miss me?" I asked.

"Do you miss me?"

"Way more than I should. I need to see you again."

"Need to?"

"Let's spend a whole day together. How many sick days do you have left?"

"I don't know."

"You should find out so we can make plans. Maybe we can take a Friday and spend the entire weekend together."

"You snore," she said.

"So do you."

"I do not."

"Maybe you don't. I'll have to spend the night again to make sure."

I went to the kitchen and began microwaving the lasagna she'd given me the night before. I stuffed a fork full in my mouth then started devouring the rest.

"What are you doing Mr. Bass?"

"I'm eating your stuff," I replied with bloated jaws.

"I thought you did that last night and quite well I might add. Well, how does it taste?"

"Wonderful. I knew it would though, especially after I threw a little hot sauce on it."

"Hot sauce? Uh uh…no you didn't drown all my hard work in hot sauce."

"Don't be offended, love. I put it on just about everything I eat."

"That could be kind of hazardous."

"Well, there are some exceptions. Some things come with their own seasoning and don't need any additives. That's the kind of meal I could just dive in and eat every day!"

She chucked.

"Did you enjoy yourself last night?" I asked.

"Greatly. I had no idea it could feel like that."

"I'm gonna make you a promise. If you just give me the next six months of your life, I'll disappear afterwards and won't bother you ever again. I would like to think we could still be friends though, no strings attached."

The phone went silent.

"You there?" I asked.

"I'm here. I was thinking about what you just said. No strings, huh. I'm not sure that I wouldn't want to hold on to a string or two."

"To be honest, I'd want to hold on to a lot more. How about we just go with the flow and don't assign meaning to our connection unless it becomes absolutely necessary. That way, nobody gets hurt."

"How do you know nobody will get hurt?"

"Because I'm willing to do whatever it takes to keep our connection intact, strings and all until you tell me you don't want to play anymore. Deal?"

"I'll think about it. I better go get ready for work. What time will you be in today?"

"I don't know. Soon."

"Don't forget we're going to lunch."

"How could I forget that? I'll see you later."

"Okay baby," she said before hanging up. Damn. I'd been elevated from Mr. Bass to baby and was on cloud 12, but was surprised by the lack of concern I felt about being involved with two women simultaneously. I hadn't quite figured out my next move, but knew it would include getting closer to Skyla and keeping the two worlds separate.

I laid down for a couple of hours then got up and got dressed for work. Thoughts of the previous night were still zooming through my head and I let them possess me until I was transformed into a cheerful, whistling hype in search of his next fix.

###

I stepped off the elevator and continued to my desk.

"Well, look at you—smiling and whistling like you just won some money. You sure are in a good mood for a Monday."

"Morning Sonya. I'm always in a good mood."

"Yeah okay, and I'm about to convert to Islam."

"Maybe you should. You'd have to give up the chitlins though."

"Don't start with me Jonathan."

"I'm sorry. I was just kidding. Believe me, I have no intention of starting anything with anybody today. Life is too short and God is too good."

"God? Okay, what have you been smoking?"

"Have a good one Sonya."

Once at my desk, I began reviewing my notes on the hearing I'd written over the weekend.

About an hour or so later, a pair of shapely, sexy legs in sheer black stockings and black stilettos appeared at my side. I recognized them and began smiling uncontrollably.

"Morning Mr. Bass," Skyla said, peering down at me with a half smile while her bangs dangled in her eyes. I wanted to rip all her clothes off and take her right there on my keyboard. "I just wanted to stop by and give you your check stub," she said.

"Check stub? Doesn't Bree normally pass these out?"

"She does, but I'm doing her a favor. That's what friends are for."

"And it sure is nice to have a friend as kind and as uh, giving as you are."

"Call me," she said, gently pinching my chin before turning and walking away.

I jumped up and began tormenting myself by following behind her and watching her ass as she walked.

"Where do you want to go for lunch?" I blurted out.

"Shhhh. You don't want people to get suspicious," she turned slightly and whispered.

"I don't care about them."

"Well, you should care."

She went down a less traveled corridor and we ended up in a secluded spot behind a row of lateral file cabinets. At first, we just stood there with folded arms, grinning at each other like first crush adolescents.

"Casa Diego," she said.

"Casa Diego what?"

"That's where I wanna go for lunch, if that's okay with you?"

"If you wanted to go to the moon, I'd find a way to make it happen."

"I don't think we'd be back in time."

"Probably not, especially the way we blast off."

She began blushing.

"1:00pm?" I asked.

"Can we make it noon instead?"

"You must be hungry."

"After last night, I'm starving. I didn't eat breakfast."

"Noon it is then. Meet me at the elevators."

Before she turned to walk away, I couldn't resist pulling her close and swirling my tongue around hers while she caressed my back. Then she stopped.

"See you at noon," she said, backing away and disappearing down the hall.

Chapter Ten

Tailoring the Fit

When I returned to my office, Bree was sitting in my chair waiting for me with her feet on my desk as usual. I shut the door then laid my back against it with my hands folded behind me.

"Bree, help! I tripped and fell," I said.

"Oh no! What happened? Are you okay?"

"Yeah, Jonathan's dick broke my fall."

"Whaaaat? So that's why you wanted his check stub from me. Get your ass over here and give me the tea." She stood, offering me my seat back, then rushed around and sat down in front of me.

"So, how was it?" she asked, eagerly awaiting my response.

"It was—it was…"

"Damn, it was that good?"

"I just never knew sex could be like that."

"Like what?"

"Like, I went somewhere. When we were joined, I left this planet and went to a place I'd never been before. It was like savoring the most exotic flavor and listening to the most melodic sound while being engulfed in the most euphoric scent. Then once he was done arousing every cell in my body, we talked for hours and he set my mind ablaze!"

"Daaaammmmm! Did he eat the muffin?"

"Like it was his last meal on death row!"

Now we were both snickering like preschoolers.

"Well good for you! I'm glad you got you some out of this world dick and got it out of your system. Now you can move on and find a real rebound man."

I stood up and grabbed a stack of papers and started filing without a response.

"Sky?"

"Huh?"

"Oh no, he did it didn't he. You can't even look at me."

"Did what?"

"Whipped your ass in one night. Ugh, I knew this would happen. Sky, you've got to forget about him. He's engaged, rumor has it to a looney tune at that."

"I don't want to marry him. I just want to spend some time with him. Besides, he's not sleeping with her."

"Oh my God, is that what he told you and you believe him? Girl, that's what they all say."

"Bree, why can't I just keep seeing him until he leaves, then we'll be out of each other's lives for good."

Just then, my phone rang.

"Can you hit the speaker button for me?" I asked her.

She let out a loud sigh and smacked the phone.

"Hello," I yelled out while continuing to file.

"Have you been getting my text messages?"

"Yes, Phillip. I've gotten all menacing 47 of them."

"Look, I don't know who you think you're fucking with, but I ain't playin' with your ass. Now, I mean it Skyla. I'm not gonna let you put my life on hold. Either you bring your ass home by the deadline I gave you or I'm filing. I'm dead serious!"

"Like I told you, do whatever you gotta do Phillip."

"Alright. Don't think I'm gonna pay your attorney's fees either. We can just use my frat brother, Hank Spaulding and let him handle it. I'm sure you've seen his commercials."

"You must be out of your mind if you think I trust you enough to use one attorney—an attorney that you recommended. I have my own attorney."

"You're so fucking stupid! I'm trying to do you a favor. But if you wanna continue being a stubborn ass bitch, go right ahead. I don't give a fuck anymore!"

Just then, Bree hit the speaker button hanging up the call.

"Girrrrrl, what a complete and utter asshole! Man Sky, I mean I knew you were unhappy, but now I really see why. You told me about the cheating, but I had no idea you were being verbally abused too. You never talk about it."

"Why would I want to talk about that?"

I went and sat back down.

"You know what, I take back everything I said about you seeing Jonathan. If he makes you happy, then you keep right on letting him take you to dick Disneyland and you go on all the rides you can with him. You deserve it."

"What? I thought you weren't a fan of the deserve system."

"Well, I was wrong."

"Knock, knock," Jonathan said, poking his head in the door. "Hope I'm not interrupting but it's 12:30pm, love."

"Oh hey Jonathan, come on in. Here take my seat," Bree said, hopping up.

"Thanks Bree," he said.

"You're welcome. Well, let me get outta here. Don't wanna keep you two from your plans. Have fun Sky and be careful. Some of the rides at Disney have a height requirement," she said, waltzing out the door with laughter.

"Height requirement, what's she talking about?" Jonathan asked.

"Nothing. Come on, let's go."

Before exiting, something caught his attention.

"Nice flowers," he said, looking over at a side credenza where I'd placed the flowers he'd given me.

"Thanks. A handsome young man gave them to me the other night."

"Yeah? And what did you give him in return?"

"Stimulating conversation."

"Umph, poor sucker."

Once on an empty elevator, we couldn't wait to kiss again. We walked outside and he caught my hand.

"You wanna take a cab?" he asked.

"It's not so bad out today. Let's just walk."

"Okay. Besides, you've got me to keep you warm. I'll call in our orders. What do you want?"

He pulled out his cell phone and started to dial. After ordering, he put his arm around me while I clasped his waist.

"So what were you and Bree so engrossed in earlier? Looked intense."

"I was just giving her the circumference of your dick, that's all."

"That better be a joke." He gave me a quick peck to my lips.

"Jonathan?"

"Yeah love?"

"What would you do if Mia rolled up right now and caught you frolicking with me?"

"I don't think there would be much for me to do. The universe would have already made a decision and I would just respect it. Then I would try to stop her from scratching your eyes out and you from knocking the rest of her teeth out."

Chapter Eleven

The Wrong Side of the Fabric

When Skyla and I got to the restaurant, it was just about empty except for a woman and what appeared to be her young son of around age seven. She was trying to get him to eat some beans by yelling and smacking him on his hands.

"Some people should really have to pass a test before having kids," Skyla whispered to me as we passed them.

"I know, right," I whispered back.

I found a booth and hung up our coats on a nearby stand then motioned for her to slide in before me. As she did, her skirt scrunched up, exposing her thighs. She saw me staring and bashfully tugged it down. As I scooted in and sat next to her, she looked surprised but pleased. My hand seemed to naturally land on her knee and she drew my head towards hers and kissed me passionately. After wiping lipstick from my lips with a napkin she said, "Now, let's see what you've got."

I looked at her longingly and licked my lips.

"Stop it. You know what I mean," she said.

I began fumbling through my briefcase while she searched through her bag. Then the waiter showed up.

"I preordered under Bass," I said to him.

"Ok, be right out."

Skyla pulled out a folder and placed it on the table while I continued looking through my briefcase.

"Dammit! I don't believe this. I left my notes at work," I said.

"Awww babe, we're running out of time."

"I know, I know."

"Okay let's just wing it and maybe you can recall some of what you wrote."

The waiter came and placed our meals in front of us, then left.

As I cut my burrito, Skyla began attacking her chicken tacos while bits of tomatoes and lettuce fell from her mouth and landed in her lap. She caught herself and stopped.

"I'm sorry baby, but I'm hungry as hell," she said with a full mouth.

"Now this is the woman I've been waiting to see. You weren't fooling anybody with that little docile, dainty nibbling act you were pulling at the Signature Room the other night."

We flashed flirty glances back and forth as we ate. Then, she leaned in and slowly licked my chin.

"What?—you had a piece of cheese right there and I didn't want it to fall and get on your pants," she said.

"Uh, huh. Keep it up and we're gonna end up inside a locked broom closet when we get back to work."

"Speaking of work, let's get down to business." She pushed her plate aside and wiping her hands with a napkin.

She opened a folder and began reading Angelica's complaint out loud:

"On November 28th, I called one of my subordinates, Jonathan A. Bass."

She paused.

"Jonathan A? What's the A for?" she asked.

"Aristotle."

"Really? Corny, but kinda sexy."

"Oh yeah? And what's your middle name?"

"I don't like it, so I'm never telling."

She continued reading with a smirk.

"….who was in the field conducting surveys and told him to report to the office immediately to go over some incomplete assignments. After outright refusing to honor my request, Mr. Bass exploded over the phone and began yelling and cursing at me. I told him to calm down and he said, quote, 'No bitch, you calm down!'"

I frowned, throwing up my hands. I mean these were outright lies! Skyla flashed me a look of reprimand before continuing.

"I repeatedly asked him to lower his voice, but he then became even more belligerent. I said, 'Look, you need to stop what you're doing and come into the office right now.' He responded, 'Kiss my ass and suck my dick, you fat, white bitch!' I was shocked and didn't understand why he was reacting like this.

I demanded that he stop addressing me with that language and come into the office at once! He then yelled, 'Fuck you! I'll come in when I'm ready and if you call me one more time, I swear I'll kill you,' and hung up the phone. I repeatedly tried calling him back, but assumed he'd turned his phone off as all of my calls from that point on went straight to voicemail."

She put the document down, folded her arms and stared at me. I returned the stare with a stern look of frustration.

"Well?" she said.

"Look, none of that is true. Doesn't it sound made up? I swear, she's lying."

"But why would she lie on you Jonathan?"

I sighed long and hard.

"I don't expect you to understand this, but Angelica is just pissed because I won't give her any attention."

"What kind of attention? Are you saying she sexually harassed you?"

"I wouldn't call it that exactly. Look, sometimes some women, women in certain walks of life…"

"You mean, women of other ethnic groups."

"Exactly. Anyway, no matter what they look like they automatically expect a brotha to be attracted to them. They'll do things and if he doesn't respond the way they think he should, they'll get pissed, especially if they're in a position of authority. That's exactly what's going on between me and Angelica."

Skyla looked shocked. Then she broke into laughter, even bending to one side while cachinnating.

"Oh, you think this is funny?" I asked

She couldn't stop herself and snorted a bit between giggles.

"This really ain't funny Skyla."

"I know…..I just."

"You just what? You don't believe me?"

"Oh, I'm sure it's true. But let's be real Jonathan. I mean, your defense can't be, I'm sexy and I know it and that's why she's lying on me."

"I'm not saying that. I may not be wording it right but this is what I'm feeling. It started after I helped her do some painting around her house one weekend shortly after our last manager left and we all got transferred to her team."

"Umph. That was helpful of you."

"Well, I'm a helpful guy….sometimes too helpful I guess."

She covered my hand with hers.

"I'm sorry for laughing baby. But, there's got to be something else. Something we can use that won't make you look like a narcissistic idiot."

I leaned forward, folded my hands on the table and hung my head. She began rubbing my lower back.

"You know I love this Mexican food but it comes with a free side of bubble guts. So, I'm gonna go to the ladies room and when I get back, I want you to tell me your version of what happened. Okay?"

"Alright."

While she was gone, I started in on my burrito, but became distracted by the woman and boy at the table we passed by earlier. She had now ramped up the coercion by cussing and hitting him upside his head. As she continued this tactic, a mixture of tears and snot formed at the crease of the little boy's mouth and I drifted to another place in time.

I myself had tasted that same concoction on several occasions as a boy before my grandparents rescued me. Only mine contained a few additional ingredients—mainly the taste of metallic. Since then, I'd done the work, read the books and healed enough to become a productive, functioning human being. But one particular memory still glowed so vividly in my mind.

It was Halloween and I'd just scored the motherload of all candy bags. Seeing as how it was almost dinner time, I ran in the house and dumped the confectionery loot on the kitchen table while mom stood at the stove cooking pork chops and smothered cabbage. As she sang along to the tunes on her favorite oldie station, I listened closely while cornering the miniature Snickers bars off to themselves and putting the rest back in the bag. I loved it when it was just me and her in the house. She was calm, happy and well—normal.

"Mom, can I have one before dinner?" I asked.

She looked at me with a loving smile and said, "Okay, but just one. I don't want you ruining your appetite."

I peeled the wrapper off and tore into my favorite treat. Then the door swung open, changing the wind and shifting the atmosphere.

"Damn, you still cookin'? You should have been done by now. You know what the hell time I get home!" Lamar, my stepfather barked.

He plunked his toolbox down on the table right on top of my candy bag and removed his jacket. I quietly tried to ease the bag from underneath it when his toolbox tipped over sending screwdrivers, wrenches and nails scattering all over the kitchen floor.

"Look what you did you little stupid motherfucka! Clean it up! And you betta not miss a nail! What the hell where you doing anyway?" he screamed. Then he glanced at the table and saw the bag of candy and the empty Snickers wrapper.

"Oh, I see. Why the hell is he eatin' this shit before dinner?" he turned to my mom and shouted. She ignored him and started to shake while continuing to turn the pork chops over.

As I scrambled to place all of the items back in his toolbox, he grabbed me by my shirt and smacked me in the face, ripping open my bottom lip. Blood began pouring down my chin and dripping onto my shirt.

"You betta not get no cavities, cause I ain't got no money to be paying for no dentist. You know you shouldn't be eatin' that shit!" he bellowed.

"But momma said I could have one before dinner," I muttered.

"Oh, she did, did she? Why the fuck did you tell him that? Huh, huh? You hear me bitch!" he roared at her. Then he grabbed her by the back of her hair and slammed her head into the upper kitchen cabinets. Her nose and forehead split open and started gushing blood while she screamed and cried like she always did. I stood back trying to figure out how to get to the skillet and soak him in hot grease. But before I could get up the nerve, he turned his focus back on me.

"Oh, what you wanna do something? Try it you little piece of shit, just try it!" he yelled.

He wrapped his hand around the back of my neck and began choking and dragging me to the kitchen table then shoved me into a chair.

"Since you like this shit so much….trying to make me pay for shit I ain't got no money for….I'mma teach you a lesson."

He dumped all of the candy on the table and stood behind me clamping my neck with one hand.

"Now eat it! Eat all of it!" he demanded.

"Lamar, don't….," my mother came close and begged. He backhanded her propelling her to the other side of the room where she landed on the floor.

His grip around my neck increased as he scooped the candy in front of me.

"I said eat it asshole!"

While my mother moaned and sobbed in the background, I began eating each piece until there were no more wrappers to unwrap. The smell of burnt meat filled the air while my mouth was engulfed with the fusion of blood from my lip, salt from the tears, snot streaming from my nose and sugar from the candy. My stomach began cramping severely. From the corner of my eyes, I could see my mother crawling to the stove. I felt like passing out and wanted to just disappear.

Then, the contents of my stomach was suddenly on the table and floor. Finally, my neck was free and I had control of my movements again.

"You see what this motherfucka did?" Lamar turned to my mother and growled, pointing at the vomit. He grabbed her arm and yanked her to her feet.

"Now you clean this shit up! I'm goin' out and it betta be up before I get back," he howled. Once he left, my mother and I sat trapped in helplessness. But we were relieved that we were free from his presence if only temporarily.

"Jonathan, babe, you alright? You need some water?" Skyla shook my arm and asked bringing me back into the present. My eyes were still on the little boy and the scene in front of me. Suddenly I stood and began walking towards their table. I could feel Skyla watching me in confusion. As my feet kept moving, I wasn't quite sure what to do. I just knew I had to do something to impede the blows the mother was giving to her son.

About midway, I stopped a waiter and asked if he could bring some maple syrup over to their table. He agreed and I kept going until I was seated in front of them. The mother looked shocked and irritated.

"So you don't like beans, huh," I folded my arms on the table and asked the boy. He looked at his mother then back at me and shook his head no.

"I didn't either when I was your age. In fact, I hated them until my grandmother taught me a trick."

Just then, the waiter appeared with a small carafe of syrup. I looked at the mother as if daring her to move. She watched me and didn't object to any of my actions.

"Now, sometimes, things can seem really nasty or bitter until something sweet gets added to them," I said pouring a small amount of syrup into the beans. "Plus, beans have iron in them. You need the iron to make you strong." I stirred the beans with a spoon as he watched. "Is he allergic to anything?" I asked his mother.

She shook her head no. I scooped up a spoonful and tasted them.

"Mmmmm. These are delicious. Here, you try some." I handed him a clean spoon.

He frowned and shook his head no.

"Brian eat the damn beans!" his mother shouted.

"Shhhhhh, ma'am please," I said motioning for her to calm down. Suddenly, Skyla was scooting me over and sitting next to me.

"You're missing out little man," I said, continuing to taste the beans.

Finally, he gave in and began eating, only stopping when his plate was clear of them.

"See, you never know what you'll like until you try it," Skyla said. The mother was now smiling. Skyla grabbed my hand and pulled me in the direction of our table.

"Come on love, we better get back," I said helping her with her coat.

Chapter Twelve

Cutting Out the Excess

Once outside, we quickly noticed the drop in temperature and decided to cab it back to work.

"115 S. Franklin," Jonathan told the cab driver when we got in.

Although he held and rubbed my hand, he seemed a bit preoccupied and I wanted to know why.

"You didn't eat much of your lunch," I said.

"Wasn't really that hungry," he replied, staring out the window. I touched his cheek and turned his face towards mine.

"Is that because you ate my stuff last night?" I asked.

His smile returned as he laughed, then kissed me.

"Probably. You got the kind of stuff that can keep a brotha full for days."

"That was a great thing you did for that little boy."

"It wasn't great. But, it was necessary."

"What makes you so compassionate towards kids? Were you picked on when you were little?"

"I guess you could say that."

"Well then, you were picked on to be picked out. God has something special for you to do."

Just then, he looked down at his watch.

"Hey man, if you turn left at the light, it will shave ten minutes off of our trip," he said to the cab driver.

I snuggled in close and placed my head on his shoulder. He put his arm around me and kissed my cheek.

"We didn't get very far with your rebuttal and the clock is ticking," I said.

"I know."

"You wanna come over tonight and work on it?"

He looked at me with surprise.

"You want me to?" he asked, smiling.

"I just invited you didn't I?"

"You certainly did and you can't renege now. What time?"

"I don't know, about eight?"

"Let's make it 7:30pm. Now we've got work to do, so don't be parading around with no panties on again."

Just then, his grin was replaced with a grimace.

"Dude, I told you to make a left. Where the hell are you going?" he asked. The cab driver just ignored him.

"Hey, I'm talking to you! We should be almost there by now and you're all the way on Chicago Avenue."

"I go where you say," the cab driver replied in a heavy West Indian accent.

"You're going where you want to go, cause I ain't said nothing about being way over here. Turn around and take us to 115 S. Franklin like I told you. Turn here. What—what the—where the hell are you going now? Turn around! Did you hear me? I said turn the fuck around!" he screamed, kicking the back of the cab driver's seat.

"Jonathan baby, calm down."

"Stay out of this," he dismissively ordered.

"Look, just pull over. I said pull over!" he screamed. "Come on baby, let's get out," he said as the cab driver finally pulled over to the curb. "Man, open the door and let us out!" he demanded, yanking on the handle of the locked door. "I said open the fucking door!" he screamed, pounding on the cab driver's headrest.

Suddenly, the door locks popped up and he jumped out with the cab driver following after him.

"You pay. You pay for trip!" the cab driver looked up at him and yelled with his hand out.

"Man, you must be outta your damn mind. I'm not paying for you to get lost and bring us way over here!"

"You pay or I call police!" the cab driver shouted.

I crawled out of the back seat and rushed to Jonathan's side.

"Baby, come on, let's just get another cab," I said, tugging on his hand.

The cab driver grabbed his other arm and said, "You pay first!"

"You betta let go of my arm. Get your damn hands off me!" Jonathan yelled, pushing him forcefully against the door.

"Baby, let's just go," I pleaded.

Just then, he grabbed the cab driver by the throat and began choking him, slightly lifting him in the air. The cab driver's eyes began to bulge as he labored to breathe.

"Jonathan! Let him go!" I yelled, struggling to get between the two men. "Baby, what are you doing? Stop it! You're gonna kill him!" I screamed.

Jonathan suddenly looked into my eyes and released the man. I turned and started walking in the opposite direction.

"Skyla, Skyla!" he shouted, jogging after me. I continued on without a word. I felt angry and confused as he caught up and walked next to me. I could see him watching me from the corner of my eye as we continued walking in total silence.

Once back in our building, we boarded an empty elevator and he stood directly in front of me. I folded my arms and avoided looking up at him.

"So, you're not speaking to me?" he asked softly.

I kept silent. He leaned in and tried to kiss me but I turned my head. The elevator doors opened and I stormed off, causing Sonya to look up and notice. I went to my office, locked the door and hung up my coat. My desk phone began to ring.

"Hello."

"Hey Sky. Listen, Candice has been calling trying to reach you. She wants a Skype session with you."

"Okay, thanks Sonya."

I logged into my account and waited.

"Well, look at you. You look great," I said when she appeared on the screen.

"Liar. I feel like a fatass."

"Nonsense. You're glowing."

"How's it going? Any closer to finding out what really went down between Angelica and Jonathan?"

I sighed. "Not quite. Let me ask you something. I know I need facts, but what's your opinion? Do you think Jonathan actually did what she said he did?"

"Personally, I'd have to say no. I've never even seen the guy frown, let alone blow up at anybody."

"Interesting. Guess I'll just have to dig a little deeper."

"You do that. Everything else okay? The divorce and all?"

"Oh, that. It's as okay as a divorce can be. I'm meeting with my attorney next week so I'll keep you posted."

"Ok. I'm gonna let you get back to work, but you call me as soon as the hearing is over and let me know how it went."

"Will do. Take care."

I got up to go to the ladies room. When I came out, Jonathan grabbed my arm and pulled me into a conference room across the hall.

"Don't act like this, love. Talk to me," he said, eyes pleading for mercy.

"What the hell was that Jonathan?"

"I know. That was fucked up. I'm sorry baby. That was just me having a moment—a very bad moment, that's all."

"Ugh…," I grunted, turning and walking back to my office.

A few minutes later he came in, closing and locking the door behind him. He sat on the couch leaning forward with folded hands and a guilt-ridden puppy dog look. I came and stood looking down at him with folded arms.

"I was wrong. I shouldn't have snapped off like that. I've just got so much on my mind," he said, staring at the floor. I sat next to him with my hands in my lap. He reached over and firmly hooked his hand into mine.

"How am I supposed to be objective with the display you just put on?" I asked.

"Aw love, please don't let your mind go there. What happened today has no bearing on the Angelica situation. Those are outright lies she's telling. Deep down, you know that."

I stared into his eyes and felt his sincerity.

"I believe you. But when this hearing is over, you're gonna have to tell me where all that came from today."

"I will. I promise."

He pulled me into his arms and kissed my forehead.

"Look at us. What a pair we make. You go around knocking peoples teeth out and I lose it and yoke up cab drivers."

We laughed, then kissed ardently.

"So am I still coming over tonight?" he asked.

"I guess so."

###

Later that evening, I arrived home around 6:00pm. After changing into some black leggings and a fuchsia tank top, I worked out and ate a salad. Soon, the doorbell was ringing. I opened the door and Jonathan slinked in wearing the same shameful puppy look he had earlier.

"Hey love," he softly said.

"Hey. I see you've got your briefcase. Are there notes in there?"

"Yup."

"Good. Let's hash this out."

He sat on the living room sofa while I went into the kitchen.

"You hungry?" I yelled out.

"No, I'm good."

I got two glasses and stood at the sink filling them with water. Suddenly he was standing behind me.

"You smell good. What's that scent you're wearing?" he whispered in my ear.

"Workout funk."

He chuckled as I handed him a glass of water.

"I need something a little stronger than this. Where's that bottle of Merlot I bought?" He sat the water down and opened up the bottom kitchen cabinets.

I took the wine from the fridge and handed it to him.

"Daaaamn! You might wanna call your sponsor and find out when the next meeting is," he said.

"Shut up. That bottle hasn't been touched since you left last night and you know it."

"I know, love. I'm just playing—trying to joke my way out of the dog house I guess."

"You're not in the dog house anymore."

"I can't tell. You haven't given me any sugar and I've been here for at least five minutes."

I reached up and hugged him. He embraced me back and kissed me tenderly.

"Okay, let's stay focused," I said, pushing him away. I took two wine glasses from the cabinet and started toward the living room. I felt a firm smack on my ass and turned to find him staring at it with a half smile while carrying the Merlot.

As we sat next to each other, he filled the glasses halfway.

"To tomorrow," he said, glass clinking mine.

We took a couple of sips. He removed his boots and tossed a pillow into my lap before laying on it and looking up at me.

"Let's have a silent word of prayer," I said, closing my eyes. A few minutes later, I opened them to find him staring straight at me.

"Did you pray and ask God for help?"

"I asked God for a lot of things."

"So, from the beginning, tell me what happened."

"Well, I arrived at the house of one of my study participants around 3:30pm. I had interviewed close to ten families that day and was looking forward to that being my last case. This one involved a little boy around nine years old living with his on/off crackhead momma in the projects. Momma running around with a rag on her head talking loud on a cell phone while her son sits emotionless on the floor in front of a TV screen. Anyway, I introduce myself to the momma. She pretty much ignores me and won't let go of her cell phone long enough to hear anything I have to say. So, I went and sat down on the floor next to the little boy."

"Wow baby. That's really sad that she didn't even care enough to find out more about you or what you were there for."

"Yeah, most of these cases are sad. But this one has a glimmer of light. I started in with my interview questions and his answers were so thoughtful and well spoken, I could hardly believe this child had come from the same woman who answered the door."

Just then his Blackberry started to vibrate in his pocket. He acted as though he didn't hear or feel it and continued.

"I asked him what he wanted to be when he grew up and you know what he said?"

"What…..A doctor? Lawyer?"

"No, he said he just wants to be a good father to his kids so they would never know how it felt to be lonely."

"Oh God, you're gonna make me cry."

"I was almost in tears myself. So we go through the rest of the questions and I'm just about done when the crackhead momma gets a visit from some guy. They go huddle up in the corner and the next thing I know, she's telling me she has to leave and asks if I could watch her kid for a couple of hours. I was pissed that she would even consider leaving her child with a complete stranger and started to tell her, hell no! But then I looked at the kid, who was now back staring at the TV as if waiting for someone who really cared about him to magically crawl through it."

His Blackberry was going off again, and again, he ignored it.

"So, what did you do?" I asked.

"Well, I couldn't just leave him there—not like that. So, I told her I'd watch him. Then her and the other crackhead looking dude up and left. I remember looking at my phone and had 16 missed calls all from Angelica in a matter of hours. But the kid said he was hungry, so I didn't bother checking messages right then.

Instead, I went and looked in the fridge only to find some molded cheese, a couple of packets of ketchup and something that looked like it used to be a pack of hotdogs. I mean this case really disturbed me and I felt extraordinarily affected by it."

His Blackberry was buzzing again.

"Shit!" he growled, quickly sitting up in frustration. Finally, he pulled it out and answered it.

"What!" he shouted. "Look Mia, I told you I'm working on my rebuttal. I have to get this done tonight. What don't you understand? Alright—Okay--Whatever. I'm not—I told you no—shit, so stop asking me!"

I got up and went into the kitchen and started putting the dishes away, but continued listening.

"Look, don't threaten me! If that's the way you feel then just do it!" he shouted before hanging up and tossing his Blackberry on the sofa next to him.

I came back and picked it up, then sat. His call log was still on display. I stared at it, then turned it around, showing it to him.

"What's this 3084 number next to Angelica's name? Is that incoming and outgoing?" I asked.

"No, it's just incoming. You have the same company issued Blackberry that I have. Don't you know how to read it?"

"None of my contacts have ever had a number that high next to their name, smartass."

I lightly tossed his Blackberry onto the table.

"I'm sorry, love. I didn't mean to be curt with you." He placed the pillow back in my lap and resumed his spot.

"So she's called you 3084 times? You've only been on her team for six months. Does she call you on weekends too?

"Yup."

Just then, a bright wattage bulb clicked on in my head and I began grinning at him. Our thoughts silently merged and he smiled back.

"See, that's why I'm so damn attracted to you. You're smart, you're beautiful and you're turning me on right now," he said.

"How does she expect you to get any work done if she's calling you that much?"

"Exactly, not to mention her emailing me all day."

Our minds were communicating again as we exchanged a look of excitement. He sprang up and retrieved his laptop and opened Outlook. I leaned in to get a closer look at the folder entitled, Angelica Incoming and as I did, my breast mashed up against his arm, drawing his attention to my protruding nipples.

"Look, she's emailed you 4247 times in six months," I said, pointing to the screen. But his eyes were still fixed on my breast. I gently grabbed his face and turned it towards the screen.

"Now, you feel my pain," he said.

"I do and from where I sit, something is definitely wrong."

He smiled, placing his laptop on the table.

"Now, we've got something to work with. Did the crackhead momma ever call you to say thanks for watching her son?"

"Believe it or not, she had enough sense to at least do that and left a message."

"You still have it?"

"Yup."

"Good. That proves that you were actually working and weren't just out tricking off somewhere."

He chuckled.

"Did you just say, tricking off? Whoa, what would Jesus think?" he said.

I playfully punched him in the arm.

"Come here," he said, slowly crawling on top of me. As we kissed eagerly, his hand found its way inside my panties and wandered deep into my forest.

"Damn I want you," he whispered.

"I want you too."

"I can tell."

He lifted my tank top and his lips traveled to my breast while my fingertips massaged the back of his neck.

"You should probably go, so we can stay focused," I softly said.

"You don't want me to do that," he replied, eyes returning to mine.

"No I don't. But, I don't think you should stay either."

"But I need you. I need to release some of this frustration and stress."

"Some stress is good for you. Keeps you on our toes."

"I don't want to be on my toes. I want to be inside of you," he said, raising up and undoing his pants.

I sprang up.

"No! No baby. We can't."

"What do you mean, we can't. Why not?"

"'Cause we both need a good night's sleep so we can be our best in the morning."

"This is how a good night's sleep is created."

"Jonaaathaaaan," I whined.

"Alright," he conceded, zipping and buckling his pants back.

He sat next to me with one arm folded behind his head and sighed.

"You're just punishing me for that cab shit earlier," he said.

I climbed on his lap and straddled him.

"Now why would I do that? To punish you would be to punish myself 'cause I'd be missing out too."

"Alright," he said, sitting up and sliding on his boots with me still on his lap.

I got up and took his hand, pulling him to his feet.

"I'm gonna use your lavatory before I go," he said.

"Okay, you know where it is."

While he was gone I sat staring at his Blackberry, fighting off the urge to pick it up and discover the mysteries it contained in the message log I'd noticed earlier under the name, Mia. I wondered why she wasn't bestowed a more prominent name like, My baby, My dime or even Boo for that matter. Then, I thought about how pissed I'd be if we shared the name, love and felt downright covetous of it.

He returned, packed up his things and we headed for the door hand in hand.

"Listen, although you always look nice, I want you to look extra sharp tomorrow, so wear a suit and tie," I said.

"I want you to look extra fine too so wear a thong and no bra. I'm kidding. You know I like it classy."

He grabbed me and gave me a bear hug, leaning backwards while my feet left the ground. We kissed long and slow before he lowered me.

"Thank you so much Skyla for all your support. You don't know how much I appreciate it," he said.

"You're welcome baby."

"Guess I better go."

"See you tomorrow at 8 o'clock sharp."

"I'll be there at 7:30am." He gave me a quick peck to my lips before leaving.

As he walked to his truck, I stared out the window and couldn't take my eyes off him. I wanted to run out and call him back. But, my earlier prayer for help and strength had worked and instead, I said a prayer of thanks and decided to go the extra mile by Googling, excessive email/voicemail from boss. The search just yielded a bunch hostile Tweets and blog posts from disgruntled employees bashing their bosses—nothing legally concrete that we could use. Guess we're just gonna have to rely on prayer and our wits. It usually works for me, I thought.

Chapter Thirteen

Adjusting the Tension

As I drove home, I thought about how it'd been my idea for us not to assign meaning to our connection. But, my heart was quickly revolting, implementing its own plans with Skyla being the driving force behind them. Although I wanted to stay, she was right. I needed to sleep, focus and rejuvenate for the task that lay ahead. After all, my future depended on it. Question was, who would I be depending on in my future. I thought about all of my conversations with her from the time we met until my head hit the pillow. It had been a while since I had such frictionless dialogue with a woman and I couldn't wait to see her again.

The next day, my phone started ringing early. While still in bed, I smiled and reached for it anticipating hearing Skyla's voice.

"What, you don't trust me to get up on time?" I said, grinning.

"Hey baby. No, I know what a punctual man you are."

I shot straight up.

"Mia, oh…hey."

"Hey baby. Look, I'm not gonna keep you. I know you've got a lot on your plate today. I just wanted to wish you luck with everything and I also need to stop by and pick up a prescription I think I left in your medicine cabinet."

"Well, let me go take a look. Hold on."

I went to the bathroom and opened the medicine cabinet.

"There're a couple of bottles in here with your name on them,"

"Can I swing by this morning sweetie? I really need them."

"I'm leaving at 6:45am, so you've got to be here before then."

"Well, I'm already up and out so I'll be there in about twenty minutes, if that's alright with you."

"That's fine."

After hanging up, I glanced at the clock which read 5:50am. I went to the closet and selected a black suit and light gray shirt with a matching tie and headed for the shower. As I sang the tune, Let's Get Closer by Atlantic Starr, I thought about calling Skyla when I got out, but decided to wait.

Afterwards, I wrapped a towel around my waist then the doorbell rang. I took Mia's prescriptions from the medicine cabinet then hurried over to answer it.

"Hey."

"Hey baby," she said, prancing in and looking around with a McDonald's bag in her hand.

"I figured you wouldn't have time to eat, so I brought breakfast."

"Thanks." I placed her prescriptions on the table then opened the bag.

She continued to the kitchen and started opening cabinets.

"Wouldn't you know it, just as I was placing my order, they ran out of coffee. So, I'll make you some."

She got a bag of Gevalia and starting a fresh pot.

I unwrapped an Egg McMuffin and bit into. But, it needed something so I went to the fridge. While bending down searching for the jelly, her coat dropped to the floor next to my foot. I stood, trying to keep my eyes from traveling her form as she posed wearing nothing but a pair of black pumps.

"We need to talk," I said, turning away and pulling up a chair at the kitchen table.

"Do you like my outfit?" she asked, coming over and massaging my neck.

"Look, you've got to stop this. Do you think you can just say the shit you said last night and walk in here this morning like nothing ever happened?"

I got up and grabbed her arm then scooped up her coat.

"Ouch, you're hurting me," she said, snatching away.

"You need to leave now Mia!"

I tossed her coat to her and walked over to the door. She began walking towards me with tears in her eyes. But I couldn't control my eyes from roaming her bare frame.

"Don't act like you don't know what's really wrong," she stopped and said.

"I know what's wrong. I just can't deal with it anymore. I can't believe this shit," I mumbled, getting her prescriptions and shoving them into her hand. I grabbed her arm again and began rushing her to the door.

"Jonathan wait. Now just wait a minute!" she screamed, jerking away and facing me.

"You know what, on second thought, fuck you!" she yelled, putting on her coat. "Don't treat me like I'm stupid. I know damn well what this is about!" she shouted. "It's about a new piece of ass! Look at you, you're not even officially enrolled yet, but you're already testing the pussy pull of that Princeton degree! You don't give a damn about me. You were with some other bitch last night, weren't you! I don't think you ever really loved me."

"Are you serious? Why the hell else would I have put up with your crazy ass for this long? Oh, yeah….it's because I like to argue and fight all the damn time. And I love your fucking mood swings. Oh…and I especially like only having sex with you twice a year. And as if that wasn't enough, you had the audacity to go to my job and make a complete ass out of you and me! I'd forgotten what a great catch you are! Thanks for reminding me Mia!"

She just stood there and started laughing.

"You wanna hear the truth about why we only have sex twice a year Jonathan? Maybe if your sex wasn't so wack and you actually came close to satisfying me in those two times you're complaining about, I'd be willing to fuck you more often! It's a goddamn waste for you to have all that dick and not know what the hell to do with it! You think you're so damn smart, don't you. You're nothing but a fucking user. You made me fall in love with your ass and now all of a sudden you don't want to be with me anymore. I should have seen this coming. You're no different from any other man I've been with. You might know bigger words and have better diction when you feel like it, but you're still full of shit!"

She continued cursing and berating me so furiously that her words almost became inaudible. Her verbal blows hit and stung and she went way further below the belt than I felt my actions had warranted. She became louder and more pugnacious with every word spewed from her mouth. And in that moment, I stood there and wondered how I'd gotten to this place with a woman I'd contemplated spending the rest of my life with.

I watched her mouth move as she hurled insult after insult at me. But, as bad as the situation in front of me was, it was also familiar. The circumstances were different, but the feeling was exactly the same. That helpless sense of not being able to control what was happening to me had returned. But this time, I was a grown ass man, not a cowardly child who became gripped with fear whenever his abusive stepfather looked in his direction.

Realizing that she'd probably gone too far, she suddenly stopped talking for a minute.

"I'm sorry baby. I didn't mean any of that. Please, I don't want this to end this way," she said, removing her coat and placing it on the floor. "Look, I love you. It's the disorder that makes me this way. I'll start taking the medicine every day, I promise. That's why I came over here."

She moved in closer and gently kissed me.

"I need you," she whispered in my ear while wrapping her arms around me and kissing my neck. "I'm getting better. Just please, be patient with me."

I stared into her eyes and felt nothing.

"Think of what we've been through….what we mean to each other. I…I know you could find another woman if you wanted to, but I don't think she'd love you like I do," she said, then began kissing my chest, slowly inching down to my stomach. "I mean…who else would be willing to do the things I do for you—things like this," she whispered, glancing up at me while removing my towel and continuing to lower herself. Her jaws were now surrounding my flesh. I watched her as my logic became locked in a battle between the erotic and the unethical and soon the unethical won out. Suddenly she stopped.

"I know you still love me," she said, slowly stretching out in front of me and spreading her legs.

My mind briefly flashed over the arguments, her insane accusations and insults. And when it finally stopped whirling, I decided she owed me something—and I was about to collect.

Chapter Fourteen

Zigzag Stitching

The next morning I rose extra early and started my routine. When it was time to get dressed, I remembered my request for Jonathan to look nice and committed myself to doing the same by selecting a fitted, knit light gray dress with a cropped black jacket. After putting on matching jewelry, I rushed out the door, skipping my usual cup of tea.

I got to work around 7:20am. As soon as the elevator doors opened, I saw a huge crowd including Chase gathered around Sonya at the front desk. When Sonya saw me, she immediately stopped talking and made exaggerated eye movements to alert the crowd of my presence. Chase turned around first. Then everyone else stopped talking and looked in my direction.

"Oh....hey Skyla," Chase said as I approached.

"What's up everybody? Is today National Chill Out day or something? Seems like nobody's working," I replied.

People began to scatter, returning to their desks.

"So, how you doin' today?" Chase asked following me down the hall.

"Fine and you?"

"I'm alright."

We walked into my office and I hung up my coat.

"Good. Have you seen Jonathan?" I asked.

"Not since yesterday."

"Okay. I don't mean to be rude Chase, but I really gotta get to work."

"I understand. Talk to you later," he said, turning and exiting.

I stood slowly twirling, examining the room. Then I began looking on top and underneath my desk. Suddenly I began to panic and started frantically searching through my bag. "Damn. I don't believe this," I whispered to myself with my hands on my hips still looking around. I'd left the other bag containing my notes for the hearing and my laptop at home. Now, I really needed to speak to Jonathan. I walked around the entire floor and saw no sign of him. So I went back to my office and waited.

Then, my phone started ringing.

"Hello."

"Yeah, hi Sheila."

"It's Skyla, Angelica."

"Oh…well…you know what I meant. I'm stuck in traffic and might be a few minutes late."

"Not a problem. Just call me when you get in."

"Is Jonathan there yet?"

I paused for a minute.

"You know… I'm not sure. He could be."

"Well, I've been calling him all morning and he hasn't answered or returned any of my phone calls yet again. See, this is exactly what I mean."

"Look, we'll deal with all that when you get here. Are you in the car, because you really shouldn't be talking on the phone if you're driving."

"You're right. I'll be in shortly."

"Okay. See you then."

I glanced at my watch and saw that it was now 7:50am.

"Shit….where is he?" I whispered, picking up the phone and dialing his number. It went straight to voicemail.

I emailed and texted both his work and personal accounts and sat nervously waiting for him to get back to me. I tried to relax, but became more anxious with each passing minute until the sound of a familiar voice distracted me.

"Where is he? Let's do this," Angelica popped her head in my door and said before continuing to her office with two shopping bags.

I got up and walked slowly behind her. My heart sped up with every step as I tried to devise a plan to stall until Jonathan arrived.

As we approached the elevator corridor, I felt as if I was moving in slow motion. About midway through the corridor, the dinging sound of the middle elevator caught my attention. With heavy anticipation, I turned my head in hopes that Jonathan would emerge. But, a hurried messenger stepped off instead, causing the muscles in my stomach to tighten. I began to feel angry. How could he miss this? How could a man—a black man—totally blow off an opportunity to attend Princeton? I felt that if he didn't care, then I didn't care either and he deserved whatever his fate turned out to be.

Angelica was now a car length ahead of me.

"Let's speed it up, missy. I ain't got all day," she turned around and said to me. And, at that moment I knew the meeting was doomed. Without Jonathan, there was no point in wasting mine or Angelica's time. I had to call out to her and put an end to this charade. I opened my mouth, but became startled by the sudden swing of a stairwell door opening up beside me as I walked by.

"Hey…am I too late? I didn't miss it, did I?" Jonathan nervously asked, falling in step with me while straightening his tie. I felt a rushing sense of relief, but anger still kindled within me.

"Where the hell have you been?" I whispered as we began to walk faster.

"You don't want to know."

"Never mind. On top of everything, I left my bag at home with all of my notes in it." I threw up my hands.

"I have your notes. They must have gotten mixed up in my stuff last night."

"Oh, Good. Angelica is pissed. She didn't think you were gonna show up either."

"Either? You mean you didn't have any faith in me?"

"Look, you knew what time you were supposed to be here. I can't imagine why on earth you'd be late to something as important as this."

"I'm here now and that's all that matters. By the way, you look wonderful," he said, looking me up and down.

I cracked a partial grin.

"So do you Mr. Bass. You'd think we'd planned this," I replied, referring to our matching outfits.

We all entered Angelica's office in a single file line. While me and Jonathan sat, Angelica took the opportunity to stand back and catch her breath. She seemed exhausted. Her messy hair hung from different angels on her head while sweat streamed down her face and landed on the oversized dingy, black top she had on.

"You need help with any of that?" Jonathan stood and asked, reaching for her bags.

"Nope. I got it," she said, sitting them down on the floor.

One tipped over from the fullness and a green and white box of Krispy Krème donuts tumbled out. Jonathan politely picked it up and put it back with the other dozens in the bag.

She then proceeded to squeeze herself around the narrow space between a file cabinet and her desk, finally plopping down in her chair and exhaling deeply.

"So kids….what game shall we play today…huh?" she asked, leaning forward with folded hands as her eyes shot back and forth between me and Jonathan.

"You know the routine. I have to tell you that this discussion is being recorded for evaluative purposes. Why don't you start by going over your complaint against Jonathan," I said, placing my Blackberry on her desk and activating the voice recorder app. She opened a folder and began taking out papers.

"Well Jonathan, you know what the problems are. I've been over this with you time and time again. I'm to the point where I can't tolerate your behavior anymore. Something's gotta change or you're gonna have to find yourself another job."

"Now hold on, Angelica," I said. "There's a process we have to follow. We can't just yell out threats off the top of our heads. Let's examine the facts and follow the guidelines set forth by CRED. Just to refresh everyone's memory, I'll read your complaint against Jonathan. On November 28th……,"

"Wait…wait…..hold on a minute. I know damn well what I wrote and Jonathan knows too. The bottom line, Jonathan, is that you're rude, disrespectful and dismissive." Angelica said, pointing at him.

"I……"

"Wait Jonathan. What do you mean by, dismissive, Angelica?" I interrupted and asked.

"I mean that when I call him, I expect a goddamn answer, that's what I mean. I'm your manager, so I should take priority over anything else you've got going on."

"Speaking of expectations, exactly what are your expectations of him as an employee?"

"Well, I expect for him to respond to me in a timely manner. I expect for him to communicate with me in a tone that's conducive to a boss/employee relationship and I expect for him to get his fucking work done…...every day! That's it. Simple. And, if he can't do that, then I'm gonna have to…"

"Let's take these expectations one by one. So, you're saying that his current response rate is unacceptable to you, correct?" I asked.

"Right," she replied.

"Jonathan, what do you have to say about that?" I asked.

"First of all, as far as time is concerned, guidelines for all analysts have already been established in our handbook. We're supposed to spend two hours in the field interviewing participants, three hours scheduling appointments and two and a half hours wrapping up paperwork."

"That's right. And you're falling short of all of those guidelines, daily!" Angelica yelled.

"So Jonathan, how is your time actually being spent?" I asked.

He opened a folder and pulled out his notes. Angelica sighed loudly and pushed herself against the back of her chair.

"Well, what it really boils down to is, I'm spending three and a half hours scheduling appointments, two hours on the phone with you Angelica, and when I'm not on the phone with you, I'm spending the remaining two hours corresponding back and forth through email with you. So, the bulk of my time is being spent responding to you."

"That's bullshit!" Angelica shouted.

"Is it? Let's take a look at the numbers," I said. "Since June, Jonathan has received a total of 3084 calls from you on his Blackberry alone, office calls not include. That comes out to about 514 calls per month and roughly 17 calls per day," I said.

Angelica's mouth hung open as she looked at me. I grabbed a nearby calculator with a tape from her desk and began punching numbers into it.

"How long does your conversation with her usually last Jonathan?" I asked.

"About ten minutes," he replied.

"So, that's 170 minutes or almost three hours a day on the phone with Angelica," I said, scribbling it down on a pad of paper.

"You two are making this shit up!" she shouted.

"The numbers don't lie Angelica. Neither does his company cell phone records."

"Then, when you add in the 4247 emails I've received from you over a six month period of time, it works out to about 707 emails per month or roughly 24 emails per day. Factor in the five minutes spent on each email going back and forth about….whatever you feel like that day, I'm spending another two hours in written communication with you," Jonathan said.

"So," she replied.

"So, how can you accuse me of being nonresponsive when I'm spending over four hours a day on the phone and computer with you?" he asked.

Angelica's eyes darted back and forth between me and him.

"None of that changes the fact that he cursed me out and hung up on me! I won't tolerate that!" she yelled.

"Angelica, now you know I did no such thing. Why are you lying?" he asked.

"I don't have to lie on anyone. I'm your boss. You do what I say, when I say!"

"Depends on who you ask. Right now, the cursing out issue is a matter of your word against his," I said.

"Right and I'm the senior party in this situation," she replied.

"The Law doesn't look at it that way," I said. "And, if you pursue this further, there will be a legal investigation where things will have to be proven in a court of law."

"Are you threatening me?" she barked.

"I'm simply relaying the facts to you. You said he cursed you out. He said he didn't. Remember, that little hallmark

American principle that says people are innocent until proven guilty? The burden of proof will be on you to prove that he did. We could always subpoena the phone conversation in question from the cell phone carrier, but that will be expensive and time consuming.

Now, as for what we know to be true, we know from Jonathan's call and email logs that you have engaged in illegal, excessive contacting, to the extent that he doesn't even have enough time to complete his daily assignments. You're the cause of that, not him. Professionally, your work ethic is the one that looks suspect because of the amount of time you're focusing on him, instead of on your other work responsibilities. But, to a judge or jury, all of your calling and emailing will most certainly look like Corporate Bullying or some other form of harassment. They're going to want to examine your management history to see if anything like this has occurred in your past at other companies you've worked for. Are you really ready for them to go digging through your life like that?" I asked.

She turned beet juice red in the face.

"So you tell me....how do you want to proceed, given the facts of course?" I asked.

She folded her hands and leaned forward while staring at me with daggers in her eyes.

"I want you both to get the fuck out of my office and I want him off my damn team!"

"Done. So, we can forget about this little uh.... misunderstanding?" I asked with a smirk as I handed Jonathan her handwritten complaint. She didn't respond.

"I'll take that as a yes," I said.

Jonathan ripped up the complaint and laid it on her desk in front of her. We stood and exited while Angelica mumbled something under her breath.

"What did she say?" I asked him on our way back to my office.

"I don't know....I think she called you a black bitch or something," he teased.

We both began laughing hysterically.

"Shhhh," Jonathan said, closing the door behind us when we entered.

"Ha ha! We did it baby!" he shouted, hugging and swinging me around.

"Yes!" I shrilled.

"You got your Law & Order on today baby! Excessive contacting? Really, love? You were just makin' shit up, but it sounded good! I love it!"

We chuckled softly, trying to catch our breath.

"Thank you. Thank you so much love," he softly said, grabbing my hands and looking into my eyes.

"I didn't do anything. You were the one who kept me organized."

"Yeah, whatever. We both know you saved my ass and I just want you to know that I really, really appreciate it."

"Well, you're welcome, if it makes you feel any better."

Just then, there was a knock on the door. Jonathan opened it and Chase walked in.

"Wassup homies? Man, what did y'all say to Angelica? She round here stompin' and fartin' and shit. Y'all must have really pissed her off. So, how did the meeting go?"

"Fantastic, thanks to Skyla. She really did her thing."

"I can't take all the credit. Jonathan really stayed focus and kept us on track."

Chase looked at us suspiciously.

"On track? So, did y'all get off track or something? I mean, was y'all having trouble focusing?" he asked.

"No, no. I just mean that he was really instrumental in the outcome too," I said.

"Oh....okay. Well, why don't I take y'all to lunch to celebrate."

"I think I'm gonna pass on lunch. I've got way too much shit to do," I replied.

Chase was staring at me again with a peculiar look on his face.

"What....What's the matter?" I asked.

"You cursed. I've never heard you curse before. See, a couple of days hanging out with this dude and he's got you cussin' and shit. He's a bad influence on you."

"Chase, I do curse occasionally."

"Uh huh. What else has he got you doing?" he asked.

"Man get outta here. I need to talk to Skyla alone for a minute if you don't mind," Jonathan said.

"A'ight," Chase replied before leaving.

Jonathan closed and locked the door behind him.

"Come here love, let me talk to you for a second," he said, taking my hand and pulling me next to him on the couch.

"What's the matter baby?" I asked.

"Nothing. I just—I've got some things I need to say to you."

Chapter Fifteen

Going Against the Fabric Grain

"God you're turning out to be a blessing to me," I said, getting lost in her eyes.

"You wanna come over tonight and celebrate?"

"I wanna celebrate with you love." I pushed her bangs back. "But in a different way. Look, I've begun to feel a certain type of way about you and I know you feel the same for me. I want us to start spending quality time together to really see where this is heading."

"I thought that's what we were doing."

"Yeah, but we've been doing a whole lotta other stuff too. Look, our relationship didn't start out on the purest of paths and that's my fault. I kind of let my desire for you govern my actions. And though I won't apologize for it, I will attempt to correct it. So, I think we should chill out on the sex."

Skyla's mouth curled to one corner and she immediately gave me a look of wariness while slightly scooting away.

"Is this new found restraint because your significant other has suddenly solved her bedroom issues?" she asked.

"No, no… Look, it's like I said. I want to continue to see you, even more than I had been, but I don't want our physical relationship to skew our judgment."

Her eyes searched mine for truth.

"If you want to end this Jonathan, then just say it. But, don't play games with me."

"Love, are you listening to me? I'm not playing games. I really, really dig you and I'm trying to make things right between us. I care for you deeply Skyla and I want, no need, for you to trust me. I never want you to feel like I'm using you. It would just kill me if you ever lost that sparkle in your eyes when you look at me or ever regarded me with disdain."

"As long as you're honest with me, I would never do that Jonathan."

I kissed the back of her hand.

"Well I wanna make sure," I said.

Trust returned to her eyes.

"Okay, I see where you're coming from and I can respect it," she said.

"Good. Listen, there's an exhibit at the Art Institute of Chicago called The Sacred and the Profane. I think we should check it out tomorrow. Can you get away for a couple of hours during the day?"

"Sure. I love art museums and galleries."

"Then that's another thing we have in common."

I pulled her into my arms and sucked and kissed her lips. I tried to stick my tongue in her mouth but she wouldn't let me.

"Uh uh. If we're going to go on the don't do it diet, then we'll have to cut out the snacks," she said.

"I didn't agree to that. In fact, I didn't even say when this sex diet will begin."

"You have to agree or it's gonna lead to a failed diet."

"I'll take my chances."

"Well, what about me? Don't I have a say in this?"

"Not really."

"We'll see about that…."

###

Later that night, I lay in bed staring at the ceiling and thinking about the pact me and Skyla made and struggled at the mere thought of it. I suddenly got an inexorable itch to hear her voice, so I called her.

"Hello."

"Hey love. It's me."

"Hey you. What time is it?" She yawned.

"It's about 11:45pm. I was just thinking about you and wondered if you wanted some company."

"Umm, did you forget about our diet? Plus it's already so late baby."

"I just need to see you—hold you and watch you sleep."

"Yeah, right."

"It's true. Why don't you go put the key under the doormat so I can just come in and not have to disturb you."

Wait for it, wait for it....

"Okay. How long before you get here?"

YES!

"The usual—around 45 minutes."

"Okay, see you then."

Fuck the booty calls. This woman had me making cuddle calls. Now I knew I was sprung, making this diet all the more challenging. But, I told her I would let her sleep and I meant it. I could feel my swag shrinking, but for her I didn't mind.

Shortly thereafter, I pulled in front of her house and took a huge box out of my back seat. I took the key from under the mat and let myself in. I began creeping up the stairs carrying an iPod Home System I'd bought her as a house warming gift, while trying to avoid the creaky areas on the steps. Once in her room, the sight of her asleep while completely naked made me almost drop the box. This was gonna be harder than I'd thought. Using only the light from the hallway, I put the box down as quietly as I could and began to open and connect the system while being careful not to wake her. After it was all assembled, I pulled out the iPod I'd pre-loaded for her and placed it in the cradle.

While removing my jacket, my eyes diverted to her nude frame causing me to drop it on top of the remote, accidentally turning the system on.

Loud music began blasting through the room shaking her out of her sleep. She jumped up and began running around like an escaped Bellevue patient. Had I not swooped her up and held her, she probably would have run out the door and into the streets butt naked.

"Baby it's me," I shouted over the music before grabbing the remote and turning the volume down. I could feel her heart racing a mile a minute as I sat down on the bed with her on my lap.

"Shit, you scared the crap out of me! What the hell were you doing?"

The look on her face made me laugh.

"I'm sorry, love. Thought I'd surprise you with a gift, but this wasn't the outcome I expected."

"You surprised me alright."

After calming down, she gave me a look of welcome.

"Hey baby," she said before kissing me deeply like only she could. "What's this? An iPod Home? Ooo, thank you! Thank you so much!" she said, pouncing on me and kissing me all over my face. I leaned back and hooked my hands behind my head as she sat straddling me.

"You're welcome. I know how much you enjoy listening to music, so I wanted you to have what you needed."

Her lips began moving but I honestly wasn't listening to a word she was saying. Instead, I was laying there thinking, hmmm, we've never done it like this before. This was a different view and I wanted to see her body parts move from this angle. Suddenly, my hands were gripping her ass. It was round and firm like a volleyball and fit perfectly in my palms. And she had the kind of breast women took out loans to buy, yet the creator had given them to her naturally. I loved the way they spilled through my fingers when I cupped them.

"Are you listening to me?" she asked.

"Shhh. I'm really hungry."

"Me too, but people on diets shouldn't eat this late," she replied, looking at me seductively.

"How about we start our diet tomorrow."

She unbuttoned my shirt and unzipped my jeans.

"Did you get on anything yet?" I asked, wiggling completely out of them.

"No."

I gave her a firm smack on her ass.

"Jonathan, that hurt!"

"Well, you disobeyed me. Didn't I tell you to go and get on something?" I said with a playful smile.

"But, that was before this diet."

"The diet isn't gonna last forever. Plus, we're already about to fall off the wagon."

"I was only kidding. I got on the pill. But you still have to use something 'cause I haven't been on them long enough for them to work."

"Okay, I will. I'm glad it's the pill cause I've knocked a couple of IUD's out of whack in my day."

"I don't want to hear about all the women you've been in before me," she said, rolling onto her side and spooning me from the front.

"Well, you're the only one I want to be in now."

I reached over and grabbed my jeans, getting a condom from my pocket. I only intended to use it if she made the offer, which she did—kind of. As we lay in a loving, fixed gaze she said, "I love your completion. It's beautiful. You're almost rust colored. I know you were born in Texas, but do you have Native American in you?"

I flipped her over pulling her on top of me and replied, "Yup and now you're about to have it in you."

She sat up smiling and looking down at me.

"Since you're driving, you put it on," I said, handing her the condom. She unwrapped it and slowly rolled it on with a sexy stare. I smiled back in anticipation.

In my experience, fine women had a hard time with this position. I theorized that because of their beauty, they were used to men doing all the work while they sat mounted on top like pretty, perched peacocks. And although Skyla's hips and thighs rocked my soul when they danced against me in other positions, the way she was handling my wave confirmed that she was no different from her peers. But, she was about to learn.

I sat up, grabbed her hips and readjusted our fit before lying back down.

"Lean back on it," I instructed. And like a good little student, she did exactly what I told her to.

"Now, open your legs wider," I coached.

"Like this?" she softly asked in an eager to please tone.

"Yeah baby, just like that."

I gave her a slow, deep kiss for encouragement before reclining again.

"Now ride it. Go slow at first—yeah—that's it—just like that."

Our rhythmic strides became one as her face contorted with pleasure and I let her take control. Soon, she was galloping with no hands, breast bouncing up and down giving me an eyegasm. While her movements carried me to soaring points of ecstasy, I became amazed at what a quick study she was. Not only had she mastered her lesson, but she was soon winning achievement awards and had even become the summa cum laude. As her flesh bounced against my stiffness, my body blasted into erotic oblivion and I yelled, "Yes, Yes!" like a bitch as graduation day came.

After simmering down, we kissed and she lay covering me. And as any good professor would do, I offered positive reinforcement and whispered, "You were so good baby," while stroking her hair and kissing her forehead.

A few minutes later, she made a graceful dismount.

"I'm gonna go tidy up," she said with a sexy, just been fucked strut on her way to the bathroom. I got up and cleaned up as well then laid back down before she returned to my arms.

"I've got to find something to wear tomorrow. I wish it was Friday so I could just put on some jeans," she said.

"You always look sexy to me no matter what you wear."

"And, what is your idea of sexiness?"

"Well, I don't want to see it all, unless we're alone together like we are now. But in public, I find it sexy when a woman leaves something to be desired. When she shows just a flash of cleavage, a sliver of thigh, teases my eyes with her curvy silhouette or romances my spirit with a hairdo that uniquely frames her face."

"I'll have to remember that."

Soon she drifted off to sleep while I lay spooning her as close as possible from behind. She felt warm and slightly sweaty. I couldn't resist stroking her left nipple. It was the one that always came out to play. The right one was somewhat shy and needed a little more coaxing. She slowly turned over to face me and began kissing me gently, letting her lips travel down my chin onto my neck and chest. Then, against my silent wishes, she stopped and settled back in my arms.

"Damn, you're taking me somewhere—somewhere I've never been before," I said, peering into her eyes.

"You're taking me there too."

"Good, cause I don't like traveling alone."

Her eyes invited me to enter her again. But, I wanted her hunger to build and swell to near famine levels before feasting one last time. So, we went to sleep until her voice woke me a couple of hours later.

"Babe, wake up. You're talking in your sleep," I said, gently nudging her shoulder. "You alright?" I asked, sitting partially up and looking over at her.

"I guess," she replied, still half asleep.

"Who is Tylin?"

"What?"

"Tylin. You kept telling him to hurry up or he was gonna be late for school."

A look of despair invaded her eyes. She sat up and drew her knees into her chest, hooking her arms around them.

"That was the name I picked had my baby been a boy," she said, voice quivering and fading.

I began rubbing her back while she rested her chin on her knees. Then suddenly she sprang to her feet.

"I'm gonna get some water."

She left the room and returned with a glass for me as well. Mine had a wedge of lemon in it.

"Thanks love," I said, glancing at the glass and then back over at her.

"Have you always been like this?" I asked.

"Like what?"

"All thoughtful and considerate."

"You mean the water? I would hope that's just part of my character."

She sat on the edge of the bed with her back to me and took a sip. I heard her sniffle while she wiped her eyes and refused to let her sink into the darkness.

"Come here," I urged softly, sitting my glass on the nightstand.

She sat her glass down and nestled herself between my legs with her back against my chest. I wrapped my arms around her and kissed the top of her head.

"Listen to the words in this song. They express exactly how I feel about you," I whispered, taking the remote and pointing it to the iPod. Soon, Prince's Adore, filled the room.

As the music played, I laid my head atop hers and gently rocked her to the rhythm. I felt her teardrops on my arm and kissed the side of her head while gripping her tighter.

When the song finished, she looked up at me with tear stained eyes and said, "Thank you Jonathan," before kissing me tenderly.

"You're more than welcome, love," I whispered back.

She leaned into me again relaxing herself.

"When was the last time you took a vacation?" I asked, attempting to shift her mood.

"Last year. Me and Bree took a girls trip to Aruba."

"Wow, that must have been fun."

"Well, Bree had more fun than me, but I still enjoyed myself. It was warm and sunny everyday with white sandy beaches between crystal blue skies and waters."

"How come Bree had a better time than you?"

"She was single and I was married. Believe me, if I'd known then what I know now, it would have been a completely different trip."

"Oh, so you would have gotten down with big dick Dexter that you met on the beach?"

"Maybe."

She reached up and put one arm behind my neck, drawing my head down to her ear and whispered, "But who needs him when you've got jumbo, jank Jonathan," then gently squeezed my nuts.

I laughed so hard that I started coughing and couldn't stop. She got her glass of water and held it to my lips. I gulped it down then sat it on the nightstand.

"Aw man. What am I gonna do with you?" I said.

The smile on her face disappeared as she softly replied, "Love me."

We laid down spooning from the front again. As she drifted off to sleep I watched her and marveled at the profound effect she was having on me. Eventually, she opened her eyes and watched me back.

"I know I look like hell," she said.

"Hell ain't the word," I joked.

She walloped me on the arm.

"Ouch! And you're violent too," I said.

We laughed then kissed as she stuck her hand through my hair, straightening strands from their roots. The black opals were looking right through me, examining my soul.

"What's that look? I've never seen it before. What does it mean?" she asked.

"It means you've got my heart. Don't fuck it up."

"I won't. You have mine too. Is it safe?"

"It's in the safest place it could be besides your chest."

Our tongues searched and found each other, occasionally inviting our lips into the mix. Suddenly her clock began alarming. She glanced over at it.

"Babe, it's5:00am. I've got to get up in 45 minutes," she said.

"Okay. I'll leave you alone and let you sleep for a minute."

I cut the alarm off and just watched her breathe. At 5:45am, I shook and woke her.

"You gonna shower with me?" I asked, springing out of bed.

"Sure."

Chapter Sixteen

Steaming Open the Seams

He hopped in the shower and started without me. Moments later, I slid the glass door back and stepped in through the steam.

The warm water glistened on his skin, unveiling how firm and chiseled his body was. As he lathered, I couldn't resist pressing my body against his back for the sheer contrast of feeling my softness against his strength. I wrapped my arms around his waist and caressed his stomach while gently kissing his spine. He slowly turned to face me and walked me backwards until my shoulders pressed against the damp wall tile. With ease, he reached down and pulled me up to his waist. I locked my legs around him and we kissed—gently at first, then wildly as we became connected again. He closed his eyes then I closed mine while his strokes became slower and deeper, bringing my body to a thunderous release.

"Thank you," I whispered. Then his thrusts became faster and more forceful.

Time was suspended as we entered into that place that neither of us could grant a proper description. With one elongated push, he grunted loudly before coming to a complete halt. Suddenly, I was keenly aware of my senses again—the sound of the shower as water beat against the bottom of the tub, the smell of his breath as he panted—the moistness of his touch as he held me.

While pinning my arms back, he locked his fingers into mine and touched my forehead with his.

I opened my eyes and while his were still closed he whispered, "I want you in my life forever."

I kissed him softly and replied, "I'm not going anywhere."

He opened his eyes and lowered me, ensuring that my feet were stable before letting go and stepping back.

As he turned and resumed showering, I stood watching him in a trance and felt intoxicated. He turned and looked at me piercingly with a half smile—like he was proud of the spell he'd just cast upon me.

"Our diet has officially begun," he said, stepping out of the shower and wrapping a towel around his waist while grinning. I watched as he exited and felt like my heart had drifted to uncharted waters. But instead of being fearful of continuing the voyage, I wanted nothing more than to forge ahead with him navigating the way.

When I got out, he was gone. I dashed to the front window to see if his truck was still there and saw no sign of it either. I sighed then went and got dressed for work.

I was excited about our art excursion he'd planned and instead of the boring gray suit I was going to wear, I chose something else—something heavily influenced by his taste. I yanked a Vera Wang navy blue v-neck, curve clinging dress from my closet and put it on. I felt sexy yet sophisticated in it and wanted a hairdo to match.

Feeling ambitious, I attempted the messy up-do by drawing my hair up into a loose ponytail, leaving some strands out for curls. To my surprise, it came out perfect.

The dangling curls added a touch of romance and class. Now, all I needed were the right accessories.

I rummaged through my jewelry box and selected a silver chained necklace with a navy blue, druzy pear shaped pendant on the end along with matching dangling earrings. Then I spritzed myself with a couple of squirts of Donna Karin, Woman that he liked so much.

I gave myself one last review in the mirror. My inner critics had been silenced by techniques I'd learned in a book Jonathan had given me entitled, Quiet Mind: A Beginner's Guide to Meditation by Susan Piver. I got my coat and left hoping that since I couldn't have him in my bed for awhile, some of my senses would at least be stroked by hearing his voice, touching his hand or tasting his lips.

As I drove to work, Mary J. Blige's, Everything, came on the radio. I cut it up as loud as it could go and at the top of my lungs sang along.

###

The elevator doors opened and I stepped off, covertly glancing around searching for Jonathan.

"Hey girl. Woo, don't you look nice today! I love the new look," Sonya said with a smile.

"Thanks Sonya. You do too," I replied continuing on. Once at my desk, I jumped into my routine, but felt inspired. Instead of soliciting money from the usual suspects, I Googled, Top 10 grant-making foundations by total giving.

Just as I was about to print the results, the sense of hearing got crossed off my list as Jonathan's voice roared outside of my door.

"Man, you're crazy if you think the Clippers are gonna beat Orlando," he said.

"Alright. Put your money where your bullshit is," Chase replied. The two of them walked right past my open door without a word to me.

The smell of Jonathan's cologne breezed through my nostrils and my heart kind of sank. But the expectation of getting my other senses aroused resuscitated it. A couple of hours went by before I got up to re-caffeinate. As I turned the corner, there he was heading right towards me while reading some kind of pamphlet. Damn, this man could wear the hell out of a white shirt. I could already feel myself smiling even though he hadn't even looked up yet. As we got closer, my heartbeat sped up. He finally noticed me, eyes appraising my appearance from head to toe. Then he quickly turned and walked in the opposite direction.

Hmm, that was odd, I thought before shrugging it off. As the day went on, I wondered if he was still in the office. Before this sex diet, we would have been on our fifth phone chat and fourth mini hook up behind the file cabinets by now. I picked up the phone and dialed his extension, but he didn't answer. I picked up again.

"Hey Sonya, it's Sky. Can you do me a favor? Can you just pop your head up and see if Jonathan is at his desk?"

"Ok, hang on."

I began pacing while holding the phone.

"Yep, he's there," she said.

"He is? Well is he on the phone?"

"Let me see. Nope, looks like he's just sitting there."

"Ok, thanks."

Now I was really perplexed and needed to move around to clear my head. I went and boarded a crowded elevator with my lunch going co-workers and pressed the button for the 3rd floor. Right before the doors closed, Jonathan stuck his arm in causing them to retract. He got on, pressed a button and quickly perused the group before spotting me. Then, he blankly looked away, shoving himself in the corner while playing with his Blackberry.

"Damn Sky, you're looking fabulous today," a female co-worker looked at me and said, drawing everyone's attention to me except for Jonathan's.

"Yeah girl, you're workin' that navy blue dress," another chimed in.

"You sure are. And your hair is just too fierce and gone with the wind fabulous, hunty! Yaaass. You betta twirl!" a gay, male co-worker added.

"Thanks. You guys always look fabulous. See ya," I said, brushing past Jonathan and stepping off on the 3rd floor.

Some women overate when they were sad and some when they were happy. I did neither. Instead, I communed with extra calories when I was nervous or anxious about something. Therefore, Jonathan's cold indifference towards me had me tearing open my third bag of M&M's.

As more time passed without any communication from him, I couldn't ignore the fact that something wasn't right. And if anybody knew what was wrong, it was Chase. I picked up the phone and dialed his extension.

"What's up Skyla," he said after the first ring.

"Hi Chase. Listen, have you….."

"I've been meaning to bring you my expense report. But, I can't seem to find a few receipts I know you're gonna need."

"That's nice Chase. Look, have you spoken to Jonathan within the hour?"

"Yeah. He's right here. Hold on."

Chase moved the phone away and said, "Hey man, it's Skyla. She wants to talk to you."

"Tell her I'll call her later," Jonathan dryly replied in the background.

"Tell him don't bother. It wasn't important," I said when Chase returned to the phone.

My mind was now spinning with questions. Had I just been played? Was he angry with me? Did I utter something during our afterglow that was now giving him cause to pause? Had he checked my credit?

The day finally came to a close with no contact from him. He'd totally blown off our date to the Art Institute and I felt disappointed, angry and sad.

After straightening up my office, I removed my coat from the back of the door and while turning to put it on, heard the door close behind me. Suddenly, Jonathan rushed over, yanked the coat from my hands and pinned my back to the wall. I could feel his heart beating fast as he pushed himself against me and kissed me vigorously.

"Why'd you wear this dress, huh? Why'd you do your hair like that?" he growled before shoving his tongue in my mouth and thrashing it wildly around mine. "Damn you're so beautiful," he grunted between kisses and pants, holding my face between his hands. "How am I supposed to keep my hands off you when you're dressed like this, huh?" He pushed his tongue back in my mouth. "You knew. You knew what it would do to me, didn't you," he said, huffing and puffing. He spun me around and held me tightly by my waist. I could feel his stiffness pressing into me. As he kissed my neck, he stuck his hand inside my dress, squeezing my breast with one hand while running his other up my inner thigh and squeezing my crotch.

"God, I could just take you right here, right now," he whispered, grinding on my ass.

Now I was breathing hard too. Then without warning, he released me. Dazed, I turned to face him and entered into a trance again without a thought in my head.

He slowly backed up while staring at me. Then he opened the door before backing out and closing it gently. And I just stood there locked in complete longing. I swear had I not been in the office, I'd have stretched out on the couch and let my own fingers do the walking.

###

Later that night I took a hot bath and afterwards crawled into bed. A few minutes later, my phone rang. I examined the caller ID before answering.

"You owe me a trip to the Art Institute mister," I said.

"I know. I'm sorry, love. Man, you knocked me out today. But it felt like you were trying to force me off our diet. And I told you I'm serious about it, because I'm serious about you."

"That wasn't my intention."

"I'm sorry about our date. Let's go tomorrow. Can you make it?"

"Sure."

"Who's your favorite artist?"

"I have several, but of course, Paul Goodnight. I love how he uses color to express emotion."

"I feel you on that. But you can't forget about Ernie Barnes. The way he captured the mundane workings of the inner city was just phenomenal."

"I concur."

"Can't wait to see you tomorrow."

"Me too. I'll try to wear something less impacting."

"Don't do that. I'll just have to garner up some willpower from somewhere while we're on this diet. I'm getting so acquainted with my hand, think I'll send it some flowers. What do you have on?"

"Uh uh, I'm not going there with you."

"Going where?"

"You are not gonna have me on this phone having phone sex with you all night Mr. Bass. That's cheating."

He chuckled.

"Alright love. See you tomorrow."

Chapter Seventeen

Closely Knitted

Over the next several weeks, Skyla and I continued excluding sex from our connection. Instead, we went on long winter walks on the lake bundled up together, to restaurants, movies, art museums and galleries, jazz clubs and she'd even managed to get me to attend church with her occasionally. By now, I'd have gotten bored with most women. But she had touched me somewhere beyond the reach of any woman preceding her. Maybe it was because she was a little older. Or maybe it was the way we communicated both verbally and nonverbally. And then there was that tempting thought that she could actually be, the one. The one. I used to hate that term. As if God, who created 10,000 species of birds and 400,000 forms of flowers would shortchange us humans by only assigning us one person on earth to carry the happily ever after torch with. But now, I was more sold on that idea than ever before and perhaps Skyla was my forever tulip.

The holidays rolled around and she spent Christmas and New Years with her family while I headed to Benton Harbor, Michigan to visit Grandma Gladys or Momma G, as I affectionately called her. She took one look at me and said it was the happiest she'd seen me in years. I couldn't help but tell her why. She gave me her blessing and made me promise to bring Skyla back to meet her. So, a couple weeks later, I did.

"Baby, stop fidgeting. You look fine," I said as we drove.

"Thanks but am I showing too much cleavage? Maybe I should have worn something else."

"You look lovely. Momma G is gonna love you."

"But what about this hemline, is it too short?"

"No. Everything's fine, love. I don't understand why you're so nervous."

"You were just as nervous when you met my family. In fact, we were an hour late for dinner cause you kept changing clothes. But once you opened your mouth, they loved you."

"And Momma G is gonna feel the same way about you. Watch, you'll see. Just relax. Everything's gonna be fine."

She floated off to sleep leaving me alone with another woman, Anita Baker. Anita saw me through the duration of the trip until we were turning off the dirt road I used to ride my bike on as a kid. I pulled into the driveway next to the Red Brick Georgian style house and sighed long and hard.

"Skyla baby, wake up. We're here," I said, shaking her gently.

She opened her eyes and yawned then looked in the mirror.

"Good, my makeup is still intact. But I need some gum." She held out her hand in front of me.

"Here, take two."

"What are you tryin' to say." She punched me in the arm, taking the gum.

I grabbed a bag from the back seat and handed it to her.

"Here. She'll like this coming from you," I said.

"What is it?"

"It's her favorite."

We approached the porch hand in hand and I rang the bell. While waiting I said, "Relax," followed by a quick kiss on her lips.

Moments later, Momma G opened the door wearing a flowered apron over her dress and some red, fuzzy house slippers.

She stood smiling with one hand on her hip and the other holding a jelly jar of Harveys Bristol Cream Sherry.

"Hey baby!" she screamed giving me a hug as I stepped through the door. She was a large woman with long, beautiful silver grey hair. We shared the same reddish brown completion and height but her eyes were a bit more almond shaped than mine.

"Come on in," she said, sitting her jar on the table and hanging our coats in the front closet. The scent of her homemade sweet potato pie smacked me in the face and the welcoming feeling of being home overtook me.

"Momma G, I'd like you to meet someone special. This is Skyla Richards," I said.

"Hi Mrs…Mrs.."

"Just call me Momma G chile, don't even worry 'bout it. Come give Momma G a hug."

Skyla complied and gave her a cheerful embrace.

"This is for you," she said, handing Momma G the bag I'd given her.

"Thanks baby," Momma G replied, sitting the bag on the table. Then, she zeroed in on Skyla.

"Ooowee! Looka here. You dun went and found yourself a pretty little thang Jonathan," she said, grabbing Skyla's shoulders and turning her slightly while thoroughly examining her. "He's told me so much about you, but oowee, I see why you're so smitten boy. She's beautiful and look at that shape. So streamline with big ol' titties just like me and ya momma."

Skyla started to blush and bashfully looked down.

"Momma G, please. You're embarrassing her."

"Aw boy, ain't nothin' to be embarrassed about. He can be so shy sometimes Skyla."

"Please call me Sky."

"Ok Sky."

We sat on the sofa while Momma G sat across from us in her recliner, sipping from her jar.

"You know, men that grew up round big breasted women are always gonna seek that in a mate. And he's hit the jackpot with you! What you 'bout a 37/38 in the bust?"

"Momma G, when will dinner be ready? I'm starving," I said, trying to change the subject.

"In a lil while baby," she dismissively replied, turning her attention back to Skyla. "And you've got such pretty hair. Is all that yours baby?" she continued, going over and raking her hand through Skyla's hair.

"Yes ma'am, it is."

"It's beautiful baby, just beautiful. You got that Mandingo hair. It's thick, but if you put a lil coconut oil and a dab of goose grease on it, it'll shine like new money! Now, what about them titties, them yours too?"

"Okay, no more cream sherry for you until after we eat," I said, getting her jelly jar and walking to the kitchen with it. I came back and sat, putting my arm around Skyla and pulling her close.

"Aw, I don't mean nothin' by it. I was just complementing her, that's all."

"It's fine Momma G. Thanks for the tips. I'll try and remember them."

"Good, cause I want us to get off on the right foot."

"Where are Nina and Nick?" I asked. "Those are my twin cousins Momma G is raising," I explained to Skyla.

"Chile, you know these youngsters of today. I can't keep up with 'em. They ain't hardly ever here—always out with friends. And when they are here, they on that Facenote and Twister all the time."

"It's Facebook and Twitter Momma G," I said.

"Well, you know what I mean, boy."

"But, they're only 16. They should be in the house every night," I said.

"I know, I know. But you can't tell these kids nothin' today. They just runnin' wild I tell ya."

"Yeah, I know. Well, how are you feeling? You're looking good."

"Thank ya son. You know, I have my aches and pains in these old bones, but God is good. He keeps me goin' every day."

"I'm gonna go to the lavatory, love," I said to Skyla. She flashed me a loving smile and said, "Hurry back."

"Be right back Momma G."

"Ok son."

I could hear them making small talk and hurried up and finished before Momma G convinced Skyla to undress and prove that her breast were real.

"Did I miss anything?" I asked, returning to my seat.

"We were just getting acquainted," Skyla said.

"Momma G, why are all your undergarments hanging in the bathroom?"

"Oh, that's what I wanted to talk to you about. The dryer is acting up again baby. Remember how you fixed it for me last time you were here? Can you take a look at it again?"

"Sure, I'd be happy to. Be right back babe," I said to Skyla before heading to the laundry room.

Chapter Eighteen

Dark Colored Swatches

"Sky baby, come on and help Momma G out in the kitchen," she said, getting up.

"Okay," I replied, following behind her.

"Jonathan's told me all about you. He's really smitten. I ain't never seen that boy smile this much. And I see how you're smiling and lookin' at him. You're smitten too."

She handed me a head of iceberg lettuce, knife and cutting board. I began chopping the lettuce in preparation for a salad.

"I am Momma G. You've raised a wonderful young man."

"Yeah, I did. It wasn't always easy though. He had such a rough start and a lot of times, people who've grown up with difficulties reject Christianity because they just can't believe God would let them down in their time of need. But if they would just keep on livin' and believin' they would see that all them setbacks were just a setup for God to bless them in the future so they can be a blessing to others."

"Truer words were never spoken Momma G. I tell him that all the time."

"You do? Well, then he's surely found a blessing in you. Just keep prayin' for him baby. He'll be alright. God's got a plan for his life. Just look at what he's already doing—about to go to Princeton, can you believe that?"

"I know. It's awesome!"

"It shole is, especially having been through what he's been through."

"He told me about his Mom."

"He did? Well then he must really trust you. He keeps things so locked up and hidden deep down inside. But I'm glad he's finally met someone to share it with. Have y'all been to visit her yet? She needs all the encouragement she can get."

We'd given Momma G a bottle of Harveys Bristol Cream as an arrival gift. But I was starting to wonder if it was time to close the bar cause she was getting a little goofy.

"Um…no ma'am, we haven't been to the cemetery. But maybe I can talk Jonathan into going one day," I replied.

"The cemetery? What are you talkin' bout chile?"

"Well, Jonathan told me she died when he was very young."

"He did, did he?"

"Yes ma'am."

I dumped the lettuce into a bowl and starting in on the tomatoes she'd placed on the counter.

"Chile, his momma ain't dead."

Just then, I sliced into my flesh, accidently cutting my finger with the knife.

"Ouch!" I shouted as blood began seeping through my skin.

"Uh oh, come here baby. Let Momma G clean you up."

She got a band-aid from a nearby kitchen drawer then held my finger under cold running water. Afterwards, she dried it off and tightly bandaged the wound.

"There you go, you're all set," she said.

"Thanks Momma G. Now about Jonathan's mother."

She went and sat at the kitchen table.

"Chile, I can't believe he told you that. His momma is alive and well and residing at the Christina Crain Women's facility unit in Texas."

I felt like someone had kicked me in the head as I staggered over and sat in a chair next to her.

"I guess that boy is still too hurt to deal with the truth. Let me ask you this. Do you love him?"

"I do Momma G, with all my heart."

"Does he know it?"

"I try to show him every day."

"But have you told him to his face?"

"Well, no."

"Tell him. Tell him as often as you can. And even if he doesn't say it back right away, keep tellin' him, ya hear me. You don't know what that boy has witnessed."

"Why don't you tell me what he witnessed."

She looked at me apprehensively, then found trust in my eyes.

"Well, his stepfather Lamar, was an abusive ass drunk and I hate him. He beat that boy and his momma daily from the time he entered their lives until that tragic night."

"What happened?"

"My daughter, Barbara, simply couldn't take no more of his shit. I told her not to marry that bastard. But, she didn't listen. Jonathan's real father died when he was two and she just wanted a man in his life. That following year, she married Lamar and the beatings started. I begged her to leave him—even tried to get custody of Jonathan. But that just made matters worse, cause Lamar took out all his anger towards me on them. The best I could do was let Jonathan spend the summers with me and his grandpa. Broke our hearts whenever he had to go back to that house of hell. Anyway, from what I could make out from Jonathan and the police, Lamar came home drunk one night and started slappin' and beatin' my daughter. And when my little Jonathan tried to stop him, he started in on him—choking that boy and was about to kill him when Barbara went and got her .45 pistol and put four bullets in that bastard's head."

"Oh my God. And Jonathan saw all of that?"

"He did. He was only ten at the time, but he did. So, when I got the call from the police that night, I knew what I had to do. Without hesitation, me and his Grandpa John took him in and I've just tried to drown him in love every since. So, if you really wanna be with him, you've got to do the same."

"What happened to Grandpa John?"

"He passed about six years after Jonathan came to live with us. Complications from diabetes. But he was a kind and loving man. Taught Jonathan everything he knew. That's why he's so handy."

Shortly thereafter, Jonathan returned.

"Everything's all good Momma G. You can take all your stripper gear from the bathroom and throw it in the dryer now," he said.

She howled with laughter. "Thank you baby. You're so smart. I don't know what I'd do without you," she said.

"Looks like you two are hitting it off. What were you talking about?"

"Oh, I was just giving Skyla some vital information about you."

"Yeah? Like what?" He pulled up a chair and sat next to me with a smile and kiss to my cheek.

"About what you like to eat and how to season it, you know…..things a woman should know about a man."

I sprang to my feet. "Well, I've got a salad to finish," I said.

"And, I've gotta get dinner on the table," Momma G said, springing up after me.

"What can I do to help," Jonathan asked.

"Why don't you set the table baby," Momma G said.

"Alright," he replied, standing next to me and getting plates from the cabinet.

"You alright, love?" he asked.

"I'm fine," I replied, lying to him.

I was anything but fine. My heart ached for him after what Momma G had just told me. But everything I had been feeling was also clearly confirmed and I knew that I would love him forever.

We all sat and while sharing a delicious meal and light conversation. I was able to keep my new found discoveries under wraps. Still, I was dying to confront him about his past. But Momma G had explained his layers to me and I made a vow to myself to unravel them gently.

"Thank you Momma G. That was scrumptious. I could take a few lessons from you," I said after dinner.

"Nonsense. Skyla's a great cook Momma G, but that was delicious."

"I'm nowhere near the cook she is baby and you know it."

"Well, anytime you want to come up here and cook or if you need recipes, just phonemail me. Jonathan has my address."

"You mean email Momma G," he said.

"Boy, stop correcting me. You know what the hell I mean."

We all laughed. Then I yawned.

"Excuse me," I said.

"It's alright baby. I'm sure you're both exhausted. Why don't you go on upstairs and turn in for the night. You can take Jonathan's old room in the front. Just make a left when you get up them steps. Jonathan baby, you can sleep in the back room at the opposite end."

"Momma G, really? You're gonna make us sleep in separate rooms?" he asked.

"Boy, you know I don't allow no forn-if-a-catin' in my house."

"But what about Nina and Nick? What if they come home? We're gonna be in their rooms," he said.

"They don't even sleep upstairs no more. They be down in the basement apartment. Got blue lights in the sockets and funny smoke sailing all through my basement."

"Funny smoke? What does it smell like?" he asked.

"Kinda like burnt leaves," she replied.

"You should have rented that apartment out like I told you," he said.

"I know, but people are just so crazy nowadays. I ain't too keen on havin' a stranger livin' in my house."

"I understand. I'll have a talk with them next time I see them," he said.

"I shole would appreciate that baby. Now go on and show Sky where she's sleepin'."

"Okay. Come on love," he said.

"Aw, that's so sweet. Y'all shole make an attractive couple. Gone give me some pretty grandbabies one day."

Jonathan showed me my room then went and got our bags. He brought mine in and closed the door. We stood kissing sensuously before I slightly backed away as not to ignite a fire that would lead to us breaking our diet and fornicating in Momma G's house.

"You don't have to pull away tonight, love. I'm so damn tired, I couldn't bring the thunder if I tried," he said.

"Oh you could, if I made you."

"And how would you do that?"

"I've got my ways?"

"I'm sure you do, but you ain't showed them to me yet."

"Well, I'll be damned if I'm gonna show you up in your grandmother's house."

We chuckled.

"You're right. Get ready for bed and sleep well," he said.

"I will. Jonathan," I called out as he turned to leave.

He stopped and faced me.

"Yeah love?"

"Nothing. Have a good night."

"See you in the morning."

I changed clothes, climbed into bed and went to sleep. A couple of hours later, I felt hands cupping my breast and turned to find someone spooning me tightly from behind.

"Jonathan? What are you doing in here?"

"You know I can't be this close to you and not touch you."

"But what if Momma G walks in. She'll never like or trust me again."

"That's not gonna happen. After four jars of cream sherry, she passes out for hours."

I cut on the lamp and rolled over to face him. Damn he was fine, even half asleep with drool leaking from the side of his mouth. He opened his eyes and looked back at me.

"Did you have a good time tonight?" he asked.

"I did."

I gently started sucking his lips. He perked up and began kissing me back. He stopped and rolled on top of me, laying his head on my chest as I stroked his hair.

"You were a hit. I knew you would be," he said.

"I don't know if I was a hit, but Momma G sure is fond of my titties."

"She's not the only one."

"Baby?"

"Huh?"

"You trust me don't you?'

"With my life."

"Good. So you know you can tell me anything, right?"

"I know, love."

"And I want to be able to tell you anything too."

Suddenly I lost my nerve. But his response brought it to the surface again.

"I want you to know me inside and out and I want to know you the same way. I've never felt this way about anybody Skyla and I'm determined to continue down this path with you."

"I'm glad you feel that way. Jonathan?"

"Yeah love?"

My pause was so long that I almost lost my nerve again, until he rose up and looked into my eyes.

"I've fallen in love with you," I said.

"What took you so long? I fell in love with you the moment I held you, when you were smearing your snot all over my Armani sweater."

"Why didn't you tell me sooner?"

"I wanted you to say it first."

"Why?"

"'Cause I didn't want you to think I was just saying it to get some."

"Get some what?"

"Some peanut butter, what do you think."

"You miss my peanut butter, don't you."

"Immensely." He laid his head back on my chest. My fingers resumed their voyage through his hair.

"Well, now that we've admitted to being in love, can you put the peanut butter back in my life?" he asked.

"Maybe. Are you sure you want it back? Might make things a bit sticky between us."

"I want to be stuck with you forever…."

We fell asleep and I awoke the next morning to Momma G singing, Jesus Is On the Mainline, loud and off key.

"Baby, wake up," I said, shaking and waking him. "Momma G is already up. You better get back in your room quick!"

He stumbled out of bed and darted out the door. A few minutes later, I heard footsteps creeping up the stairs.

"Jonathan? Sky?" she called out. "Get up babies. Time for breakfast."

"I'm up Momma G," I hollered out.

"Me too Momma," he piggybacked from down the hall.

"Okay, I'mma finish up breakfast. Y'all come down when you're ready," she hollered.

We showered separately, got dressed, ate and helped her with the dishes afterwards. Then we packed up in preparation for our trip back to Chicago.

"Momma G, thanks for everything," Jonathan said, giving her a hug of gratitude. "It was good seeing you as usual and we had a wonderful time."

"We did, thanks again Momma G," I said with a hug and kiss on her cheek.

"Aw, y'all are welcome. Anytime. Come back and see me soon. Take care of each other," she said, opening the front door for us.

"You drive," Jonathan said, tossing me the keys.

As we drove, he kissed the back of my hand and gripped it tightly, smiling at me with his head against the headrest.

"You look happy," I said, returning the smile.

"Man, you just don't know."

"Tell me then."

"I'm happy." He let down the passenger window and shouted into the wind, "I'M HAPPY!" causing me to giggle.

After letting the window back up, he selected Musiq Soulchild's, So Beautiful, on the CD player.

While driving, I wondered if there would ever be a good time to bring up his past and unfold that one thick layer of pain. I had to know where his head was in terms of his mother, so I had to say something. But now was simply not the time.

Chapter Nineteen

Patching & Pressing

It was such a relief for the two women in my life to meet and actually like each other. Momma G emailed me and told me how much she enjoyed meeting Skyla and that she was noticeably good for my life. Her opinion meant the world to me and was in sharp contrast to how she felt about Mia. She hated her. In fact, the last time I resumed our engagement, I didn't even tell her 'cause I didn't want to hear her mouth about it. But as far as I was concerned, Mia was a thing of the past. Eventually, she'd get it. All my efforts were focused on solidifying my emotional connection to Skyla now. Sometimes I found myself just staring at her like you would a refreshing drink on a hot summer's day when wondering what was in it to make you feel so energized. And although we had paused our physical attachment, we were committed to the discovery process in each other—so much so that the only heat being generated between us was clearly coming from our cell phone batteries.

"What are you doing," she asked.

"Talking on the phone with you."

"Besides that."

"Writing you something."

"Read it to me."

"It's not ready yet. When it is, I'll give it to you."

"I'll write you something back."

"I'd like that."

"Maybe I'll give it to you on Valentine's day. You know it's coming up."

"You mean the man made holiday designed to siphon money from gullible, pathetic consumers?"

"As romantic a man as you are, I'm surprised you feel that way."

"I just don't think romance should be whored out for profit. It should be celebrated every day by making the one you love feel special, the way you do me."

"And you do me right back."

I stopped writing and sighed.

"What's the matter?" she asked.

"See, now I've got to go 'cause we ain't made love in forever and you've got me thinking about doing you."

She chuckled.

"You know I didn't mean it like that."

"Well, whether you did or didn't, thoughts are in my head and I better go before I end up coming over there."

"If that's the case, then yeah, we should say goodnight."

"See you tomorrow at work, love."

"Goodnight baby."

The next day I came into the office early. I had transferred to a new team and had a new manager. Juan Gutierrez was a young Hispanic brotha and was cool as hell. We got along great and now I had a second reason for enjoying my job. But calling my first reason was always top priority whenever I arrived.

The phone rang a couple of times and I was just about to hang up when she said, "Skyla Richards speaking," in her best professional black woman's voice.

"It's me, love."

"Oh, hey baby. Sorry, I was just changing my pantyhose and wasn't looking at the caller ID."

"I ought to come back there and take them off so I can dip my chocolate in your peanut butter."

"If you do that we'll definitely blow our diet. You know how fattening peanut butter is."

"I know, but I haven't had it in so long. A little taste won't hurt."

"A little taste will lead to us emptying the whole jar."

"You're right. Well, what are we doing tonight?"

"Since it's Friday, I thought I'd hang out with Bree and catch up. We haven't done that in a while and I miss her."

"Ok. Maybe I'll hang out with Chase then, since I haven't hung with him in a minute either."

"Maybe afterwards, we can hookup and go have an early breakfast at that all night hole in the wall diner on the west side that you like so much."

"Sounds like a plan. I'll call you when I'm done."

"Ok baby."

Later on that evening, I called Chase and he was totally up for it. In fact, he was already at the bar, so all I had to do was show up.

I spotted him as soon as I walked in sitting and flirting with a female bartender behind the bar.

"JD and Coke," I told her, sliding on a stool next to him.

"Hey man, what's up?" he looked up and said.

"What's up with you?"

"Man, guess who called me last weekend?"

"You know I can't keep track of all your freaks."

"Ahh, but you know this one, as in the biblical sense."

"Who?"

The bartender came and sat my drink in front of me.

"Thanks," I told her.

"Guess," Chase said.

"Man, just tell me."

"A'ight, Mia."

I chuckled.

"But she was looking for your ass. Called me at 2:00am last Saturday. Said she still had my number from the time you used my cell phone to call her. Man, why'd you do that girl like that?"

"Like what?"

"She said she hasn't heard from you in months and you won't return any of her calls. She actually broke down on the phone. Almost had me crying too."

"Mia's crazy and you know it. You went to Hampton with us. You remember how it was."

"I know but damn, you could have let her down gently."

"This coming from a man who cracks and discards women like eggshells."

"Well, I am the Captain Marvel of pussy. But you're the Captain Save-A-Ho, so what happened?"

"Skyla Richards happened, that's what."

"Ahhh. I should have known. What, y'all in love?"

"As a matter of fact, we are. Fate brought us together and fate will keep us together."

"Damn, it must be good cause she got you up in here singin' Captain and Tennille and shit. My grand momma used to listen to that shit."

We laughed.

"Seriously though man, I'm happy for you. I knew you had promoted her out of jump off status when you told me you took her to the Signature Room. Shid, my jump offs are limited to Harold's Chicken or maybe Pizza Hut if she gives good dome. But, never the 95th floor of the John Hancock building."

"Man, she was never my jump off."

"Oh, a'ight. Don't get offended. It is what it is. Besides, all anybody has to do is see you two together to know what's up."

"I'll take that as support."

"It is. Hey, if you're happy bro, I'm happy. Say, ain't that Ortiz over there?"

I turned to look where Chase was pointing.

"Yeah, that's that asshole."

"Hey Ortiz!" Chase shouted.

"Man, don't call him over here."

"Too late now."

Great, now Mia's ex-boyfriend, Cortez Ortiz, was walking over to us. He hated me and I hated him for what he used to do to her before we hooked up.

"Hey Chase. What's up?" he came over and said while grinning.

"Hey man, how you doin?" Chase replied.

"Hey Jonathan. How you doin' man?"

"I'm good," I replied, looking straight ahead.

"Good. How's Mia doin'? You two still together?"

"Nope."

"Seriously? I'mma have to hit her up on Facebook when I move back here in a couple of months. I'm just in town visiting my boys over the weekend."

"That's right, you stayed out there in Virginia after we graduated," Chase said.

"Yeah man, but it's just too damn slow. I gotta get back here where the action is. Well, I see my boys are here so I'mma run. Good seeing you guys."

"Same here man. You look good," Chase said as he left. "Man he looks bad," he then turned to me and said. "Remember how skinny he used to be in college? Must be all them enchiladas," he said.

"All I remember is how he used to beat the shit out of Mia."

"Yeah, he was a violent motherfucka. On a lighter note, what are you and Skyla doing for Valentine's Day?"

"Not you too. Man you know I ain't down with the bullshit."

"I know that but does she know it? All women expect something from a guy on that day. Even third tier hoes be havin' their hands out. So if you wanna be happy, then you betta make sure she's happy."

"Well, she knows how I feel about it and she knows ain't nothing happening."

"You sure bro, I'm just trying to keep you from making a crucial mistake by ignoring it."

"Man, I run this."

We sat, catching up until my Blackberry began to vibrate. I looked down and examined it.

"Gotta go man. Skyla's waiting for me."

I got up and tossed him the money for my drink. He broke into laughter.

"What's funny?" I asked.

"Nothing man. Go on and handle your business Mr, I run this. You don't wanna be late," he said, continuing to laugh.

Chapter Twenty

Permanent Stamping

My favorite holiday besides Thanksgiving had rolled around and my man was rebelling against it. But, that was his hang up, not mine. So I put on my baddest red dress and matched it up with a tube of MAC Divine Night red lipstick and headed off to work.

I just didn't understand why Jonathan was so sour on Valentine's Day. It was a day for true romantics to celebrate our everlasting belief in love and I wasn't about to let him ruin it. I didn't expect anything special from him that day and that was okay. I still felt grateful that love had visited me again, even though my significant other refused to donate 24 hours in its honor.

"Morning Sonya. I love your red pant suit. Girl, you're looking fierce today," I said, going behind her and checking my mailbox.

"Thanks Sky. You're lookin' especially jazzy too. Oh, hey…Jonathan was here earlier and before he left he asked me to tell you to call him on his cell."

"Okay, thanks."

I knew whatever he wanted had nothing to do with the spirit of the day, so I didn't rush to return his call. We weren't going to dinner. In fact, we had no plans to see each other at all, so I overlooked the folded note in my mailbox with my name on it in his handwriting and opened the more pressing things instead.

Once at my desk, I began editing a proposal, which kept me busy for hours. I didn't even realize it was past noon until my stomach started growling. Then, Sonya called.

"Hey, Jonathan's on the line."

"Ok, you can transfer him."

"Hey love," he said.

"Hey."

"Did Sonya give you my earlier message?"

"She did."

"Sooooo, were you gonna call me back?"

"I was, when I got a moment. Been kinda busy today."

"I see. Did you get my note?"

"I got it, but haven't read it yet."

"Well, make sure you read it. Look, I want you to spend the night with me tonight. I think it's time we officially end our diet."

"Oh really."

I was already a little miffed about not celebrating the day. But now I was pissed that he had the nerve to call me with such a selfish request. Men.

"Why should you get what you want when I'm not getting what I want today? You know what, I'm really busy. Bye." I hung up abruptly. A few minutes later an email from him popped up on my computer screen.

"You're acting like a spoiled brat and being mean to me today and I don't like it!!"

I quickly deleted it and went searching for the note he'd left to see how else he could irritate me.

I opened it and after reading it, instantly melted.

"Ooo girl, you look like you're about to cry. What's up?" Bree said, walking in the door. I grabbed a tissue and wiped the corners of my eyes.

"Nothing. It's just my allergies. I'm always leaking and dripping all over the place," I replied.

"Yeah right."

She snatched the note out of my hand.

"Bree, give it back!"

"Nope."

She proceeded to read the note out loud:

"My dearest Skyla:

You knew one day I would hunger for your existence, so you prepared a feast of love and you fed me. You knew I would be submerged under the weight of my own sorrow, so you lit a candle that led me to your touch and you restored me. You knew I was weary from being lost in an arctic land of unfamiliarity, so you allowed me to lay in your warmth, and you loved me.

So grateful that we met. Love Always, Jonathan Aristotle Bass.

"Daaaaammmmnnn girl! Ain't no man ever wrote me nothing like that! The closest I got was in the first grade when Timothy Wallace sent me a note with a booger on it that said, do you like me, circle yes or no. This sounds like he's in love like a motherfucka! You two romantic saps belong together. Bet y'all are gonna have a really special time tonight, huh."

"Wrong. He thinks Valentine's Day is just a capitalistic holiday designed to make the rich richer and the poor bigger suckers."

"That's too bad, but he might be on to something."

She handed the note back to me.

"What about you and Mike? What are y'all getting into tonight?"

"Definitely not each other. His auntie's bunion got infected and he's gotta go take care of her."

"What? Bree, you're an intelligent woman. Do you really believe that?"

"Well, yeah…I do. What?"

"Nothing. Nothing girl."

"Since you're not doing anything and I'm not doing anything, let's hookup and do nothing together."

Chapter Twenty-One

Mending the Tears In the Fabric

It was clear that my views had caused some tension between us. So, the onus was on me to straighten it out. The only reason the day had any significance to me is because it was important to her. And since she held it in such high esteem, I decided to let it become important to me regardless of my opinion. I made a few phone calls then popped in to see her.

"Hey Bree. How you doin'?" I asked, walking through the door.

"I'm good Jonathan."

Skyla looked at Bree and tilted her head a couple of times towards the door.

"Oh, hey…listen Sky, guess we'll get together and do nothing some other time."

"Okay girl. Bye." Skyla stood and locked the door behind her.

She came and embraced me, slowing moving in for a kiss.

"Uh uh. You must have read my note. Now you want a kiss. Nope."

"Shhh. Come here baby."

She gently showered my face and neck with kisses.

"You were being all mean to me earlier."

"I know. I'm sorry baby," she whispered.

"I should bend you over that desk and give you a spanking right now." I forcefully smacked her ass.

"Ooo, that hurt….and I liked it," she whispered, then kissed me zealously.

Afterwards, I took her hands and held them for a second before placing one on my forehead. "I don't feel so well," I said.

"What's the matter babe?"

"I think I'm coming down with something. And if I've got it, then you probably have it too. We should probably both take off tomorrow—stay in and work on ourselves."

She chuckled, shyly looking away.

"Come on, you wouldn't want to infect our co-workers with whatever we've got, would you?"

"Oh noooo. I wouldn't want to do that. So, when will we be hit with the full blown version of….whatever this is we're getting?"

"I don't know, but we should stay in and quarantine ourselves as a safety precaution."

I put my hand on her forehead and then on the side of her neck. "See, you're getting it too. But yours feels much worse. Let me take you to my place and nurse you back to health."

"What time?"

"About Sevenish?"

"Let's make it Eightish. I'm expecting some papers to arrive in the mail, so I have to go home first."

"Pertaining to the divorce?"

"Yep."

"Hmmm. Well that's important. Yeah, you go and handle that. Why don't I just swing by and pick you up then."

"Ok."

I turned to leave but before exiting looked back at her and said, "And bring a change of clothes….enough for a couple of days."

Over the next several hours, I conducted a number of interviews. Then, I headed to the car wash and got my truck detailed before going home to prepare for the night's unsupervised playdate. I wanted everything to be perfect. Our diet had accomplished its goal. We'd shed the casualness of our relationship and gained a stronger, everlasting bond. So I saw no need for it to continue.

But the night got off to a bad start. I was an hour late getting to her house. Not on purpose though. I'd ordered a special flower arrangement for her and even though these flowers were rare and out of season, the florist swore he could have them ready for me by 7:30pm. Not! But, they were able to pull it off by 8:30pm.

I quickly parked. But before I got out, my phone started ringing. Thinking it was Skyla wondering where I was, I answered without looking at it.

"Hey sexy," I said.

"Hey baby. I miss you. Where are you? What are you doing? I cooked you something special. What time will I be seeing you?"

Dammit!

"Look Mia, I have other plans." The phone went silent. "Mia? You there?"

"Yeah, I'm here. You know what? Don't worry about it. This is my fault. I should have talked to you first before I went ahead and cooked you a four course meal. I can just put it up and bring it over tomorrow."

"Uh, I don't think that's a good idea. Look, I gotta run."

"Well, who are you hanging out with tonight? Is it Chase?"

I was already an hour late and knew that if I told her the truth, she would have me on the phone arguing for another two hours or worse—be waiting outside to ruin my night with Skyla. So I did what any man trying to escape from the clutches of his old woman into the arms of his new one would do. I lied.

"That's exactly it. Me and Chase are just gonna hit a couple of clubs tonight. You know how I hate Valentine's Day anyway."

"Yeah, I do. Well, have a good time and don't drink too much."

"Alright. Talk to you later."

I hurried to the door with foliage behind my back and had to ring the bell three times. Figured it was payback for my tardiness. When she finally answered, her appearance blew me away.

"It's about time. Are you gonna be on CP time for your classes at Princeton too?" she said.

"Hey love. These are for you." I handed her the flowers and kissed her on the cheek as I walked in. "Sorry I'm late," I said.

Her eyes expanded as she completely unwrapped the arrangement and gasped.

"Awww…..these are beautiful baby!"

She reached up and kissed me.

While she went and got a vase, my eyes became cemented on the bottom half of her pink sweat suit with the word, Juicy, spread across her ass. When she came back, she sat the flowers on the table in front of us. I sat down and pulled her onto my lap facing me.

"Look at you. You're adorable without makeup. And those bangs and ponytail make you look like a 16-year old girl. Got me feeling like a lecherous old man."

"Mentally, you are a lecherous old man."

"Shhh, don't tell anybody. I have an image to uphold. You like your flowers?"

"I love them."

"Good, cause I picked them out just for you. Each kind has a special meaning."

I scooted up, leaning forward with her on my lap while she turned slightly towards the arrangement. "You see these right here—these are Yellow Jonquils. They symbolize, desire. And these ones are called Purple Larkspurs and they represent an ardent attachment—And the white ones are Syrian Mallows, better known as the Rose of Sharon."

"Oh, like in the bible."

"Uh huh. The giver of Syrian Mallows is said to be consumed by the love of their recipient. And the Rose of Sharon grows in dry, unfavorable conditions—kind of like my heart was before I met you."

Her eyes were bursting with compassion and she kissed me soulfully.

"You're really trying to get up in that peanut butter jar tonight aren't you," she said.

"Uh huh. I'm 'bout to rip it open! Come on. Let's go."

Chapter Twenty-Two

Give & Take in the Fit

I got my overnight bag and we headed out the door. There was something I needed to say to him and the drive to his place gave me a chance to share it.

"Babe, I have a confession to make," I said.

"What's that, love?"

"I kind of stopped taking my pills."

"What? Why?"

"They were making me so nauseous."

"Why didn't you just call the doctor and have them adjusted?"

"I meant to, but never got around to it."

Silence filled the air.

"Don't be mad," I said.

"I can't get mad at you. You're the hostile one in the relationship."

"Uh, did we just conveniently forget a certain incident involving you and a cab driver?"

"You're right. Guess we can both get a little turnt up. Seriously though, it's no problem. I'll just stop and get some condoms. Might as well pick up one of those home testing kits too."

"I think that's a good idea. We should know our status. What did you do with the condoms you had before?"

"We weren't having sex, so I got rid of them."

"Uh huh, you had better not been swirling your chocolate around in somebody else's peanut butter jar."

"Come on love, you know me. I'm picky and choosey brothas choose Jif."

We stopped at Walgreens then proceeded to his place. Once inside his apartment, he took our coats and hung them up.

"Excuse the place. It's a little messy," he said.

"Stop playin'. Your place is always neat. I'm way messier than you."

"I wouldn't say that. You're just a little unorganized, that's all. I'm gonna go and check on some stuff I put in the dryer earlier."

He left and headed to the lower level laundry room.

I sat in a recliner waiting for him to return while looking around. Although it was only a one bedroom apartment, it was always immaculate without any traces of clutter. My eyes continued wandering—stopping first at the recently waxed hardwood floors, then at the recessed bookcases housing dozens of books—then over to the evenly placed African American art on the walls and then-down to his music collection.

Even though we lived in a digitized world and Jonathan was always glued to his gadgets, I loved that he had tons of books and CD's. I walked over and examined his CD's closer, noticing their musical range from Bob Marley to Pat Metheny. My own collection included many of the same artists, confirming our similar tastes. Then, his cell phone started blaring on the table right next to me.

It was as if God had given me the perfect opportunity. Jonathan was gone and his phone was giving his text message alert tone from a sender named, Mia. I couldn't resist and picked it up.

We'd voluntarily exchanged passwords, so I had no logical reason to distrust or doubt him. Still, I couldn't help clicking on her message:

Hey baby. I miss you. While you're out having fun, I just hope you're thinking about the last time we made love. I've thought about nothing but. I understand what you're going through. In fact, no one understands you better than me. You don't have to verbalize it. As the wedding gets closer, I can feel you getting cold feet and pulling away. That's normal. It's okay if you need a little time, 'cause I know you'll be back. And when you return, we'll resume our plans to be one forever. Love Mia.

Just then he came back, arms filled with folded comforters. I quickly put his phone down before he looked over at me.

"Sorry it took so long, love. They needed a few more minutes. You hungry," he asked, putting one comforter down and taking the other into his bedroom. He came back and began spreading the comforter out on the floor. I studied his expression. He looked back at me, trying to decipher mine. I knew what we had and wasn't threatened by Mia's fantasies. We had the real thing and in that moment, I felt kind of sorry for her and wondered why she was still calling him. Had he ended things the proper way with her? Or had he left things up in the air, creating a twisted gray area in her brain that she delusionally interpreted as encouragement. I knew somewhere later in the night, I'd have to find out.

"Yeah, I'm kinda hungry," I replied.

"Good, 'cause I'm going to cook for you."

"Okay. I'm gonna go pee. Be right back," I said.

When I came out, he was in the kitchen starting dinner.

"Need any help?" I asked, sitting at the kitchen table.

"Nope. Just sit there and look pretty."

"You sure? I'd feel better if you let me do something."

"In that case, I guess you can go select some music and when you come back, you can pour us some wine."

"Ok."

I trekked back into the living room and rummaged through his CD's. Reasons, by Earth, Wind & Fire began to play as I walked back into the kitchen.

"Awww, yeah. That's a good one baby," he said.

"The old ones always are. They just don't make song like this anymore."

"I know, right."

I opened a cabinet and got the wine glasses, then the wine from the fridge, along with an opener from one of the drawers. After filling his glass with Merlot and mine with Unoaked Chardonnay, I sat and watched as he seasoned a pan of salmon fillets and placed them in the oven. Then he got a large mixing bowl and started dumping ingredients in it.

"I don't feel like I'm assisting much," I said.

"Well come over here."

He handed me a whisk and the bowl. I began whisking what was turning into some kind of sauce while he went in the living room and began placing throw pillows on the comforter he'd spread out on the floor.

He came back to the kitchen and poured Ziti pasta into boiling hot water, then went back into the living room and strategically lit candles all around the room. He dimmed the lights and came and stood next to me.

"I'll take this," he said, taking the bowl of sauce and pouring it all over the salmon.

"Look at you, Chef Home Boyardee. Not only is he smart, handsome and sexy, but he cooks too!" I joked.

"And don't you forget it," he said, smiling.

"Never, but I'm still the prize."

"God knows there's no disputing that."

Now Drake's, Special, from his first mixtape was playing. As I rapped along to it and adlibbed, he smiled while getting a bowl and dumping the mixture of salmon, sauce and pasta into it. Then he took the bowl into the living room and placed it in the center of the floor on top of the comforter before returning. I slid over next to him doing my best hip-hop rapper bounce while getting silverware from the drawer. He began bouncing to the music too while taking the silverware out of my hands and placing it back in the drawer, keeping only one fork. I continued bouncing and rapping, then took the few plates he had from the cabinet. He came and took the plates out of my hand and put them back in the cabinet. I stopped moving.

"What are you doing babe?" I asked.

"It's called a community bowl. We're going to eat out of the same dish with the same utensil. It's a custom over in Africa."

He took our wine glasses into the living room and placed them on the floor, sitting Indian style with his legs folded and sticking the fork in the bowl. I came and sat across from him in the same manner.

We said Grace and just before he fed me the first bite, I said, "African custom my ass....you just ain't got no damn dishes." We laughed, then I tasted his creation. "That's really good, babe! What is it?"

"Thanks, love. It's Ziti with honey mustard salmon. I'm glad you like it."

"You're just full of surprises."

"So are you. Whacha know about Drake old lady."

"I know plenty."

After we finished, he grabbed a pillow, put it under his head and stretched out on the floor. I climbed on top and lay covering him.

"You ready for dessert?" he asked.

"Depends. What's on the menu?"

"Peanut butter."

Chapter Twenty-Three

Piping Around the Edges

The night was full of passion as I got reacquainted with Skyla's peanut butter sandwiches. My memories were a weak match for her actual touch. Still, there was something I wanted from her that she hadn't offered me yet. Unlike my past behavior with women, everything I did for her I did sincerely from my heart. I never gave to get, never uttered anything to evoke some ego stroking response from her in return. So, I couldn't help but wonder why a passionate woman such as herself hadn't visited me in a particular way yet. Even though my tongue had roved her tender places numerous times, she still hadn't returned the deed. But, I loved and respected this woman and wasn't just gonna clobber her with, hey……when are you gonna suck my dick? I was a patient man and would wait until she felt inspired to sing to me.

The next morning I called off and lay watching her. She slowly opened her eyes and smiled.

"Morning gorgeous," I whispered.

She reached over and grazed my lips with a kiss before turning to look at the clock.

"Shit, I'm late for work!" she said, springing out of bed and quickly starting for the bathroom down the hall. But her steps were arrested by a jolt like movement before continuing at a slower pace.

"Calm down baby," I hollered out. "I called Bree earlier and told her you wouldn't be in today. She said she has keys to your office in case anyone needs anything and that she'll call you later."

The toilet flushed and she emerged walking way gingerly than usual.

"Oh, okay," she said, climbing in bed next to me.

"I just wanted you all to myself today. We're sick remember."

"That's right. I forgot we've got some mysterious illness that won't let us keep our hands off each other."

"You okay? I noticed you walking a little different."

"Well, you did kind of rearrange my anatomy last night. I think my ovaries are where my appendix used to be and my liver and kidneys are now a threesome."

"I'm sorry, love. It's just that the sight of me inside of you from behind takes me to caveman levels. Tell you what, I'll run you a hot bath later on and try to lay off of it for a day or two."

"I didn't ask you to lay off of anything. I've never been a big fan of doggie style, but you made me a believer last night."

"You just hadn't been humped by the right dog, that's all."

She leaned over and kissed me.

"Maybe I should call Bree."

"Can't you do that later?"

"Ok. Well then I'm gonna go to the bathroom and journal."

"Why can't you journal right here?"

"I need a little privacy baby." She climbed out of bed and grabbed her overnight bag.

About 15 minutes later, she returned to my arms with a smile.

"You feel better now?" I asked.

"Much. Thanks for understanding."

"Of course I understand. Actually, I really dig that you have that as a passion. Now it's your turn to understand that I gotta take a leak."

Once in the bathroom, I noticed her bag lying on the floor with her journal sticking out of it. Jonathan, don't do it man—don't invade her privacy like that. She wouldn't do that to you, I thought, eyes glued on her journal as I took a piss. Like hell she wouldn't, I then reasoned.

I washed and dried my hands, then carefully slid the journal out of her bag. While opening it, part of me felt guilty. But the other part that wanted to know her completely felt justified as I quickly read her last entry:

Last night, Jonathan's tongue awakened nerves I didn't even know I had. As it caressed my folds, I wondered how he knew the exact places to apply pressure and tenderness to. Damn his phone! I could have stomped the shit out it for messing up the flow and abruptly ending his service session, even if it was Momma G. Afterwards, I thought about giving him all of my ATM and credit card pin numbers if only he would go back down and finish what he started. Instead, I settled for his smile which ignites fireworks in my heart. I love how he looks at me as if I were made for him. But lately, there's a hint of a question in his gaze and I know he's been waiting for this. So there's no befitting time than now to celebrate the death of that damn sex diet by granting him his silent wish. After all, he's earned it. Aside from his kindness and generosity towards me, he has the kind of dick that you want to please—let it go wherever it wants to go—do whatever it wants to do, feel whatever it wants to feel and I'm honored to be its tour guide. I want to sing to it until it swoons, then demands an encore for which I will gladly return to the stage.

Damn!!! It's about to be on and poppin'! Let me hurry up and get my black ass back in that bedroom, I thought, closing her journal and sticking it back in her bag.

When I returned, she was on her knees at the foot of the bed.

"Come here," she softly said.

"What are we about to do, pray?" I asked.

"No, but one of your prayers is about to be answered," she said patting the bed in front of her with a seductive stare.

I tried to be cool as I sat down. Then, with diva like confidence, she grabbed my mic and opened her mouth.

She started off gently humming to me in a slow, melodic tone. Soon, her tongue was traveling up and down my scale as it vacillated between flat and sharp notes while doing sweeping riffs. But this was no run-of-the-mill pop song with mediocre, auto-tuned vocals. This was an Italian aria supported by the strength of a full string orchestra with perfect pitch. But there was nothing sad or tragic about the story she was weaving around my loins.

As her jaws took me in further, she sped up the tempo sending me into symphonic bliss. The warmth of her mouth against my shaft swelled my anticipation and at the point where most audience members cried during an opera, I wanted to blindfold myself from her performance to keep from surrendering to her passion too soon. But, like the tearful opera goers, I couldn't restrain myself and exploded with liquid applause during her finale.

My body immediately went limp and I felt drained.

"Did I get you?" I asked as she stood and grabbed a washcloth from atop the dresser.

"A little," she said, tossing the cloth to me after she used it.

"I'm sorry baby."

"Don't be sorry. I'm not."

She went into the kitchen and shortly returned with a glass of ice and a Peach Mango Snapple.

"Here," she said, filling the glass and offering it to me.

"Thanks, love. My mouth was a bit dry."

"Thanks to your little spill, mine wasn't."

I chucked and took a sip. While sitting with my back against the headboard, she crawled into my arms and rubbed my stomach."

"Ah, this is so good. You sure you don't want some? Here just taste it," I said offering her my glass.

"I just did. You want me to taste it again?"

We laughed and I sat the glass down before we settled into a tight embrace.

"I do," I said with a kiss to her forehead.

"You do what?"

"Anything you want me to. I know how much you like Mexican food. I'll go rob a Taco Bell right now just for you—get you all the Fresco Tacos you want."

She burst into a cackle.

"I'm serious," I said.

"I don't want you to do that. All I want is for you to not change once you get your fancy doctorate degree."

"My life may change, but nothing will ever change the way I feel about you."

"We'll see."

"You still don't trust me do you."

"I trust you. I just don't trust your nature. Men always do something to fuck things up, be it intentional or unintentional."

"Wow, that's harsh. If I could change anything about you, I would remove that thin layer of doubt coating your heart so you could be completely vulnerable to me. Maybe then, you'd see how much I really love you."

"I love you too Jonathan. And, I'm only able to say that because I am completely vulnerable to you. Now, as long as you're removing things, how about you completely remove Mia from your life."

"What are you talking about? I have."

"Since when?"

I lifted her chin and fixed my eyes on hers.

"Since I looked into your black opals and felt something I've never felt before—since you've reacquainted me with the euphoria of making love instead of perfunctory fucking—since I felt you touch me on the outside and somewhere deep…..I mean deep on the inside in a place I wasn't aware existed. That's since when."

"But…."

"Shhhh."

I placed my finger over her lips then kissed her sensuously, hoping to evict the seriousness from her conversation.

"Jonathan?"

"Yeah love?"

"Does Mia have any inkling that it is definitely over between you two?"

She was determined to chew this subject up and grind it down to mush. So, I figured I might as well humor her and be done with the Mia talk once and for all.

"She should. We had a huge fight and I haven't seen her in months. I even got a COB form from Sonya and made the necessary changes."

"That's great but what about communication…have you told her it's over?"

"Well, no. I haven't said those exact words."

"So you're just gonna leave raggedy edges like that? I mean, you were going to marry the woman. Don't you think you owe her at least a conversation for clarity sake?"

"That's how my relationships always end."

"That doesn't make it right. Don't just let things fade to black. Put on your big boy belt and cut the damn lights out. Get clear, no questions, end of story."

I realized she was absolutely right.

"I will, love."

"Now, about that other woman in your life…"

"Who, Momma G?"

She took a long pause.

Chapter Twenty-Four

A Checkered Pattern Past

We'd shared a lovely meal the night before, exchanged sensual affections and engaged in meaningful dialogue. Now, it was time to launch out into those ugly corners and spaces where his hurt sat balled up in a hardened, crusted callus of pain. So, I said a silent prayer, took a deep breath, then went in.

"No, your real mother," I said.

He slowly unraveled from my embrace and sat on the edge of the bed with his back to me.

"What did Momma G tell you?" he hesitantly asked.

I sat up and scooted in close, wrapping my arms and legs around him from behind. As I held him, he covered my arms with his.

"You should have told me. Why'd you lie to me about her being dead baby?" I softly asked.

"Believe me, I wanted to tell you. It's just that I've worked so hard to distance myself from the memory of that night that I just don't like talking about it. Whenever I do, it's like it's happening all over again—not just that night, but the entire first ten years of my life."

I gently kissed his shoulder.

"Baby, whatever happened to you wasn't your fault. You were born perfect and you're still perfect to me."

"Thanks, love."

"Did you go and talk to someone, I mean professionally?"

"Yeah, my grandparents made sure of that."

"Did it help?"

"It did, but their love and support helped more."

"How can I help?"

He turned and looked at me, eyes showering me with tenderness.

"Are you kidding me? Just being with you every day has helped to clean the stain of that tragic memory."

"Then, we'll keep creating new memories until no trace of the stain is left in your mind."

He moved in close and we shared a loving kiss.

"Would you ever want to go and visit her?" I asked.

"I'm just not ready. Seeing her would only bring it all back. Besides, she'll be out in five more years. I'll just deal with it then."

"Okay. I love you Jonathan."

"I love you too Skyla."

I continued to hold him while pondering the journey by which we all come here. I thought about how some of us are gently handed to loving and loyal parents and some of us are dumped into the muck and mire of abuse—covered in the thick, sticky residue of cruelty and chaos. But who decides our paths? My brain started to hurt and I surrendered to the only common denominator between the two journeys and prayed that Jonathan would be healed beyond what eyes could see or mouths could ask for. Then I prayed that we'd both be forgiven for all the peanut butter jars we'd emptied in the past and times to come.

Over the next few months, he'd started flying to Jersey in preparation for his move. He'd completed his Masters and secured a future start date at a Jersey Boys and Girls club as a Program Director. But, there was still so much more to get done. So, he appointed me his little personal moving manager.

He'd found an apartment, but I was in charge of furnishing it, which was kind of fun. Since I was too busy at work to travel with him most of the time, we relied heavily on phone pics of the furnishings I'd selected before charging them to his credit card. But in the midst of all our busyness, we still found quality time for each other.

Chapter Twenty-Five

Fastening, Buckling & Buttoning

For once, I was grateful I had a full plate because it kept my mind off of the fast approaching separation we'd have to endure. But when things became too hectic and overwhelming, Skyla and I knew how to retreat from it all.

We lay on opposite ends of her sofa, legs garbled together in a twist. As the rain beat against the windowpane, she journaled while I read, Down, Up & Over: Slave, Religion and Black Theology by Dwight Hopkins. Even with the onslaught of modern technology, I still loved the feel of paper between my fingers and the whipping sound pages made as they turned. Skyla had similar views, preferring ruled journals with psychedelic covers and a pen over a MacBook. I placed my book on my chest and studied her instead. She looked up and caught my gaze.

"What?" she asked.

"I've been thinking…"

"About what baby?"

"You know I'll be leaving for Princeton soon."

"Are you trying to depress me on purpose?"

"No. I just want to maximize our time together before I go."

She sat up and placed her pen in her journal before tossing it onto the table.

"Okay, keep talking," she said.

"Well, you know it kills me when I have to leave you and go home."

"And it kills me when you go or when I have to leave your place."

"Exactly. Then there's the financial aspect of us paying rent at two spots."

Her eyes lit up and she cracked a half smile.

"So, I was thinking that maybe we should move in together for the next couple of months before I leave. I could sublet my place and move in here since you have more space. But as a man, my pride won't allow you to pay the rent. I would have to pay it."

"I think that's an excellent idea, except that my pride won't let me relinquish control and let you pay my entire rent."

"It wouldn't be just your rent anymore. It would be our rent. Look, why don't we compromise. Would you feel better if I paid the majority of it, say a 70/30 split?"

"What about 50/50?"

"Can't do it. How about 60/40 and all the other bills 50/50?"

"Deal. I'm sorry baby. This is shit creeping up from my past. My ex paid for everything, so he controlled everything leaving me completely powerless in that relationship."

She crawled between my legs, folding herself into me before kissing me.

"I would hope you know by now that I'm not him," I said.

"Thank God for that."

"Now, let's see—when can we officially start cohabitating."

I leaned over and grabbed my phone from the table. I examined my calendar and became stuck on the date, March 23rd, as it was marked with a capital "P."

"Uh, love? Is everything okay?" I asked.

"Yeah. Why?"

"You didn't request your monthly backrub from me yet."

She moved to the opposite end of the sofa and folded her arms.

"Skyla, is there something you want to tell me?"

She looked down and then back up at me.

"I'm late," she said.

"I noticed. Two weeks to be exact."

"You keep track of my periods?"

"Yup. Look, I know what you're like when you're PMSing....snappin' at me for nonsense. A brotha needs all the warning he can get. Now, should we be registering at Target for Onesies and Huggies?"

"I don't know."

"What do you mean, you don't know?"

"I haven't taken a test."

"Why not? What are you waiting for? Aren't you excited to know? I'm excited and it hasn't even been five minutes."

"So you'd be happy?"

"I'd be ecstatic! But I need to know how you'd feel about it."

"Honestly Jonathan, I'm terrified."

"Of what? You're healthy aren't you?"

"Um...yeah."

"I'm asking because I'm not sure if I told you, but I'm a Sickle Cell trait carrier. But as long as you're not, there won't be a problem."

"I'm not, but that's good to know. I'm scared that I might be pregnant and at the same time, afraid that I can't be because of the miscarriage and all. So, I've been treating my fears with procrastination."

"Ahhh. Well, that's no way to handle it, love. But, I understand where you're coming from. What did the doctor say after you miscarried?"

"She told me that I'm still young enough to have kids."

"Well let's choose to believe her then. Look at me."

I placed my finger under her chin and guided her face to mine.

"I'm here for you and with you. I mean that," I said.

"I know you do."

"Let's just go get a test right now."

"No. Drugstore tests are too unreliable. I want to go to my doctor and find out for sure."

"Okay. Well, can you make an appointment today for my sake?"

I offered her my phone.

"I will," she replied, taking it and dialing.

Chapter Twenty-Six

Clashing Textiles

A few days later, Jonathan and I headed to the University of Chicago Hospital to get an official pregnancy test from my gynecologist.

"You okay?" he asked as we drove.

"No, but I will be eventually."

"God is with you and so am I."

I looked over and kissed him on the cheek. He kissed the back of my hand and held it tightly.

We pulled into the lot and finally found a spot after driving around for what seemed like hours. On our way into the building, I inhaled deeply and exhaled.

"It's gonna be okay, love," he said, squeezing my hand.

I checked in at the desk and we sat quietly in the waiting area. Jonathan gave me a reassuring glance before cracking open a book. I felt melancholy as I thought about the outcome of my test. If I was pregnant, I would be elated but overwhelmed by how our lives would have to change. And if I wasn't, I would be relieved but paranoid about being able to have children, especially with the man I loved.

"Skyla Richards," the nurse appeared from a side door and called out.

"Right here," I said, standing and following her down a brightly lit hallway with Jonathan closely behind. She gave me instructions and a cup and I went to the bathroom and followed them.

A few minutes later, I came out, handed her the cup and we went and waited in an office for the results. The doctor finally came in with my chart.

"Good to see you Skyla. How are you?"

"Fine Dr. Marsh. How are you?"

"I'm good. About to get my last kid off to college and become an empty nester. I can't wait!"

"Oh, bet your husband can't wait either. This is Jonathan Bass, the man in my life."

"Pleased to meet you Jonathan. I've been taking care of Skyla since she was a young girl."

"Nice to meet you Dr. Marsh. Glad to know that you and Skyla have such a long standing history."

"We do. Speaking of history, let's discuss something that could change your history together as a couple and talk about these test results."

My stomach was in knots and I felt like throwing up.

"Give it to us straight doc," Jonathan said.

"Alright, well with that being said Skyla, you are not pregnant."

The first feeling that hit me was relief. But to my surprise, tears began streaming down my face. Jonathan hugged me tightly.

"Aw, it's gonna be okay," Dr. Marsh said. "Were you taking your pills correctly?" she asked. But I couldn't speak.

"Not always Dr. Marsh," Jonathan answered for me, pulling me even closer.

"I see. Well, there's nothing in her chart that will prevent her from becoming a mother."

"You here that love, it's gonna be alright," he said as I continued to cry. "Thank you Dr. Marsh," he said.

"You're welcome. I'm gonna leave you two alone. Skyla, I want to see you in a month and we can talk more in depth about your plans. Nice meeting you Jonathan. Keep the faith. It'll happen," she said before leaving.

Afterwards, Jonathan hugged me and wiped my tears with his thumbs.

"Aw love, it's okay. It just wasn't God's time, that's all," he said.

My thoughts had become more aligned with his and I became audible again.

"Thanks baby. You're right."

He gave me a peck on the cheek and then kissed me passionately.

"Come on. Let's go," he said.

Before exiting the building, I stopped him.

"Babe, I need to go to the ladies room."

"Okay. I'll wait here."

When I came out, he was standing by the water fountain speaking to a woman. It seemed as if they knew each other. Truth was, she looked a little familiar to me too.

"I'll meet you in the car babe," I said, passing them and continuing to the parking lot.

"Okay love, be there in a minute," he replied.

I got in the passenger seat of his truck and started it with my spare key. About five minutes later, he climbed in beside me.

"Give me some sugar," he said. I leaned over and took in his tongue as we kissed.

"Who was that you were talking to?" I asked afterwards.

"That was Mia."

"Really? Whoa, she's gained weight."

"I know. I hardly recognized her. That's the heaviest I've ever seen her."

"Did she recognize me?"

"Kind of."

"Well, what did she say?"

"She just asked if you were the woman she got into it with at my job."

"And what did you tell her?"

"I told her I wasn't exactly sure who she got into it with because I wasn't there."

"Why didn't you tell her the truth?"

He looked at me like I was annoying him.

"Look, you know how unstable Mia is. Although she seemed more rational than I've seen her in years, why send her off the deep end by telling her that the woman who Mike Tysoned her is now her replacement," he said.

"Guess you've got a point. See what your breakup did to her. Got ol' girl eatin' donut and ice cream sliders."

"It's all your fault. You came along and just snatched a brotha."

Chapter Twenty-Seven

Splits, Slits & Cuts

The time had passed so quickly and I'd be leaving soon. We'd gotten so close and I didn't know how I would do it—live without her. But I knew the Creator would give us grace and assist us both with the transition. Still, it broke my heart every time I thought about leaving and the only thing I knew to do was make every second count. So when the weekend rolled around, I planned to somehow put a forever stamp on what started as a temporary arrangement.

After breakfast, we lounged crosswise in bed—me reading, Colored People: A Memoir by Henry Louis Gates Jr., with her head propped against my stomach as she journaled listening to music with headphones on.

Suddenly she put down her journal and took off the headphones. She picked up a pillow and hurled it at me, knocking my book out of my hands. After quickly mounting me, she grabbed another pillow and walloped me again.

"Oh alright, you wanna play, huh." I grabbed a pillow and bopped her in the head with it.

"Yep, I wanna play." She giggled while smacking me again with the pillow.

I grabbed it from her and rolled her over on her stomach.

"I see what you need." I partially pulled down her sweats and whacked her on her ass.

"Ouch!"

"Uh huh, you need to be tamed."

She wiggled out from my grip and jumped on top of me, jabbing me in the chest with her fist.

"Damn, those baby hands hurt!" I grabbed her fists and held them.

"Shut up. Don't be hatin' cause you've got big ol' Goliath hands."

She laid her head on my chest and snuggled close to me.

"They're just right for palming your ass. Seriously though, I'm gonna have to find a jewelry store with an infant section to get your ring."

She sprang up, eyes examining me pensively.

"Don't do that," she said.

"Don't do what?"

"Say things to me that create expectations."

"I can say what I want as long as I plan on fulfilling those expectations. Did you really think I'd go away and leave you in Chicago with all these thirsty brothas without sealing my commitment to you?"

Joy gleamed across her face in the form of a wide smile.

"Marry me Skyla. I know this is backwards, but I…."

"No it's not. It's perfect."

She kissed me stirringly.

"I love you so much Jonathan."

"I love you too. So is that a yes?

"Of course it's a yes!" She hit me in the chest again.

"Look, stop punching me with those midget hands. Let's go shopping next weekend. I want you to pick out three rings you like and I'll select from the three. That way, you won't actually know which one you're getting."

"Baby are you sure?"

"I've never been more sure about anything in my life. Of course, a few things have to happen before you become Mrs. Jonathan Bass."

"Like what?"

"Like your divorce being final and me finishing school."

"Well, I anticipate my divorce being final real soon."

"Good. Then all you need to do is be patient and supportive, the way you've always been. Would you do that for me?"

"I'll do that and anything else you need me to do."

"For now, I just need you to get in that kitchen and fix me a samich!"

###

Finally my last day at CRED had come and it was bitter sweet, but mostly bitter. I'd be leaving in a week and for the most part, loose ends had been tied up and things were in order. I'd finished my internship and it was time for change. I wasn't just leaving a job though. I'd be leaving a place where I found my future—a future at Princeton and a future with Skyla.

I came into the office with all my things and went straight to see her.

"Knock, knock," I said, tapping on her open office door.

She looked up and smiled. God I was gonna miss her.

"I was looking for a Skyla Richards? I have some items to give her," I playfully said, putting my things down and closing the door.

"That ratchet chick? What do you want with her?" she joked, coming over and hugging me.

"I've got some equipment to give her."

"Umph, and I heard you've got some good equipment. I'm gonna miss you so much baby."

She embraced and kissed me.

"Me too."

I squeezed her tighter as we gazed at each other. Tears welled up in her eyes and mine.

"Ok, let's see what you've got," she said, abruptly stepping away.

"Well, here's my laptop, here's my Blackberry and here's my keycard and keys."

"You sure you don't have anything else?" she asked, running her hand across my crotch.

"Nope, that's it," I said, smiling.

I took her hand and we sat on the couch.

"How do I do this, love?"

"Do what?"

"Leave the woman I love."

"I don't know, but we do what we have to do in life. Stay focused on your goals and think of all the kids you're going to help someday. At least that's how I plan to deal with it."

"You're right. This is only temporary."

I kissed her hand and glanced down at it.

"In all my running around, I haven't had time to check on your ring. If you weren't so picky, I could have went back and gotten it that day."

"I know, but they were all starting to look alike. I just wanted something unique that we both liked. I'm glad they're able to create my design."

"Yeah, but now it's gonna have to wait until my first trip back. You cool with that?"

"Of course."

"Good. Guess I better get out of here and let you get some work done."

She got up and walked to her desk.

"Umph, Umph, Umph," I groaned.

"What?"

"Just admiring my work, that's all. All that peanut butter stirring I've been doing has made your ass a little bigger."

"You're so nasty."

She came over and handed me a folded note while sitting on my lap.

"This is for you. But promise me you won't read it until after you leave—maybe on the plane ride to Jersey," she said.

"Why wait until then? You read it to me."

She reluctantly took it back and began to read:

My want is not just for a man, but for your being, with your intellect. I seek not just to be held, but to feel the substance of warmth, tenderness and adoration embedded in your embrace. I desire not to be bedded down, but to be made one with your flesh and your spirit. I long not for an experience, but for a period held captive in time with you. Love Skyla L. Richards.

"You wrote that just for me?"

"Yep, just for you."

"I'm absolutely speechless."

"Well, kiss me then."

We shared a rousing kiss until she stopped.

"Thank you, love. That was beautiful. You've turned out to be so much more than I could've ever imagined. I've definitely met my match in you," I said.

"You're welcome baby. Guess I should let you get outta here."

She got up and went to her desk.

"No goodbye kiss?" I asked.

"Don't say that word. I can't even think about how I'm gonna say goodbye to you."

"I promise I won't say it again until we part before I board the plane."

"Are you kidding? I'm sorry baby, but there's just no way I'm gonna be able to say goodbye to you in an airport. They'll have to wheel me outta there in one of those airport wheelchairs."

"I understand. Since my truck will already be in Jersey, I'll just cab it to the airport."

"I'm glad you understand."

"See you at home tonight."

I walked over and kissed her before exiting.

###

The day before I left, Skyla had taken off and we spent most of it just being together. Later that night she cooked my favorite dish, this time adding crabmeat to the lasagna like Momma G had suggested and it turned out perfect.

Afterwards, she cleared the table and stood at the sink rinsing dishes. I came and embraced her from behind.

"You were kind of quiet tonight. What's on your mind, love?"

"I don't know—it's just hitting me that you'll be leaving in the morning."

"I will, but I'll be back in a couple of months."

I brushed her hair to one side and kissed her neck.

"I know," she said before a long sigh.

"And we'll call, text and Skype all the time."

"Yeah, but it won't be the same. I won't be able to touch you or feel you next to me."

"Why don't you go lay down. I'll finish the dishes."

"You sure?"

"Yeah, it's cool."

After cleaning the kitchen, I headed upstairs to join her. She was standing at the top of the stairs wearing nothing but my white button down and a pair of white bobby socks.

"Now that is truly sexy," I said.

She came and grabbed my hand then led me into the bedroom.

While she took off my button down and stretched out on the bed, I selected a playlist that would capture the essence of the night and what it meant to us.

As Atlantic Starr's Send For Me, began to play, I got undressed and climbed on the bed and went in for my last supper. I wanted the night to last and took things slow. Once inside of her, I kept my eyes on hers as we were swept away by the intensity of our union. Our bodies pushed into each other until it became too much for us to contain and soon, tears were leaking out of her eyes, draining into her ears. I kissed and wiped them until they were replaced by my own as they fell and splashed against her face.

"I can't bear to watch you leave," she whispered afterwards.

"Then you won't have to. I'll leave while you're asleep and in the morning when you awake, I'll be gone."

We fell asleep adjoined and a couple of hours later, I woke up and watched her sleep one last time. But before calling a cab and heading to Midway Airport, I got up and put the final finishing touches on my departure.

###

After checking in at the airport, I headed to the departure gate and on my way spotted a familiar face.

"Jonathan? Wow. What are you doing here?"

"Hey Mia. I'm heading off to Princeton."

She looked even larger than she was the last time we ran into each other.

"Today?" she asked.

"Yup."

"Well this has got to be fate, 'cause I've been meaning to call you every since we ran into each other at the hospital. You have time for a cup of coffee?"

I looked at my watch, but knew I had a couple of hours to kill. I thought about how Skyla had challenged me to get clarity with Mia, which I hadn't made time to do. So, now seemed as good a time as any.

"Sure," I said.

We found a coffee shop and she ordered a decaf tea while I ordered a small, black coffee.

"So what are you doing here?" I asked.

"Remember Cortez Ortiz from college? I was just dropping him off. He was visiting me from Virginia, but he'll be moving here soon."

"You're kidding right? Mia, have you forgotten what he put you through?"

"He's not like that anymore Jonathan. He's changed."

"I don't believe it and neither do you."

"I do believe it."

"So, is that what you wanted to talk to me about?"

"Not quite."

Then, she opened her oversized black trench coat and a protruding belly stuck out, causing my heart to race. I opened my mouth, but nothing came out.

"It's yours Jonathan—conceived the last time we made love. It was the day of your hearing when we had that terrible fight."

"How….how do you…"

"I know it's yours. I haven't been with anyone else."

"But Cortez, you just said he…"

"He and I just reconnected two months ago. I'm six months pregnant with your child. For a long time, I wished—prayed that things would be different between us….that you would come back to me and things could be like they used to be. But when that didn't happen, I decided to let go and move on. Now, Cortez and I are engaged. But don't worry. I don't want anything from you. He knows it's yours and he still wants to marry me before the baby is born. Just thought you should know in case you ever want to be a part of your child's life."

My eyes shifted from her belly to her ring finger, which was stuffed into an engagement ring.

"So you're telling me that you're just going to up and marry Cortez, a man that used to put you in the hospital on a regular. You're gonna place a hostile, abusive, batterer over my child. Mia, that's not gonna happen. You can't do that. I won't let you!"

"I'm sorry Jonathan, but you really don't have a say in what goes on in my life. I thought you'd be happy for me."

"Really? Really Mia? You thought I'd be happy to know that my child is gonna be raised by a cowardly, violent asshole like Cortez?"

"I told you he's not any of those things anymore. He's changed. I know it's only been a couple of months, but I can tell he's different. We're different together. Whatever happened back then is in the past and I'm willing to give him another chance."

"Well just date him then. Give the monster time to reappear. Don't marry him."

"I'm going to marry him Jonathan, no matter what you say!"

"Ok, listen. I'm not trying to tell you what to do, Mia. Believe me, I want you to be happy. But, I have my reasons for objecting to you marrying Cortez."

"I knew it, this is personal. You just don't like him. You've never liked him!"

"No, that's not it."

"Well, then what is it Jonathan?"

"Look, I know men like Cortez. My stepfather was just like him and I can't allow…. Listen Mia, I'm begging you, please don't do this. Don't place our child in a volatile situation like that. What do I have to do to make you change your mind?"

Chapter Twenty-Eight

Double Sided Patterns

When I opened my eyes the next morning, the weight of the sadness shrouding my heart was as heavy as the blanket covering me. I pushed through it and rolled over only to find rose petals sprinkled in the shape of a heart with a framed picture of me and Jonathan in the center of them. It was from the night we went to the Signature Room—our first date so to speak. I sat up and smiled then went to the bathroom to brush my teeth. I opened the medicine cabinet and there was a note card in his hand writing taped to the toothpaste:

What can I say love….The moment I saw you, I wanted to know you. The moment I held you, I wanted to have you. The moment you kissed me, I wanted to feel that fire in your soul that burns for only me. The moment we were joined, I wanted to be with you forever. I made a playlist of all our love making songs. It's entitled S & J. Play them often and think of us. Love, JAB (Jonathan Aristotle Bass)

Suddenly, I could feel his spirit and knew I'd be okay.

I headed down to the kitchen and put some water in the tea kettle. I opened the cabinet and lo and behold, another handwritten note card was taped to my favorite box of green tea:

Everything I do, I do for you, for us, for ours. Everything you do, I feel, I absorb, I cherish. This simply is our truth and nothing can ever change that. Another playlist of songs we liked to chill to is entitled, Being with SR……Love JAB.

Now I couldn't stop smiling and it felt like he was standing right next to me. I got dressed for work and headed out the door.

Once in my car, I discovered yet another note card taped to my steering wheel:

Alas my love, please put the lid on my peanut butter jar and screw it on tight until I get back!!! Love JAB.

I went to work floating on the vapor of his essence and where I'd anticipated creases of sadness in my day, a smile illuminated instead every time I thought of him.

Weeks passed and I was still finding his handwritten note cards. In fact, they made up the majority of communication I'd received from him in the weeks after he left. I must admit I thought he'd be contacting me way more than three times a week through text messages. But hey, he was a black man at Princeton, so I was sure he was busy and things were hectic. And even though I sulked silently, deep down I understood.

I walked into my office and Bree was in her usual spot.

"Get your damn feet off my desk," I said, knocking her legs onto the floor.

"Ooo, ain't we cranky. Your man dun gone and left you, so as your girl, I'm gonna overlook the stank attitude you've had lately."

She went and sat across from me while I sat down.

"I haven't had a stank attitude."

"Sky, I'm your best friend. Best friends tell each other the truth, so I'm here to tell ya....you've been real bitchy lately."

"Have I girl? I'm sorry. I guess I am kind of missing my man and letting it get the best of me. It's that townhouse Bree. Everywhere I look, I see his face, hear his voice, smell his scent."

"Humph, what's that smell like, corn chips and pickles?"

"Shut up."

"Maybe it's time for a change."

My brain perked up and smiled at her comment.

"You know, you might be right," I said, growing happier by the minute. "Dammit girl, that's what I'm gonna do. I'm gonna move and find a space to create newness in!"

"Good. Glad I could help. Now that he's gone, maybe we can resume falling off bar stools together. I've missed you girl."

"Aw, Bree. I'm sorry. I've missed you too. Tell you what, why don't you come by tonight. I can cook something and we can sit up, drink wine and gossip like we used to."

"Now you're talking. About seven?"

"Sounds good."

"Alright girl. See you then."

She exited while I sat feeling better than I'd felt since Jonathan last touched me.

Later that night, she arrived right on time.

"Hey girl," she said, prancing through the door while handing me a bottle of Kendall Jackson Chardonnay.

"Girl, you're back with Kendall? I thought y'all broke up," I said.

"We did 'cause Kendall be doing me wrong in the mornings. But his stuff is so good; I just keep going back for more."

"Well, you go right ahead on. Kendall is too rough for me, so I won't be doing the threesome with y'all anymore. I'll stick to my kinder, gentler Unoaked Chardonnay."

"Girl, youza punk."

"I am and proud of it."

She went straight to the fridge.

"So what are you cooking?" she asked, opening it and sticking her head in.

"I don't know. What do you feel like?"

"Uh, I think the better question is what kind of dish you're gonna make with ketchup, Thousand Island and jelly, cause that's about all you've got in here."

"Shoot! I forgot to go grocery shopping. Jonathan was always on top of that."

"Well, he ain't here to be on top of it or you, so get your jacket and let's go. I'll drive."

As we walked to her car, gloom came searching for me and found me.

"Aw Sky, cheer up. You'll get through this," she said, hooking her arm into mine.

"I know. It's just hard, you know? I miss him so much."

"I know, but it's like you said earlier, you just gotta get into a new routine."

"You're right."

As we drove, we chatted as usual until something captured my attention.

"Wait Bree. Stop!"

"Here in the middle of the street?"

"You passed it. Go around the block!"

"What? What is it?"

"Just go around again. This time, drive slow."

"Okay." She circled back around at a slower pace.

"Okay…okay now… Right here. Pull over!"

She did and I hopped out the car. She parked and joined me as I stood looking up at a two-flat building with a for sale sign in the yard.

"This is perfect," I said.

"Girl, you must be light headed from not eating yet 'cause this is a piece of shit. I know you're not thinking about buying this crap are you?"

"All it needs is a little tender love and care and it'll be like new!"

"Girl, please. What it really needs is some gasoline and some matches."

"You don't see my vision. Shut up and give me a pen."

"Sky, maybe we should do this in the car. This doesn't look like the safest of neighborhoods. You're really considering moving here?"

"I'm not worried about the neighborhood. That's why I've got my Glock."

"What? You mean you come strapped?"

"Sure do."

"I didn't know that. How long have you had it?"

"For years, I haven't practiced in awhile though. Me and Phillip used to go to the gun range all the time."

"I wanna go. Next time, take me."

"I will."

She grabbed a pen from her purse while I rummaged through mine and got a piece of paper. I quickly wrote down the number on the sign and silently prayed.

"Uh, can we go now before we become victims of more senseless violence plaguing our community?"

"Ok, come on."

###

Once in the store, we wandered around trying to think of something quick and easy to cook.

"Ooo Sky, I've got it! Why don't you make some of that ghetto jambalaya you make. It's soooo good."

"My jambalaya is not ghetto. It's innovative, that's what it is."

"Whatever. I love it. What do we need for it?"

"For starters, we need some andouille sausage, rice, cabbage…."

"Okay, let's go," she said, dragging me over to the sausage section at the deli counter.

She took a number and got in a long line. After waiting with her for a few minutes my thoughts forced me to abandon her.

"Sorry girl, I can't be here. But here's the money," I said, heading for the cereal aisle instead. About 15 minutes later, she joined me.

"See, it didn't take that long. You're so impatient," she said.

"That's not why I left. I just couldn't be around all that thick, long, brown meat with Jonathan being so far away."

"Now, I feel you on that. Well, you betta not go roaming to the produce department either. Your ass might get kicked out for fondling the zucchini."

We laughed and finished up our shopping before heading home for an evening of fun filled girls night camaraderie.

###

As the weeks went by, I still hadn't heard Jonathan's voice. But we continued pouring our feelings into text messages and in doing so, I started noticing a pattern. Whenever I called him during the day, his phone always went straight to voicemail while our texting didn't start until the evening when I got off work. Logically, this made sense because we were both busy in the day—him with school and work and me swamped at work. But, as a woman, my gut was saying something else. So to test my female intuition, I completely stopped responding to his texts and had stopped calling and leaving him voicemails, forcing him to call me before sundown. Then I waited to see what my little plan would produce.

When Friday rolled around, I fell into my normal routine of filing while dancing and twerkin' to the music. My desk phone rang and without looking at it, I hit the speaker button.

"Hello," I said.

No response.

"Hello. Hello," I said again.

Still no response.

"Hellooooooo," I said, almost singing it.

"Damn, I'd forgotten how heavenly your voice is to me."

Finally Jonathan's voice was coming through the phone. My heart swelled with joy and I began smiling so wide it felt like the corners of my mouth were about to touch my ears.

"Weeeell, it's about damn time! Hey Mr. Man. What's been going on?"

"Hey love. I miss you so much, I wish I could just come through this phone right now and give you a big ol' hug, kiss and whatever else you need me to give you!"

"I've been needing to hear your voice. You must be super busy."

"I am, but I want to hear about you. How are you doing?"

"I'm missing you like crazy."

"I miss you too love, you just don't know."

"Tell me then."

"Well, for starters, I can't stop thinking about you Skyla. I mean, you're on my mind so much that I seriously started considering transferring to the University of Chicago."

Wow, I was shocked by what he said, but happy that he was longing for me just as much as I was longing for him.

"Pray about that baby. You just got there," I said.

"I know, but I'm lonely without you. I need to see you, touch you, feel you inside and out."

"Aw baby, I feel the same way. At least you'll be home next month."

"I know and I can't wait! What do you have on? Never mind. Don't tell me. You'll only be tormenting me. I miss my peanut butter. Wish you could send me some."

"When you come home, you can have all the peanut butter you want. How's work?"

"Good."

"And what about your classes?"

"They're cool."

"You getting used to your apartment?"

"I'm hardly ever there. I'm in the library most nights. That's why I've been texting you instead of calling. Listen love, I gotta run. But I'll be seeing you soon. I love you so much Skyla."

"I love you too Jonathan. Bye baby."

I was amazed at how powerful one brief exchange could be. Five minutes on the phone with him had erased my gloom and undid the despair of distance. I'd gotten my fix and was good until I could get another hit of him in person.

###

One Month Later.....

You'd have thought it was my wedding day the way I'd been preparing. I'd been high all week—juiced up off the very thought of seeing him. I'd taken off that Friday and spent the morning getting my hair and nails done. Figured my ring finger would be bedazzled with diamonds by the end of the weekend, so my nails had to be tight. Then I went shopping for new everything.

Once I got home, I didn't bother to cook. We were to be each other's feast for the night so there was no need.

A few hours before he was to arrive, I bathed and put on his favorite perfume, along with a new panty and bra set. Then I selected that blue dress he loved to see me in. After reviewing myself in the mirror, I suddenly took it all off. Had we been going out on the town, it would have been fine. But I wanted to stay right here between these walls until he was ready to enter into mine. So I put on the one outfit he found the sexiest on me—his white button down shirt and a pair of white bobby socks. I pushed up the sleeves, but left it open. After all, it was a special occasion. I straightened up, dimmed the lights, lit some candles and poured some wine.

It occurred to me that he might be tired and jetlagged. So, I arranged a tray of fruit and cheese and fluffed the pillows just the way he liked them. I really didn't care what we did that weekend. I was just elated to be seeing him face to face and was up for anything and everything.

Just then, the phone rang.

"Hey," I said.

"Hey girl. Whatcha doin?"

"Gettin' ready to see my man."

"Oooo girl, I know you're frantic cause you ain't had none in a couple of months."

"Girrrrll, I can't even explain how excited I am Bree!"

"I'm happy for you Sky. But I gotta take you sex toy shopping if you're gonna be experiencing these frequent droughts."

"Uh uh, girl. Nothing can take the place of my baby's dick, you hear me, nothing!"

"Hey, don't knock it til you've tried it. Girl, nowadays, they got dildos that are so dick-like, you almost wanna put a condom on them."

"Girl, shut up. Why are you messing with those things anyway? You've got Mike."

"Fuck Mike!"

"What? What happened?"

"I don't know Sky, I hate to say it but you were right. I'm done fucking with married men."

"Hallelujah! She's seen the light! But what really happened?"

"I just got tired of being alone on Christmas, New Year's Eve, New Year's day, Valentine's Day, St. Patrick's day…"

"St. Patrick's day?"

"Girl, yeah. He had the nerve to tell me he's got Irish in his family and they always get together and march in the parade every year. I told that negro to kiss my blarney stone."

"Wooo, girl that's too much. Listen Bree, you're beautiful, smart and funny as hell. Start believing it and men will believe it and treat you accordingly. But it starts with you. You are the prize, not the man—regardless of his money or accomplishments. And as soon as a man gets that twisted, then he becomes the bitch in the relationship. You just gotta make sure you're a top prize and not a Cracker Jack prize. Be a warrior, not a whistle."

The doorbell rang, setting off fireworks in my brain.

"Woo hoo!"

"Alright girl. I guess that means your man is at the door. Go on and answer it. I'll talk to you later."

"Okay. Love you girl, bye."

My stomach began to flutter as I ran towards the door and touched the knob. The bell rang again. I went and grabbed my lipstick and reapplied it before running to the mirror and back over to the door. Then I opened it and my heart exploded with excitement!

Chapter Twenty-Nine

Rips, Holes and Stains

I couldn't wait to see her—let her eyes fan the flames of my desire so we could be alone together and burn. I'd been so busy with school and she'd been busy with her life here. But finally, we could focus on each other and awaken our physical union again.

"Come here love," I said stepping through the door and grabbing her while my lips and hands traveled her body.

"I missed you so much baby," she softly said.

"Shhh."

I took off my jacket while backing her towards the sofa. Then I sat down and she climbed onto my lap straddling me the way she used to. We kissed long and slow for what seemed like hours. Finally, she came up for air while I switched to kissing her neck and breast.

"Let's go upstairs," she whispered.

"Okay," I whispered back, standing and starting to carry her.

Suddenly I was halted by a nagging thought. I wanted nothing more than to be inside of her, but I had to get this Mia business off my chest so we could enjoy the rest of our time together. I sat back down with her still wrapped around me.

"What's the matter baby?" she asked, making lanes in my hair with her fingertips. I grabbed her hands and kissed each palm before leaning my head back. I couldn't resist squeezing her ass, but forced myself to focus.

I took a long, deep breath as I looked into her eyes.

"Look love, I need to tell you something and I want you to listen and process what I'm about to say with thought instead of feeling. Can you do that for me?"

"I'll do my best. What's wrong?"

"Nothing's wrong. Things are just—different, that's all. Not wrong," I replied, pushing her bangs from her eyes. I sat up and kissed her hungrily. She aggressively returned the kiss, while unbuttoning my shirt.

"God, you're even more beautiful than my memories painted," I said.

She pulled my undershirt up and began kissing my chest traveling downward, swirling her tongue inside my navel while unbuckling my belt. As my stiffness pressed against my zipper, she unzipped my pants while her kisses continued their descent towards my groin. I became ensnared in the moment as I watched her tug at my boxers. Then her mouth grazed my shaft.

"Babe, babe, come here," I said, yanking her back towards me.

"What is it baby?"

"Nothing, I just—there's something I need to say to you and I really need for you to hear me."

Frustrated, she sighed and sat straight up on my lap.

"Okay, I'm listening?" she said, eyes searching mine for reason.

"A situation has come up, and I've had to handle it the best way I know how. You understand that don't you?"

"No, not really. Baby just tell me what you're talking about."

"I'm talking about my future—our future. Yours, mine and....his or hers."

She got up and scooted over. This was one of the hardest things I ever had to do. In the back of my mind, I replayed the memory of her saying that she could never hate me as long as I was honest with her and I prayed to God that she meant it.

"Mia's pregnant," I uttered, zipping my pants.

Her eyes popped open even wider than their natural set. She slowly stood and turned her back to me while folding her arms. I jumped up behind her.

"Love, I swear, it happened before me and you ever became a couple…I mean a serious couple."

She went and gazed out of the window. I quickly followed and stood next to her. I began stroking her hair while waiting for her to speak.

"Are you saying you still love her?" she asked, words breaking and voice cracking.

"What? No, no. I'm not saying that at all. I'm saying that this thing—something has happened that I have to deal with."

I kissed her on the neck and embraced her from behind.

"I only love you—like I've never loved anyone before," I said, kissing the side of her head as she peered out the window. "But, I can't have my seed growing up without me."

She turned and looked at me with sympathy.

"I understand that. Of course you'd want to be in your child's life. I would never stand in the way of that."

I blew a hard sigh of relief.

"Good. Good baby. I knew you would understand. So this whole marriage thing is just a formality. It gives me certain legal rights that can't be overridden."

"What marriage thing?" she asked, looking confounded.

"To Mia. I married her to stop her from marrying her violent ass ex boyfriend. I just couldn't let that happen."

The compassion disappeared from her face as she slowly walked back to the sofa and sat holding her head. I rushed over and sat beside her.

"Love, you know how I grew up. You know what happened to me. I can't risk my child going through anything remotely like that. You don't know Cortez. He's a straight up monster! I won't have my child exposed to that!"

Anger suddenly grew into her eyes as she looked at me.

"Wait, so you're telling me that you married the bitch, as in—til death do us part?"

"Well, yeah. This way, it'll be impossible for her to ever put another man over my child. But, I don't have any intention of giving you up or becoming anything less than what I already am in your life."

"But now, you can't become anything more than that either Jonathan!"

The heat in her voice shook me to the core. She had a look that I'd never seen before and I didn't know what it meant.

"Babe…love….." I said, placing my hand atop hers.

She pulled away from me, folding her hands while remaining silent and looking straight ahead.

"You are and will always be the only woman I love. You know nothing will ever change that don't you?"

I couldn't read her expression, which scared me.

"Okay, I know this is a lot to take in. I guess I shouldn't have expected you to know how to react."

I kissed her on the forehead while she sat emotionless.

"Do you need some time to process it all?"

She shook her head yes.

"Okay love. I'm gonna go and give you some space. But, I hope you won't make more of this than it really is. It's just a piece of paper that means absolutely nothing to me. Mia and I are mere roommates, at least until the baby is born. Nothing more."

"Nothing Jonathan? Nothing? You're married now. You said a vow in front of God and the whole world. You're joined to another." She was still refusing to look at me.

"God knows my heart and he knows it will always belong to you. And as far as the whole world is concerned, our love transcends societal norms and can't be bound by worldly rules and regulations. This is us we're talking about. Not two people who just met in the club. Us. We don't need a license to love."

I lifted her chin, forcing her eyes to meet mine.

"I love you Skyla and nothing in this life or beyond can change that. Everything I have belongs to you….my heart, mind, soul and body. I know you feel the same way. Please try and see my side. This marriage was just a business decision, much like an arranged marriage in other civilizations. In some cultures…."

"I don't want to hear about other cultures or any more of your intellectual bullshit Jonathan!"

The anger in her tone had crescendoed to a fever pitch and stopped just short of loathing.

"Okay look, I'm gonna go and leave you alone with your own thoughts. I guess I'll just stay with Chase for a few days. I'll call you tomorrow, love."

I stood to leave. When I got to the door I looked back at her. She was sitting so quiet—so still. I pulled the box containing her engagement ring from my pocket and opened it, placing it on the table by the door.

"This is for you, love," I said.

She glanced over at it.

"I don't want it. Give it to your wife."

"In my heart and mind, that's exactly what I'm doing."

Chapter Thirty

Heavy, Thick Material

One thing I'd learned is that I could not control a man, nor what he did. The only thing I could control was my reaction to it. So, I knew what I had to do. I got dressed, grabbed the case containing my 9mm Glock and jumped into my car.

Before I knew it, I was driving 80 miles per hour in a 45 mile zone while my heart raced and blood pulsated through my veins. As my foot pressed down on the pedal, I thought about the irony in the name, Mia—slang for missing in action, which Jonathan would now forever be to me. She had everything I wanted—the man, the baby, the life…. I had to do something and just kept going until I parked, ran to the door and began pounding on it.

"Open up, it's me Skyla!"

Nobody answered so I started kicking.

"I said open up, I know you're in there!" I shouted.

Finally, the door swung open.

"Oh hey, come on in."

I entered, looking around.

"Everything alright?"

"No, but it will be after this," I said.

I walked into an empty bay and loaded my Glock and put on my ear and eye protection. I flipped the switch and a target sheet went zooming backwards. As I pulled the trigger and felt the jolt of the bullets leaving my gun, I felt somewhat euphoric. I flipped the switch again and the sheet came flying towards me.

"Damn! Not bad for somebody who hasn't been here in over a year. Look how well you did," Pete, the gun range owner said, taking the bullet riddled sheet and examining it.

"Here, let's start another round."

"No Pete. I'm fine. I just needed to let off some steam. I'm good now."

"Ok, if you say so. Haven't seen you in awhile, but I still have your credit card info on file. You're looking really good Sky. You know I always found you very attractive. I heard about you and Phillip. Now that you guys are done, how about we hang out and spend some time together."

"Thanks Pete, but dating is no longer on my list of priorities these days."

"You sure I can't take you to lunch, dinner or hell, breakfast for that matter?"

"Pete, I'm just in a different space right now."

"Is it because I'm white? Mr. Right could be white you know."

I laughed.

"Pete, it's not because you're white. It's because you're a man."

"Oh no, you're not gonna turn gay on me are you?"

I didn't answer and just gave him a curious smirk as I left.

###

The first time my heart was broken, I couldn't cry at all. This time, I cried for three days straight after that night. But the first broken heart taught me that time really does mend all wounds and the most profound lessons are only birthed through the bitter concoction of truth and time. But if after a healthy dose of both my heart still felt raw and mangled, I simply had to place my trust in a higher power and be willing to be the one that got away. I pulled Sadie out and let whatever was within me come out:

One day when I'm stronger

I'll wonder how I became so weak
One day when I'm stronger
I'll have the courage that I now seek
One day when I'm stronger
I'll be able to lift someone else
One day when I'm stronger
I'll realize the power was always in self.
For what's behind me shapes my future,
What lies ahead creates my path,
The unknown is soon forgotten
And the truth is mine to craft.

Over the next several weeks I was in straight up ignore mode but it was no match for Jonathan's persistence. At one time I couldn't buy a call from him during the day. Now, I probably couldn't pay him to stop. His deluge of emails and texts became so numerous that they were starting to deplete storage space on my work and personal devices as I couldn't delete them fast enough.

"Ok girl look, I love you but this is getting ridiculous. Please call this man. Jonathan's called and emailed me roughly thirty times today. I'm not kidding Sky, look," Bree walked in my office and said, shoving her Blackberry in my face.

"Just ignore him like I do."

"Sky, ignoring him is not the answer. You need to talk to him."

"I have nothing to say."

"Ok, I know what he did was fucked up. But you at least know why he did it."

I stopped working and looked at her.

"And? That's supposed to make it okay?"

"No, I'm not saying that. But come on Sky, you still love him and God knows he still loves you. You two have got to come to some kind of conclusion. He knows he made a mistake. How long are you gonna keep punishing him?"

"This is not a game to me Bree. I just don't see the point in talking to him. I'm never gonna be able to trust his judgment again and I won't continue to be the ball that keeps getting dropped and bruised in his juggling act of bad decisions."

I got up and started packing up for the day.

"Where are you going? It's only 3:00pm," she said.

"Well, I'm closing on my building Friday and I've got a ton to do before then. Hey, thought you were gonna give me the name of Mike's friend, the contractor. You said it yourself. The place needs work and I need someone who can fix it up affordably."

"Yeah, yeah…I know what I said. His name is Andre. I'll text you his number."

"Thanks girl. Let's go."

I locked up and we left.

When Friday morning came, I handed the real estate agent a check and she handed me the keys to my very first home. I felt a deep sense of accomplishment. But lurking in the background was also an overwhelming sense of anxiety. It needed so much work and I felt panicked at the thought of a starting point. So, when I got to work, later that day, I picked up the phone and called the guy Bree recommended.

"Hello," he answered sounding a bit gruff and irritated.

"Hi, my name is Skyla Richards."

"Oh, Bree told me you'd probably be calling."

"Good. I wanted to know when you could come take a look at my building and give me an estimate on some repairs."

"Well, I'm pretty booked up for the next month. But Mike told me what a nice lady you are so I'll make an exception for you."

"Great. The address is 2518 S. Barkham St. Can you come by next Saturday, say 11:00am?"

"Sure. I'll see you then."

"Thanks Andre."

"Please call me Dre."

"Ok, Dre. Bye."

Just then, Bree appeared in front of my desk.

"Was that Jonathan you were talking to? He blew up my phone again yesterday."

"Girl please. I told you, I have no intention of ever speaking to him again."

"That's sad Sky. It's just downright heartbreaking."

"I agree. You should tell him that the next time he calls you."

"I get it. You need time to heal."

"No, I need time to get over his ass."

"I don't like what I'm seeing. You're becoming cold and it is so unbecoming of you. Looks way better on me. I think it's time for a girl's night out again. Since you just closed, let's go out and celebrate."

"Not a bad idea. When?"

"When are you moving?"

"Not until next Friday."

"In that case, let's go tomorrow night."

"Let's do it."

###

For once, I was more excited about going to the club than Bree was. It had been a while and I guess my ego needed a hug. So I put on the dress that would get it the most strokes.

The bell rang and I answered it all dressed and ready to go.

"Damn girl, you got the girls sticking out the sunroof tonight. I've never seen you show that much cleavage," Bree said.

"Well, there's a first time for everything."

"You look great though. That dress is so hot on you, it's only right that you be the designated driver. You can't get drunk in a dress like that. Might wake up without it."

"Okay Bree, I accept the mission. Come on, let's go."

Once at the club, Bree ordered martini after martini, holding me to my role as the designated driver. I ordered a couple of glasses of wine and basically made sure she didn't get into a car with strangers.

"Wooo, I know I'm gonna feel like shit in the morning," she slurred.

"Well, I'll just ply you with Gevalia cause we're going to church tomorrow."

"Ok, I ain't mad atcha. Look, what are you gonna do about this Jonathan thing. My finger is gettin' sore from deleting his messages. He loves you Sky. You know how hard it is to find a guy who really loves you?"

"Bree, the only person he loves is himself. What he did, he did out of pure selfishness without even thinking of my feelings. That's not love and I just can't forgive him for that."

Then, in a drunken kung fu master's accent, she said:

"Ahh young grasshoppa—listen and learn from your teacha—you make common mistake many women make during transition. You meet smart man with good dick—he take you to spinning restaurant on top of skyscrappa—write you poems and eat cream like winner of pie eating contest and you confuse intellectual intelligence with emotional intelligence."

I laughed so hard I nearly fell out of my chair as she continued:

"But grasshoppa, not his fault. He experience bad things very young—you pray for him and not give up on him. Rememba, you not perfect—you not only one hurt. You harbor unforgiveness. That's not love eitha—you have issues too young grasshoppa."

I suddenly stopped laughing.

"But Bree he…,"

"No more lessons tonight grasshoppa. Me drunk and in need of sleep. Me camp out at your place."

Once in the car, she passed out before I could pull off. I thought about what she said as I drove. Her delivery had me in stitches, but her message pierced my conscious.

She was right. I wasn't exactly an innocent party and knew deep down that my own selfishness had contributed to this whole situation. But there was nothing I could do about it now, except to leave things up to those miracle working twins, grace and mercy and their life changing cousins, wisdom and understanding.

When we got home, I helped her up the stairs and she collapsed onto my bed. I rolled her over and went to sleep next to her.

The next morning, the alarm clock failed me.

"Bree, wake up girl. We missed the 8 o'clock service so we've gotta find Jesus on TV."

I turned on the TV and began surfing the channels.

"Giiirrrlll, you know I'm hung the fuck over, just let me sleep," she woke up and said.

"No, get up. If you're gonna wake up on lean, then you've gotta watch Joel Osteen. So, get up!"

"I feel sick. But, it ain't the liquor from last night that's gonna make me call earl.

It's those Jesse Jacksonish rhymes you're making. Please stop."

"Only if you get up and watch TV church with me."

"Alright, alright. I'm up."

Chapter Thirty-One

Cuffing, Tucking & Binding

As fast as water stops when a faucet is turned to the off position—and as quick as darkness covers a room when light is taken away, Skyla's voice disappeared from my life. They say the road to hell is paved with good intentions. And if that was the case, then my misguided objective reasoning had landed me in the blistering pit of disaster.

As I sat in the library trying to study for an exam, I wondered what Skyla was doing and felt powerless to find out. I'd reviewed the events time and time again in my mind. How could I have misjudged the situation so terribly?

I felt like a lad at a baseball game whose favorite batter has just stepped up to the plate. With the crack of the bat, the ball takes flight soaring straight towards him. He stands, keeping his eyes on it with laser like focus and joyful anticipation. And just when it's within his reach, he leans into the wind, fingertips slightly touching it. Then, out of nowhere, a strange wind comes along veering the ball off course. Panic sets in as it swiftly travels in a different direction. All he can do is watch as his hope and dream of capturing the momentous prize begins to fade. And when it is but a faint view of a shadow in the distance, he is left sunken in the acerbic angst of, almost.

I had been both the strange wind and the lad in this scenario causing my mind to be racked with regret. The last thing in the world I wanted to do was cause the woman I loved pain. But I couldn't see past my own fears long enough to search and find a different solution to the problem at hand.

I packed up my books and left for a place I couldn't call home. It was where I resided—where we both resided, but my home and my heart was still back in Chicago with Skyla.

I walked in feeling drained.

"Hey? You hungry? I cooked some of that soup I know you like."

"I told you to stop cooking for me Mia. It's not necessary."

I put my briefcase down and hung up my coat.

"But I'm your wife. Wives cook. That's what I'm supposed to do."

"Oh God, don't start that shit again. Look, legally we are connected, but nothing else about us resembles a marriage. I don't need you to cook or clean for me. I don't want to have sex with you. And I especially don't want to pretend like we're a couple. All I want is for my child to grow up in a stable home, void of violence. That's the only reason I'm here."

"I know you feel that way now, but you'll change your mind once the baby is born. As long as we're on the subject of our child, the hospital called about our blood tests. Turns out, I'm also a Sickle Cell trait carrier. My adoptive parents never told me that. Guess they probably didn't know."

Great. All this effort to protect my unborn child and now I was being challenged by genetics.

"Ok. Then our next step has to be to get a prenatal genetic test to find out the chances of the baby being born with the disease," I said.

"Isn't that dangerous?"

"People do it all the time to see if a child is predisposed to certain illnesses. I'll call the doctor in the morning and make an appointment."

"Ok. But what if the doctor determines that our baby will have the disease?"

I sighed.

"We'll deal with that if and when we have to."

The next day, I found a Geneticist who also had specific experience in the area of Sickle Cell Anemia. So a week later, we went in for the test.

###

"Relax Mia. I'm sure things will be fine," I said, sitting across from her in the waiting area.

Not long after, a nurse came out and led us to separate examination rooms as this test involved biological samples from me as well. After we'd both been examined, we sat for a couple of hours awaiting the results. The doctor and his nurse finally emerged with both our charts looking worried.

"Uh, Mr. Bass? Can I talk to you privately for a moment?" he asked.

Now I was confused and concerned.

"Sure Dr. Tate." I followed him into a different room while the nurse stayed behind and spoke with Mia.

"This is extremely awkward for me," he started off. "And although I have a medical obligation to uphold these results in the strictest of confidence, as a God fearing man I also have a moral obligation to divulge the truth."

"I'm afraid I don't understand Dr. Tate."

"Well, these results show that you can't possibly be the father of this unborn child."

I felt like someone had just flung a 300 lb. medicine ball into my stomach. I slowly sat down and tried to steady my breathing.

"I'm sorry Mr. Bass. While some of my colleagues disagreed on whether or not I had the right to tell you, I know in my heart I did the right thing."

"I believe you did Dr. Tate. Thank you. I just need a moment alone."

"Of course."

My mind was racing so fast with questions it felt like my temples were about to explode. What the hell kind of game was Mia playing with me? If I wasn't the father then who the hell was? How fast could I get on a plane and run to Skyla with this news? Where could I find the nearest divorce attorney? I planned to answer all of my own questions. But first, I had to talk to the person with inside knowledge.

The ride from the doctor's office was tense. She knew something was wrong with me and I knew something was wrong with her.

We continued into the apartment in total silence. In fact, four hours later, she still hadn't been forthcoming with the truth. So I figured I better confront her before she created more lies she could use to try and wiggle out of the situation.

She was just about to go to bed and I had retired to my sleeping quarters, which was on the living room sofa.

"So, that's it? You weren't going to say anything?" I said as she started into the bedroom. She turned to me with crocodile tears and came and sat next to me while looking down at the floor.

"I'm sorry Jonathan. You had rejected me and he was there for me when I needed him. I know I was wrong. But, he…."

"I don't give a fuck about him! I don't know who him is. But I thought I knew you."

"You know him too Jonathan."

"What the hell are you talking about Mia? Who is this, him, you keep bringing up?"

She finally looked up at me.

"It's Chase's baby."

Chapter Thirty-Two

Darkest Before the Darning

I'd been in my building for about three months and life was finally starting to resemble a form of normalcy. I'd hired Dre and he was doing a pretty good job of fixing up the place. Thank God too, because every potential tenant I interviewed let me know in no uncertain terms that they weren't interested after being given a tour. I wanted to hurry up and get some extra cash coming in, so I appreciated Dre's efforts. And the barrage of calls and messages from Jonathan had finally stopped, leaving me free to regain my focus at work.

The next morning when I got into the office, to my surprise Candice was sitting at my desk.

"Oh my God, look at you! You look great!" I said, hugging her. "I wasn't expecting to see you here," I said.

"I know. You look wonderful as well. I've missed you Sky."

"I've missed you too."

"That's what makes this so difficult."

The smile on her face disappeared and excitement drained out of her voice.

"You're my best employee and I care about you as a friend, but I'm gonna have to let you go," she said.

"Let me go? Why?"

"CRED is under investigation for allowing one of its employees to assault someone on company property. Do you know a Mia Bass?"

"Oh lord. Yes, I know her."

I slumped down in a chair and felt dizzy.

"She's claiming that you assaulted her right here in the office. Is it true Sky?"

"Yes. I was just under so much pressure and she was spitting in my face and calling me all sorts of names. I know it's no excuse."

"Why didn't you come to me when it happened? I could have stopped it from getting to this level. Now it's too late. It's gotten too big so there's nothing I can do but let you go. I'm so sorry."

"I understand."

"Damn, I wish it didn't have to be this way. Here, take this," she said, handing me an envelope. "I wish I could do more, but this is the most severance pay I can give you. Hopefully it will hold you over until you can find something else. I also wrote you a letter of recommendation."

"Thanks Candice."

I stood and she hugged me firmly.

"I'll need your laptop, Blackberry, keycard and keys. Do you have them with you?"

"Yep, here they are."

As I glumly handed them over, I thought about how my out of control behavior had finally caught up with me and I felt disappointed in myself. How could I have let Mia, or anyone for that matter get me frazzled enough to strike them. Then I decided to ease up on myself after realizing that it was simply a test—a test that I'd failed miserably, kind of like Simon Peter did when he went ham on Malchus' right ear.

On my way home, anxiety kicked in and spread as I tried to figure out how I was going to hire a lawyer to get me out of this mess and continue to pay Dre for the repairs so I could rent one of the apartments and get the money I now so desperately needed. As I did the math in my head, I came to the grim conclusion that there was just no way I was gonna be able to do both. So Dre and his repairs were just gonna have to take a backseat to my legal issues.

The next day a certified letter came and shit was getting real. It stated that I'd been charged with assault and a second investigation was underway. It had some more legal mumbo jumbo in it that I needed a lawyer to interpret. So I went online in search of a good one.

When I heard Dre's truck pull up outside, I went and opened the door before he could ring the bell.

"Hey boss lady. I got the paint you wanted," he said, stepping through the door. "Why the long face?" he asked.

He was a brown skinned brotha that stood about 5'7" with round expressive brown eyes and dimples in his cheeks. He had a medium, stocky build and was as cute as a teddy bear.

"Sit down. I have something to tell you."

"What's up boss lady," he asked, sitting next to me.

"I'm not gonna be able to continue to pay you. So, the work will have to stop."

"Why, what's the matter?"

"I got fired and caught a case, all in the same day."

"Damn, that's messed up. Wanna talk about it?"

"No. I'm gonna have to hire an attorney. I'm sure that's gonna be expensive."

"What kind of case?"

"Assault."

"You?? Nooooo."

"Yes me."

"You must be tougher than you look. Well, how are you gonna rent the place with it looking like this?"

"Good question. I have no idea."

"Hmm. Tell you what—maybe we can help each other out. You need a tenant and I need an apartment. I'm going through a divorce and living under the same roof is getting crazy."

"Wow. My divorce was just recently finalized. I can't even imagine going through that and having to live with the person."

"It's straight up chaos. But listen, why don't I rent the first floor apartment from you. I'll pay you whatever you're asking for it and you can use that money to hire a lawyer. I'll also keep working on the repairs at a discount. Will that help you out?"

"Dre, that's a generous offer, but I don't want you to move to help me."

"I'm moving to help myself. I was already looking, see?"

He pulled a listing of vacant apartments he'd printed from the internet out of his pocket and showed it to me.

"You can check all my references and do a background check too," he said.

"I already did that when I hired you. Let me think about it."

"Okay. While you're thinking, I'm still gonna finish what I started, so I'll be downstairs. Hang in there, slugger."

I chuckled as he left.

A couple weeks later, I decided to take Dre up on his offer and he moved in the first floor apartment. I spent countless hours doing online job searches, sending resumes and following up on leads and in the midst of one of my job searches, Bree popped in to check on me.

"Hey girl, come on in. I'm on hold with a potential employer. Be with you in a minute," I said, hitting the speaker button.

The human resources lady came back on the line.

"Ms. Richards?"

"Yes?"

"We did receive your resume. You've got great qualifications and we think even greater potential. It's such a shame that we can't hire you though."

"Why not?"

"Look Ms. Richards, we're not looking for a bouncer. We need a grant writer—one that will keep her hands on her keyboard, not her fists through people's mouths."

She started laughing and hung up on me. I was shocked! Then the phone rang again. I hit the speaker button and answered it.

"Ms. Richards? You called about the grant writer position?" a woman asked.

"Yes I did. Is it still open?"

"It is and we would love to hire you, but we're a small organization and having you on the premises would make our liability coverage go up. We can't risk that. Sorry, but good luck with your search," she said before hanging up.

I hit the speaker button releasing the call and flopped down on the sofa with my mouth open.

"I can't believe this. How do they all know?" I wondered out loud.

"Wait a minute girl, something ain't right," Bree said, grabbing my laptop and quickly typing something. A few minutes later, she slammed it shut.

"What…what's the matter?" I asked, trying to take my laptop from her.

"It's nothing Sky."

"Bree, let me see." I snatched the computer and whipped it open.

She had clicked on a website called Chicagononprofitcareers.com and zeroed in on a post from someone named, sexymiab which read:

Looking for a smart, results driven program director and/or grant writer? Well, DO NOT hire Skyla Richards. She's an erratic, violent sociopath with no regard for the workplace. In fact, there is a legally pending case against her for a physical altercation she had with an innocent party at her current place of employment, CRED. Hire at your own risk!

"Oh my God! That crazy Mia chick is bashing me all over the internet!"

"You know you can sue that bitch for defamation of character for this shit."

"No wonder no one wants to hire me. You know what Bree, you're right. I'm gonna call my lawyer right now to see if I can counter sue."

I left a message for my lawyer and then decided it was time for a break.

"Girl, I need some air after all of that," I said.

"Okay. I gotta get back to work anyway. Don't worry Sky. That crazy heffa won't get away with this. I'll call you later."

"Okay girl, bye."

After she left I went downstairs to see how Dre was coming along.

"Ooo, that color looks great." I said.

"Didn't I tell you? You've got to learn to trust your eye more. I told you it wouldn't be too bright. Looks perfect to me."

"It does. I'm gonna go grab something to eat. You want something?"

"Thanks. I am kind of hungry. Are you going pass a Taco Bell?"

"That's exactly where I'm going."

"Can you pick me up a Fresco Burrito Steak meal with a coke?"

"Sure."

"Here, here's the money. Get whatever you want out of that too."

"Dre, I can buy my own lunch."

"What's it gonna set me back, five dollars? Quit trippin' and take the money." "Okay. Be right back."

Chapter Thirty-Three

Sewed Up, Patched Up....Messed Up

Mia moved and found a place of her own without me having to kick her out and it took about three months before my marriage to her was annulled. Within that time frame, I'd stopped contacting Skyla and tried to let time and space smother her anger towards me. At least that's what I hoped it would do. Plus I wanted everything to be in order the next time I approached her. Mia and the threat of a baby with another woman had been officially removed from our lives. Now I could go back to her with an open heart and conscious and prayed she'd be ready to embrace me with the same.

I took an early flight back to Chicago and headed straight for CRED. The elevator doors opened and Sonya met me with a wide smile.

"Hey Jonathan!" she said, standing to hug me.

"Hey Sonya." I returned the hug.

"I've got to talk to Skyla. Is she in?"

Her smile was replaced with a scowl.

"Guess you haven't heard. She got fired."

"What? When? Why?"

"You and wifey must not talk very much. It's her damn fault. She's pressing charges against Sky. Got me all caught up in the mess too. I don't like it Jonathan. I don't like it not one bit, but what can I do."

"Damn, I swear I didn't know. Where is Skyla working now?"

"I don't know. The only person who might know is Bree."

"Thanks Sonya."

I literally ran to Bree's office. I knocked on her open door and she looked up.

"Hey boy!!" she said, coming over and throwing her arms around me. "God, it's good to see you! How are classes?"

"Everything is everything. Look, I just found out about Skyla."

"Yeah. It's unfortunate, but she's strong. She can handle it. Got a good attorney too. She's just looking forward to it being over with."

"Where is she?"

"Jonathan, now after everything went down, I went hard for you. Tried to get her to call you every chance I could. I mean, I really went to bat for you. But you know how she is. When she makes up her mind, ain't nobody changing it."

"Yeah, I know. I just need to talk to her Bree. So much has happened. Where is she working?"

"She's not yet."

"What? Well, is she still out by you? The last couple of letters I sent her were returned for a bad address."

"Yeah, she moved."

"Where Bree?"

"Now Jonathan, you know you're my boy, but I can't tell you that. She made me promise."

"Bree, I've got to know. I'm still in with love her. I have to see her!"

She turned her back and folded her arms while pacing, then studied my face for a few minutes.

"Ok look, please don't tell her I told you, but it's 2518 Barkham St. Not too far from her old place."

"Thanks Bree. I'm on my way. Oh, first can you do me a huge favor. I need to type something. Can I use your computer and printer?"

"Ok, but what's up?"

"Well, just in case she refuses to see me, I think I better write her something. Got an envelope?"

"Sure. Good luck."

Bree gave me some privacy and I opened my heart and let it pour out onto the computer screen:

My dearest Skyla,

So much has happened since we last spoke or touched. The words, I'm sorry, seem so futile and so inadequate for the amount of hurt and pain I've caused you. Yet, I say them with all sincerity. Please forgive me. Turns out, the baby Mia was carrying wasn't mine. It was Chase's. Can you believe that? None of that even matters. What matters most is that I love you more now than ever and the clouds of confusion have faded and I'm able to see things clearly now. My only path is forward, but without you, I'll still have to feel my way through the darkness. Please allow these words to melt any residue of hurt you might still be feeling. I need to see you in person, so if we don't connect on this trip, enclosed are plane tickets for you to come see me next weekend. Because of what we've shared, I have faith in the future, so I'll be waiting for you at the airport. Love you now and always, JAB.

I printed it along with some e-tickets I'd purchased and sealed the envelope.

"Thanks again Bree for being in my corner," I said with a grateful kiss to her cheek.

"Boy, you know I gotcha."

I headed out and just before the elevator doors closed, a male voice hollered out, "Hey Jonathan, wait up."

But the doors closed before anyone boarded. Once on the ground floor, Chase stepped off of another elevator.

"Dude, wait up," he said, touching my arm.

"Man, get the fuck off me!" I shouted, shoving him against the wall.

"Look man, I'm sorry. It just happened," he yelled as I stepped outside.

Men like Chase came a dime a dozen where I was from. He and Mia were cut from the same cloth—people who would do any damn thing to get what they wanted. Their kind was always gonna be around. But, I had more pressing things on my mind, like getting my baby back.

Chapter Thirty-Four

Blind Stitching

On my way back from Taco Bell, I drove down my block and noticed that Dre had parked his truck in front of my building and was carrying tools and materials in. So, I parked in the garage. While walking from the backyard to the front porch, I checked my email to see if any more employers had responded to me. Just as I was about to turn to walk up the steps, I looked up and saw Jonathan jump out of a car and fly up the front steps. I quickly backed up, almost falling into the bushes as I leaned my back against the side of the building and peeped out just enough to hear his conversation:

"How you doin'? I was looking for Skyla Richards."

"She's not here. Can I tell her who stopped by?" Dre asked.

"Sure, it's Jonathan, Jonathan Bass. And I'm sorry, but who are you?"

"I'm Dre. Dre Higgins."

"Oh, looks like you're here doing some repairs. I won't keep you."

"Actually, I live here."

"Oh….I see. And Skyla lives here too?"

"Yes, that's right."

"Under the same roof….with you."

"Yup."

"Umph. Ok. Well, please give her this envelope for me."

"I sure will."

"Thanks man."

Then Jonathan left. I made sure he was halfway down the street before trotting up the steps and opening the door. I headed downstairs where Dre was mixing paint.

"Here ya go," I said, handing him his meal.

"Thanks sweetheart," he replied.

We sat on the sofa in his living room and started to eat.

"So, what did I miss?" I asked.

"Nothing. Oh, I almost forgot—some guy stopped by and wanted me to give you this."

He got up and took an envelope from the fireplace mantle and handed it to me.

Right away I recognized Jonathan's handwriting on the front of it. It said, Skyla, please read immediately! This letter explains everything. Hope to see you soon.

"Dre?"

"What's up?"

"Have you prepped your fireplace yet? I know it feels like we're having an extended summer, but it's still winter."

"As a matter of fact I have. Want to try it out?"

"Yep."

"Ok."

Soon, a warm cozy fire was burning. As I gazed into its flames, I thought about how beautiful and deadly they could be at the same time. Then when Dre went to the bathroom, I took Jonathan's unopened envelope and fed it to the fire.

SEVEN YEARS LATER

Chapter Thirty-Five

Skyla's finished Edges

As the years went by, I had come to terms with many things and searched for the common thread in all of them. My momma always said that a woman teaches a man how to treat her by what she chooses to accept from him. Lord knows I accepted way too much from Phillip, thus his perpetual cheating. With Jonathan, I wasn't quite sure what my acceptance had taught him—maybe that a small flicker of compromise can quickly spread into a wildfire, destroying everything in sight. Still, these relationships had forever changed me and I was grateful for them.

Mia never showed up to court for any of the hearings so the case was ultimately thrown out. And since I didn't have the money to keep pursuing the counter suit against her, I withdrew my complaint and dropped the case.

Despite the fact that no one still wanted to hire me fulltime, life was good, sort of. I'd started working as a freelance grant writer, which made ends meet and allowed me to work from home. But the economy had taken a turn for the worse and I was no longer able to secure grants or funding for the few large clients I had. The smaller ones were feeling the pinch too and only a few could still afford me. In short, I was broke.

"Oh my God," I mumbled. "Babe, you can't keep adding people to the guest list. We're already way over budget," I yelled out.

I went into the bathroom and pulled back the shower curtain.

"Did you hear me? This is getting out of hand. I'm starting to feel like we should just go down to the Justice of the Peace and get married," I said.

"No way. I did that once and I'm not doing it again, especially with you. I want a real wedding."

"Dre, it really doesn't matter as long as we're together."

"Can we talk about this when I get out? It's cold in here."

"Well if you wanted heat, you should have gone downstairs and showered at your place. I can't afford to have mine over 60 degrees."

"I came up here in hopes that you'd join me. But you're right, it's cold in the bathroom and the bedroom up here."

"Why'd you agree to be celibate before marriage if you're gonna keep complaining about it?"

"Look, I agreed because I love you, but I ain't got to like it."

I closed the curtain and sat on the toilet, flipping through a magazine. He got out and wrapped a towel around his waist.

"This whole, my place/your place thing is stupid. If you would just move downstairs with me, we could rent this top floor out and that would solve some of our money issues."

"I told you, I'm never going to live with a man again, unless we're married."

"Boy, the guy before me must have really done a number on you."

"Whatever."

Suddenly I gasped.

"Look at this Vera Wang wedding dress. It's absolutely gorgeous!"

I turned the magazine around to show him.

"It sure is. But that price is ugly."

"I know. A girl can dream though."

"Aw baby, one day I'll be able to make all your dreams come true. But right now, this economy is making it tough. It'll get better once my loan is approved."

"I know."

I got up and he followed me into the bedroom.

"Well, I better get dressed. Got to go find fifty dollars worth of groceries with a twenty," I said.

"Ok. I've gotta go meet a potential client. See you tonight."

"Good luck."

"Thanks."

He kissed me on the cheek and went down to his apartment and I left shortly after.

As I sat in an Aldi parking lot, I checked my wallet again—like by some miraculous occurrence I was suddenly gonna recount my money and be in surplice of $300. Instead, I had ten dollars less than I thought I had. So, I said a quick prayer that something would happen to turn my finances around.

While roaming the aisles checking prices and tossing things into my cart, a deep voice suddenly said, "Skyla Richards?"

I turned to see where the voice was coming from.

"Professor Tolliver. How are you?" I asked with a hug.

"I'm great. I'm no longer sitting on as many nonprofit boards, so I'm free to travel and enjoy life," he replied.

"I'm surprised you remember me with all the students you had at DePaul."

"Well, you were one of my brightest, so of course I remember you. How are you? You look great?"

"Thanks Professor. So do you. I'm having a few problems but I'm hanging in there."

"Ah yes. I heard about your troubles over at CRED."

"You're not the only one. Seems everyone's heard, even potential employers. I've been trying to get a fulltime job, but no one wants to risk having me on the premises."

"I'm sorry to hear that. You're so talented and bright. The nonprofit world needs you. Have you tried going independent?"

"I have, but the economy is so bad. I still have a couple of small clients, but the pay is small too. I just need something steady right now."

"Hmmm. I have an ambitious friend with some lofty but useful goals and ideas about building some inner city facilities to aid the youth. He could use a good grant writer with fundraising experience like yours. Why don't I give him a call. Do you have a middle name?"

"Yes, it's Lee. Why do you ask?"

"I suggest you use it. The nonprofit world here in Chicago is small and unfortunately, your name and that little incident has been splattered all over the internet. Using your middle name will help you at least get your foot in the door again."

"Makes sense. I would really appreciate your help Professor. I'm also going by my maiden name nowadays, which is Taylor."

"Even better. I'll set it all up and will just be as vague as possible. But I'll put in a good word for you, Lee Taylor," he said with a wink.

"Thank you so much Professor. That would be great!"

"Give me your number. I'll call you in a few weeks to give you the information you'll need for your interview."

"Okay." He handed me his phone and I typed in my contact information. "Here ya go." I gave it back to him and we shook hands.

"Take care Skyla," he said, continuing on with his shopping.

As soon as I left, I called Dre to tell him the news. I was excited and he was excited for me. A few weeks later Professor Tolliver texted me the location, time and date of my interview. I thanked him again and tried to get used to the thought of going by my middle name.

The morning of the interview, I was too excited to sleep and got up at 4:00am. A couple of hours later I showered and put on my most professional navy blue suit and white blouse. I even threw on a strand of pearls just to polish off the look. Dre had bought me a brand new pleather briefcase and came up to give me a pep talk before I left.

"Wow, you look fabulous," he said.

"Thanks. I feel….nervous."

"Don't be. I've got a good feeling about this. You're gonna do great. Just go in there and show them what you're made of. And remember to answer when they call you, Lee."

"I know. That's gonna take some getting used to. Thanks babe. I gotta run. I'll call you as soon as it's over."

"Alright. Even though I don't think you'll need it, good luck."

We kissed and I headed off to the address Professor Tolliver had given me.

I pulled up to a building in the west loop portion of downtown and was surprised that it was in a residential area. I parked, walked up to the door and rang the bell.

A few minutes later, I was buzzed in without having to give my name. Upon entering, I looked up and noticed security cameras and figured the receptionist must have seen me.

Once inside, I became even more curious as I walked into a recently rehabbed brownstone that looked like it could have been featured in Architectural Digest. The exposed brick walls surrounded the sprawling main level which was beautifully supported by glossy, mahogany wood flooring. High end furnishings were pristinely sprinkled about lending a contemporary coziness to the atmosphere. Now it was clear that this was both a business and living quarters to someone.

"Hello," I said to the receptionist, voice slightly echoing throughout the main level.

Without looking at me, she put up one finger and said, "I'll be with you in a moment."

I waited patiently for about five minutes and then cleared my throat.

"Um…my name is Lee Taylor and I'm here to interview for the grant writer position."

Suddenly, she stopped what she was doing and slowly raised her head. Her eyes began ogling me up and down.

"You're Lee Taylor? Oh, no, no, no. That can't be right," she said, shuffling papers around on her desk in search of something.

"I know I'm a little early, but my interview is at 9:30am."

She let out an irritated sigh and cut her eyes at me.

"I know what time it's for. But you're a woman. I assumed by the name, Lee Taylor, that you were gonna be a man. My bad."

"Well, I would hope my gender wouldn't be a problem."

"Did I say it was a problem?" she rudely quipped.

She got up and peeked in a large office behind her desk. Her pencil skirt was so tight that it forced her to take short, choppy steps. She sat back down and pulled out a small compact mirror and began adjusting what appeared to be a bad weave. Then, she snapped the compact closed and looked up at me.

"Well, the doctor is on the phone. Just fill out these forms and have a seat. He'll be with you shortly."

I took the papers and sat on an adjacent sofa filling them out. Now I was really confused. Did she say, doctor? What kind of doctor? I thought I was going to some nonprofit agency that wanted to help poor kids in the hood. What the heck would a doctor have to do with that, I wondered. I got up and gave her back the completed forms. Thank God I'd gotten a drivers license and state ID under the name Lee Taylor so that an employer could legally hire me.

While waiting, I picked up a Parenting magazine from the glass table next to me and began thumbing through it. As 9:30am approached, I peered over the magazine and studied the receptionist. She was now looking in the compact mirror again, smearing bright pink lipstick over her top lip. As I continued watching her closely, she stood up and attempted to straighten her tight ass skirt before walking into the large office again.

"It's time for your interview," she whispered. A minute later, she came back out and without looking at me, yelled, "He's ready for you now."

"Okay thanks," I replied, standing and gathering my things.

When I walked into the office, he was just hanging up from a call and was seated in a black, high back leather chair with his back to me. I waited for him to address me. But, when that didn't happen right away, I closed the door and went and sat in one of the chairs in front of his desk. While placing my purse and briefcase in the chair beside me, the small commotion made him finally turn around. The moment our eyes met, time froze and so did we.

We both remained speechless and motionless, until I sprang to my feet and clumsily began gathering my things.

"I'm sorry, I—I-can't do this," I said.

As I quickly turned to leave, my heel got caught in the fringe of the oriental rug and I stumbled before Jonathan ran over and grabbed me. I snatched away and made a beeline for the door.

"Wait Skyla. Don't go!"

I stopped moving.

"I have to."

I started for the door again, yanking it open.

"Wait! Please come back!"

I turned around and looked into his eyes. I shouldn't have. Even after all that time, things still happened deep inside of me whenever I looked at him.

The next thing I knew, I was dragging myself back to one of the chairs with him watching intensely.

He closed and locked the door and sat across from me in his chair with his arms folded. He didn't say a word. He just stared at me while slowly rocking back and forth. After about five awkward minutes or so, he finally spoke.

"I always wondered what your middle initial, L, stood for, but you would never tell me. Thought Lisa, maybe. Or, Linda, Lesley, Laura, or even Love… It's Lee, huh."

"Yep."

"And, Taylor is your maiden name."

"Nothing gets past you."

He looked down and zeroed in on my engagement ring, then up at me again.

I returned his stare with an icy, cold look and after about five more minutes of intense silence, he said, "So……tell me, what qualifies you for this position?"

Was he serious? He knew my background and experience, but was determined to annoy me. Hadn't he done that enough? Well, if this was how it was gonna be, then I'd serve the bullshit right back to him.

"In my previous position, I wrote numerous grant winning proposals and have contacts with key people at top grant-making foundations. I have samples, if you would like to read them."

I opened my briefcase and pulled out a stack of papers held together by large binder clips.

"This is one I wrote for Parker Memorial Hospital. They were building a new wing and I was able to secure $120,000.00 from the MacArthur Foundation for them. And here, this is another one I wrote for…."

"Why didn't you meet me that night," he interrupted.

"As I was saying, the Ford Foundation issued $75,000 to…."

"I called you for weeks—months. Why didn't you return any of my phone calls, texts, emails or letters?"

"A lot of my contacts are local. However, I have a few…."

He came around and sat on the edge of his desk in front of me, leaning forward getting just inches away from my face as I continued talking.

"I left you plane tickets and waited for you all night. Why couldn't you at least talk to me?" he asked, talking over me.

"You married another woman!" I blurted out. "You know what, this was a bad idea. Sorry I wasted your time." I jumped up and headed for the door again with my things in hand.

"You can't just run from this Skyla. We need to talk about what happened!" he said.

I turned and looked at him angrily. Then, jerked open the door and ran from his office. I kept running until I got to my car. As I stood fumbling with my car keys, tears filled my eyes and trickled down my cheeks. I could barely catch my breath. But the long ride home gave me time to compose myself and prepare for the questions I knew Dre would ask.

Once home I parked, took a deep breath, then jogged up the steps and opened the door. The lights were on, so I knew he was in my apartment.

"Dre?"

"Back here," he hollered from my bedroom. I put my things down and went to join him.

"What are you up to?" I asked.

He stood blocking the doorway with a wide grin on his face. Then, threw his arms around me and held me tightly.

"You did it baby! I knew you would!" he said, pulling me in front of the bed and pointing to it. With individual pieces of paper, he'd spelled out the word, CONGRATULATIONS, on the bed and had placed an artificial rose next to it.

"What's this all about?" I asked while smiling.

He went over to the nightstand, pushed the speaker button on the phone and dialed into our voicemail. As he continued smiling, Jonathan's voice came through the phone:

Hello Lee. This is Dr. Bass. I was thoroughly impressed with the level of experience and knowledge you displayed in your interview today and have no doubt that we'll work quite well together. Given that you're exactly what I'm looking for, I'm prepared to offer you a starting salary of $90,000. I know this might seem a bit unprofessional, leaving this kind of message on your voicemail. But, I wanted to make you an offer right away, before anyone else put a bid in for you. Call me back as soon as you can. Or, if your schedule permits, you can start tomorrow morning at 8:00am. Either way, you have my number."

"Woo hoo! I knew you could do it. Baby, we're on our way! Plus, there's more good news. That small business loan came through and now I can advertise for more clients and hire more guys. It's raining miracles today baby!" Dre shouted, cutting off my air as he squeezed me tightly.

I wanted to just crawl into bed, pull the covers over my head and stay there until this daytime nightmare was over.

"What's the matter baby? Oh, I get it. You're in shock. I understand how you feel. But, get used to it baby cause things are only going to get better from here!" he yelled.

I plopped down on the bed, getting the letters he'd placed on it all out of order. He sat next to me.

"What's wrong baby? Why aren't you excited?" He placed his arm around me.

"Dre, I can't take that job. I just don't think it's right for me."

"What? Aren't you the one who's always telling me what God has for you is for you? Baby, this is for you! You deserve this. It's what we've been praying for."

"I know, but everything in me is telling me not to take it."

He got up and began rubbing his forehead.

"So, let me get this straight. Yesterday, we were broke as hell and today, we've been blessed with an opportunity to make a joint income of over two hundred fifty thousand dollars when I factor in my projected sales. This job is in your field—it's what you're good at, or so you're always telling me, and did I mention it pays ninety fucking thousand dollars? Now baby, I love you but you're gonna have to help me understand this one."

"I know it sounds crazy."

He knelt down in front of me, held my hands and looked into my eyes.

"Think about it babe. We'll be able to go into our marriage debt free and take that trip to Paris you've always dreamed about."

I felt torn. Dre had a point. In fact, he had several points. But inside, those feelings I'd worked so hard to seal with anger were unraveling. Now memories of me and Jonathan were floating to the surface and I had no object to beat them back down with.

As I looked at Dre, all I could think about were those wrapped-around-each other walks on the lakefront, candlelit baths and stolen, rainy afternoons filled with passionate love making with Jonathan. I felt weak for acknowledging the memories. But the thought of how it all ended shot a strong dose of strength in me.

"Babe, you're right. I was being selfish. Only a crazy person would pass up an opportunity like this."

"That's my girl. Now, let's get some champagne and celebrate!"

###

The next day when I got in, Jonathan was already standing in his office doorway looking at his watch. He was still fine and wore a white shirt even better than I remembered.

"Oh hi…uh, Lee. Come on in. Let's get started," he said.

I hung up my sweater and joined him.

"First, let me just tell you how glad I am that you're here. I've got a lot of projects I'm working on and you're just the right person to help me."

This might be easier than I'd thought. He seemed so professional and focused on business that I started letting my guard down.

"Great, where do I sit?" I asked.

He opened an adjoining door.

"Well, I was going to knock out this wall and expand my office. But, now that you're here, I think I'll just leave it and create a space for you right in there."

"So I'll have to pass through your office in order to get to mine every day—interesting. Well, where do I sit in the meantime?"

"Right over here." He walked over to a desk facing his and tapped on it.

"I thought you might like to face the window," he said.

"The window behind you. Right."

"I'm going to get a cup of coffee. Do you want some tea?

"No thanks."

While he was gone, it gave me a chance to check out his credentials on the wall. He'd won a couple of awards for independent research studies he'd conducted. Then, there it was atop the cascade of other accolades in all its glory…

Chapter Thirty-Six

Jonathan's Durable Lining

It was as if she'd bartered with time, trading the years for beauty and when I returned with coffee in hand, I became trapped in the sight of her examining my degree on the wall. Her silhouette still moved me deeply and I felt grateful for being in her presence again. She must have felt me staring, because without turning around, she said, "Congratulations."

I went and stood next to her.

"Thank you. Coming from you, that means a lot. But you know what they say."

"They who? Your Princeton homies? No, I don't know what they say."

"People in general say that success is nothing without the one you love to share it with."

"So what are we, acting out scenes from the movie Mahogany now?"

"We could. Especially the one where Tracy returns to her roots and decides she wants her old man back."

She looked at me and rolled her eyes.

"So. Where do we start?" she asked.

"With getting your old man back?"

"Where do we start with work."

She strutted over to her desk to get a pen and something to write on. God I missed that strut.

"Why don't I give you the grand tour," I said.

"Ok."

We began walking side by side. I seriously had to make a conscious effort not to grab her hand, the way I used to.

"As I'm sure you've figured out, this is also my home. Bedrooms are on the top floor, the kitchen is right through there—study and bathroom over here. It's convenient and has obvious tax advantages. This room right here is where I conduct my sessions. Since my patients range in age from three to twenty-three, I videotape all the sessions for note taking purposes."

"So the room is camera monitored?"

"Yes, 24/7. Parents are aware. Every night before Tonya leaves, she downloads the sessions onto a DVD and I store them and keep a log by date, even if there were cancellations and the DVD is blank."

"Why keep blank DVD's?"

"I'm working with kids. Could be useful legally if my activity was ever called into question."

"That's smart."

I showed her the lower level, which was basically used for storage, a home gym, laundry and lounging as it had a pool table and bar. Noticeably absent from my tour was the upstairs bedrooms. Everything about her had infused my passions again and I saw no need to temp myself. We ended up back in my office and a red, rectangular box had been placed on her desk along with a smaller gold one.

"Thanks for signing for these, Tonya," I peeked out the door and said. Then I went and stood in front of Skyla's desk where she was seated. I guess my uncontrollable staring was making her uncomfortable, 'cause she crossed her legs and tugged her skirt down.

"Let me just say again how happy I am you're here. We have a lot of work to do and I would like for you to secure funding for an expansion project I'm working on. I'm trying to add a few free clinics to my practice. In fact, I have a meeting with some

MD's and artsy friends of mine at 11:00am. I'll be partnering with them to establish a medical clinic, along with an arts clinic for at risk youths."

"That sounds wonderful! I'm excited for you. I'll get started on it right away."

"I got you a couple of welcome aboard gifts. Go ahead and open them."

I watched as she unwrapped the same custom floral arrangement I'd given her years ago, only this time I ordered more Purple Larkspurs to symbolize that my ardent attachment to her was still intact. Her eyes glowed with joy. Then she opened the smaller gold box. In it contained a jar of Jif peanut butter with a white bow around it. She couldn't help but smile and laugh. I was grinning from ear to ear too. I walked over and closed the door as I needed to get one more thing off my chest. As I walked back over to her, she looked nervous, but curious. I sat on the edge of her desk and leaned in close.

"Listen. I know we have the potential to do great things together. But in order to make that happen, there's something I must say to you. I know how badly my decisions hurt you and I want you to know how sorry I am for that. I apologize from the depths of my heart Skyla."

She looked down and then back up at me.

"Thank you for that Jonathan. I think there's enough hurt to go around, so I apologize to you as well and want nothing but the best for you."

"I'm glad. With you around, I believe the best can happen. I'll be out attending meetings all morning, but I'll be back in a little while. Call me if you need me," I said before leaving.

Chapter Thirty-Seven

An Old Sentimental Garment

I could feel my heart starting to thaw as I watched Jonathan leave. While staring at his side of the room, I wondered if in all of his becoming, he'd made time or room for a lady in his life. Bree had told me about the whole Mia/Chase thing and I wondered how it had affected him. Then my phone rang, reminding me that it was none of my business.

"Hey Dre."

"Hey baby. Well? How's it going?"

"So far so good."

"What about your boss.....you think you two will get along?"

"Um....probably."

"Good. Well, I'mma let you get back to work. I love you."

"I love you too. Bye."

I went to the bathroom and when I returned, Tonya was sticking her desk phone in my face.

"Dr. Bass wants to speak to you."

"Ok. Hey Jonathan. Oh, alright. Sure. I'll get it and meet you out front. See you in a few."

I hung up and rushed back to the office. I looked in his top desk drawer and grabbed an iPhone then dashed out the front door and down the steps where he was waiting in a black BMW 640i convertible. He rolled down the window forcing me to remember how fine he looked in shades.

"Here you go," I said, handing him the phone.

"Thanks love," he replied with a firm peck on my lips. "I'm afraid I've become somewhat of an absent minded professor with the schedule I keep. This is the emergency contact phone for my patients. Can't leave this behind."

"It's no problem. Have a good meeting."

"Thanks love."

As he sped off, I thought, Really? Really Jonathan? Did you really have to give me a sensual black eye by referring to me by my old love slave name and kissing me? Stay focused Lee, I whispered to myself.

When I returned, Tonya shot me an agitated look.

"You know, I think it's really rude of you to call him by his first name. He's Dr. Bass. He's earned his title and out of respect, you should use it," she snarled.

"Well, with all due respect, you should really mind your business. If he had a problem with it, I'm sure he'd tell me. That hasn't happened so I see no need to discuss this any further."

No this twenty something, bad weave having, tight clothes wearing heffa wasn't trying to check me. She obviously hadn't caught on that me and Jonathan had history and I preferred to keep it that way. I went to my desk and got started on finding him some money. I really believed in his vision and wanted to give it my best work effort.

###

Before I knew it, two weeks had gone by and I was already receiving my first paycheck. And even though Jonathan was super busy with his patients and his projects, he always made sure he spent a couple of hours a day updating me on work related issues.

Late one afternoon after he'd gone to a meeting, my phone started ringing.

"Hey babe," I answered.

"Hey baby. I just wanted you to know that I'm stuck out here at this site. The job has to be completed by morning, so I'm afraid I'm gonna be home late—really late. I'm sorry."

"Dre, don't worry about it. It's okay."

"I'm glad you understand. Don't work too late."

"I won't. I'm the only one here right now, but I'm about to leave soon."

"Ok. Be careful."

"I will."

Before packing up and heading out, I needed to hydrate and headed to the kitchen. As I passed by the session room, the bright colors of the small children's tables and chairs caught my eye and I felt compelled to enter. One side had toys, dolls, trucks and games for the smaller kids and the other side was more maturely decorated. I went and picked up a doll, then sat at one of the small tables in a kiddy chair while contemplating.

I knew my biological clock was ticking with explosives and wondered if and when that time would ever come for me.

Out of the corner of my eye, a shadowy figure appeared and I turned to find Jonathan watching me from the doorway with his jacket tossed over his shoulder and his hands stuffed in his pockets.

"So, how've your first few weeks been?" he asked, walking over and sitting next to me in another small chair. He laid his jacket on the little table and scooted over close to me.

"They've been productive. I threw some bait out there. We'll see if it catches some of the bigger fish."

"Good."

As I sat silently staring at the doll I was still holding, he reached over and touched my knee.

"You're going to be a great mother someday. I know it."

I looked into his eyes and got lost in the compassion reflecting back at me.

"I've missed you so much Skyla. When I looked up and saw you sitting in my office, I couldn't believe it. I thought I was dreaming or having some kind of psychotic episode."

"I was in shock too."

"Looks like we've come full circle."

His hand was still on my knee and I couldn't bring myself to remove it.

"So, you're engaged now. Congratulations," he said.

"Thanks. What about you? No woman has gotten her Lee Press-Ons into you yet?"

"Well, there's been a few blossoms, but nothing deep enough to take root."

Now, his hand was no longer stationary—it was rubbing my knee with no objection from me. A few minutes later, I found the strength to stand.

"I guess I better be going," I said, walking over to a plastic bin. I bent to put the doll back and suddenly felt him against me from behind.

"I'm sorry. I just need to touch you," he whispered in my ear while slowly running his hands under my skirt and up my inner thighs.

It was as though my passions had muscle memory by the way my body responded to his touch. Now there was an ocean between my legs and I was wordless.

"I'll stop if you want me too," he whispered, hands unbuttoning my blouse and venturing inside.

My brain was screaming, Stop! No! Don't! But my body was shouting, Yeeesss! from the top of Mount Everest.

He spun me around and whisked me up and started carrying me, lowering me in front of a credenza on the other side of the room. While clinching each other we kissed passionately, the way we used to. Then I felt my skirt being unzipped and him yanking it to the floor. His kisses began journeying down to my breast, then on to my stomach while he pushed my legs apart and moved my panties to one side.

Oh no, not the tongue, not between those lips, I thought, as my desire became hostage to the pleasure of his touch until his phone starting ringing.

"Shit, that's my emergency line. Dammit!" he yelled, standing and answering it while trying to catch his breath.

I quickly got dressed and left, guilt riding shotgun with me all the way home. As I drove I decided that there was just no way possible we could continue working together. There was only one thing left to do. The next day when I got to work, I quit.

###

"Quit?? You can't quit! I won't allow it!" Jonathan shouted when I told him. This was the first time he'd ever raised his voice at me and I was completely caught off guard.

"Look, I know last night got out of hand," he said. "But, I promise it won't happen again. I still love you Skyla, but I love you enough to let you be happy with someone else, if that's what you want really. Is it?"

"Yes."

"Then okay, I'll back off. But I'm not going to lose you again now that you're back in my life. I still want your friendship."

"I'm sorry Jonathan, but I just can't stay here."

"Tell you what. How about we compromise. You can work from home as long as you come into the office and work twice a week and are available to me by phone, text, email and Skype if need be during the time in between."

Had I quit, Dre would've killed me. Plus I really needed the money.

"Okay," I relented.

"Good. Good, love."

"Stop calling me that."

"Ok, ok. I'm sorry."

Chapter Thirty-Eight

Extending the Seam Allowance

She was still my little delusional angel—pretending that she didn't feel the same way I did and thinking I would actually let her quit. If she needed me to cut her some slack, I could oblige her. But I'd never give her enough room to escape again.

I canceled all of my sessions that day and made some time for me to smooth things over with her. Things eventually calmed down and we settled into a relaxed, comfortable work day without any awkwardness between us. Soon, it was lunch time.

"Here's your corporate card," I said, placing an Amex credit card on her desk. "Your first expense will be taking me to lunch today."

"Okay, but you know I like Taco Bell's Fresco menu."

"I know. That's fine. I'm not picky, until it comes to my peanut butter. Let's go."

She picked up her sweater and was about to put it on.

"You won't need that. It's supposed to be 75 degrees today."

"This is Chicago. Supposed to doesn't count."

She put it on anyway, obstructing my view of the way her ass wiggled when she walked. Before we exited, she grabbed the mail from her mail bin and opened it in the car as we drove.

"All this sunshine and you won't let me let the top down," I said.

"But you know why. The last time you let it down, my hair was all over my head when we got to that meeting. I bet your colleagues were thinking I was a hot buttered mess."

"To be honest, your hair isn't what they were looking at."

She playfully punched me in the arm.

"I see you're still violent," I joked.

"I might be, but I know how to get on the stroll and get your money," she replied, smiling and pushing a check for $87,000 from a major foundation in my face. It took everything in me not to pull over and show her how much I appreciated it.

"Wow, it's a good thing you love Jesus cause you could really get into trouble with a skill like that. Thank you Skyla."

"You're quite welcome Dr. Bass."

Then strained silence zoomed around us.

"What did you do with the ring I gave you?" I asked.

She didn't answer.

"Skyla? I said what did…."

"I heard you Jonathan. I thought about pawning it after Mia trashed me on the internet and I couldn't get a job. But something wouldn't let me."

"So you still have it."

"I do..I mean, yes. You want it back?"

"It's yours. It belongs to you. What about all the playlists I made for you? Did you keep any of them?"

"Those I deleted."

I wanted to say more, but promised her I'd keep my feelings, hands and tongue to myself. So I let the conversation fade.

We went to lunch and she indulged in her favorite and afterwards, we headed back to the office. I liked our time alone in the car and looked forward to it.

"Look at you, listening to gospel music," she said.

"I listen to it all the time. One of the many residual effects of being involved with you. I also still pray and I even go to church and read my bible, all because of you. Thanks for what you taught me and thanks for lunch today. I enjoyed it."

"Good. Next time, I'll take you to the Olive Garden, since I know how much you like Italian food. You know I'm kidding."

"I'm a humble man. It's not like I wouldn't eat at the Olive Garden. I'm just glad you remembered what type of food I like."

"I remember everything Jonathan. That's the problem."

"Would you rather forget?"

She took a long pause, then said, "No."

Once back in the office. I cranked up a playlist on my computer while we worked across from each other for the next several hours.

"I like that song. What is it?" she looked over at me and asked.

"It's called, Bossa Blue, by Chris Standring. I'll burn you a copy of my playlist."

"Why don't we just share it on iTunes?"

"Uh uh. I'm gonna give you a CD," I said, inserting a CD into my computer and proceeding to burn the songs on my playlist. "That way, you can't just delete it and get rid of it like you did all the other playlists I made for you. Let's see. I'm gonna call this collection of songs, A Chi Love Story." I got a case out and wrote on the label before ejecting the CD.

Just then, Tonya entered.

"Excuse me Dr. Bass, but here's yesterday's DVD. I forgot to download it before I left. So, I did it this morning."

"Ok, thanks."

Normally, I always reviewed the DVD's before storing and securing them. But Skyla was standing at her desk bending forward looking for something and my eyes found her cleavage as it bulged through her white sundress and I became pleasantly distracted. While continuing to observe her, my mind drifted back to a time when I was allowed to do way more to her than just watch. I began multi-tasking—gazing at her cleavage while putting the CD into its case. She suddenly looked over and caught my eyes fully locked on her bosom. Then she looked down at her dress and pulled it up, abruptly stopping the show.

"I think I'm going to head out. You need anything before I go?" she asked.

After that show, I need a whole lotta things, I thought.

"No, I'm good," I said.

"Ok. See you on Thursday."

"Alright. Oh hey, here's the CD I made for you. Don't destroy it. I want you to keep it for a long time."

"I will. Good night Jonathan."

Chapter Thirty-Nine

Trusting the Master Tailor's Design

On the drive home, I felt calm—finally at peace. I was happy that Jonathan and I were able to come to some sort of agreement and I got to keep my job and my paycheck. I was certainly willing to do my part and as long as I was determined to keep us on track, I was confident that he would respect my boundaries.

When I got home and walked into Dre's apartment, he was rummaging through his movie collection.

"Hey babe. What's up?" I asked.

"Well, I thought we could have movie night, the way we used to do before we became semi-ballers."

"I love that idea."

"Good. The only problem is I can't seem to find a movie that we'll both want to watch. I love horror and you love romance so it's kind of hard to find something that combines both."

"Well, keep looking. I'm sure you'll find something. I'm gonna go up and change my clothes and afterwards I'll come down and make some popcorn."

"Alright baby."

"Oh Dre?"

"Yeah babe?"

"I bought some wine, but forgot to bring it in. Can you get my car keys and get it from the car?"

"Sure, be right back."

When he returned, I was in his kitchen microwaving popcorn. A few minutes later, he seemed to have found a movie and was inserting it into the DVD player when I joined him on the living room sofa with a bowl of hot buttered Pop Secret.

"So, what movie did you find?" I asked, snuggling up next to him while tucking my legs beneath me.

"I don't know. I got this off your car seat. The label on the case says, A Chi Love Story."

At first, it didn't register in my head until moans of ecstasy were soaring through the room as lusty, erotic images of me and Jonathan filled the TV Screen. Without knowing, Dre had indeed chosen a movie that blended the odd pairing of horror and romance—the horror of betrayal coupled with the romance of two brazen souls whose ties resisted all attempts to be severed and would forever be intertwined.

I became immobilized while my brain began stringing together the sequence of events that had brought me to this point—The tender yet fiery tryst between me and Jonathan that made us forget cameras were rolling the night before—Tonya's late session room DVD download that captured our heat on film—the unspoken passion that caused Jonathan to become distracted and place the session room DVD in the CD case instead of the music CD he'd made for me—my refusal to acknowledge the feelings that had driven me straight to the center of this altered state. All this had led to the look of despair Dre's eyes were now casting upon me.

As my own sensuous groans provided the soundtrack to this treacherous event, I sat motionless—no explanations—no excuses. I just sat cradled in the belly of unbridled truth that had chiseled its way through layers of denial and carved out a path that I could no longer ignore.

CPSIA information can be obtained at www.ICGtesting.com
Printed in the USA
LVOW04s2251100215

426544LV00013B/209/P

9 780996 084444